LYNX

The man ran.

Now and then, he would glance to his right, a look of fearful expectation upon his face; but he continued to run, his mind focussed upon a line of trees some distance ahead. Behind him, half a kilometre away, the wreckage of his burning helicopter sent oily plumes into the sky.

Like a black, cruising shark, the Mil Mi-24 helicopter gunship, bearing no insignia, kept station with him some yards away, a mere fifty feet above the ground.

The man's breath came in great, chest-heaving sobs. He had thought he had made it; but the gunship had caught him in the open. Now, his eyes looked upon the distant trees with a mixture of hope and despair.

Were they drawing closer fast enough? He tried to will them forward, to confirm his hope.

Why didn't the gunship do something?

ABOUT THE AUTHOR

Julian Jay Savarin learned about flying as a pilot in the R.A.F. He is the author of six successful thrillers, including *Waterhole* and *Wolfrun*.

He was born in Dominica of African, Mayan and French ancestry. Savarin was educated in Britain and took a degree in History. In the 1970s he toured with his rock band, Julian's Treatment, and recorded two albums. Thereafter he settled down to writing and composing. *Gunship*, his latest work, comes from NEL next year, and is every bit as gripping as *Lynx*.

Lynx

Julian Jay Savarin

NEW ENGLISH LIBRARY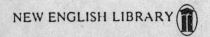

First published in Great Britain in 1984 by
Martin Secker & Warburg Limited

Copyright © 1984 by Julian Jay Savarin

First NEL Paperback Edition April 1986

NEL Books are published by
New English Library,
Mill Road, Dunton Green,
Sevenoaks, Kent.
Editorial office: 47 Bedford Square, London WC1B 3DP

Printed and bound in Great Britain by
Hunt Barnard Printing Ltd, Aylesbury, Bucks.

British Library C.I.P.

Savarin, Julian Jay
    Lynx.
    1. Title
    823'.914[F]   PR6069.A937

    ISBN 0-450-39009-8

PROLOGUE

"You're joking!" Fowler said. He stared, appalled, at his Head of Department. "You've had a mission running, something like this especially, without letting me know? I thought I was supposed to be number two around here." He looked outraged.

Kingston-Wyatt rose slowly from behind his big, inlaid desk, walked over to his favourite window that looked down upon a sleepy London square.

"I didn't want you involved, Adrian, in case this thing blows and the shit hits the fan. I want you smelling of roses. I have recommended that you take over the Department should I become er " Kingston-Wyatt gave a grim smile, ". . . unpopular." He did not look round.

Fowler said nothing. The two of them had worked together for years. He had plenty of respect for the sometimes machiavellian Kingston-Wyatt. They were friends of long-standing too.

"If things do go wrong," Kingston-Wyatt was saying, "I want you to get hold of Pross. If anyone can do it, he can."

"You don't expect the man you've sent to make it?"

"Who knows with these things?"

Fowler felt a chill descend upon him.

Kingston-Wyatt still did not look round.

The man ran.

Now and then, he would glance to his right, a look of fearful expectation upon his face; but he continued to run, his mind focussed upon a line of trees some distance ahead. Behind him, half a kilometre away, the wreckage of his burning helicopter sent oily plumes into the sky.

He had discarded all his gear, and now he ran in his olive drab flying suit, wanting only to get away. He'd not made it to the pick-up zone. Something had gone wrong. They'd been waiting for him. He ran as if the devil himself were at his heels. The devil might well have been.

Like a black, cruising shark the Mil Mi-24 helicopter gunship, bearing no insignia, kept station with him some yards away, a mere fifty feet above the ground. Its elongated sensor boom, a malevolent proboscis, protruded from its bulbous nose. Sometimes, when the sun caught it in a particular way, it would look like a huge bloodsucking insect.

The man was not thinking of huge insects as he ran. He was thinking only of making it to the treeline. The gunship did nothing, but continued to keep station.

The man's breath came in great, chest-heaving sobs. He had thought he had made it; but the gunship had caught him in the open. Now, his eyes looked upon the distant trees with a mixture of hope and despair.

Were they drawing closer fast enough? He tried to will them forward, to confirm his hope.

Why didn't the gunship do something?

The man gave a loud sob. They were playing with him; the trees and the gunship. The gunship was letting him run until it was time for the kill. He wanted to yell at the unfeeling machine; to scream at it.

But he continued to run in silence.

Without warning, the gunship pointed its nose into the sky, seemed to heave itself backwards, climbing at the same time. It rose with startling swiftness.

The man could not believe his luck as the sound of its rotors began to fade. Were they really leaving him? He braced himself as he ran, expecting at any moment that the bullets would come ripping into his back. But nothing happened. The sound of the motors continued to fade. Why?

Even as the question formed itself in his tortured mind, the man urged his body to greater effort. The trees were drawing nearer, and the gunship had left him at last. That was all that mattered. Whatever the reasons, he was relieved.

His feet pounded towards salvation. He was not interested in the direction in which the gunship had disappeared. He paused momentarily, thought he could detect a faint hum. There was no direction to it. He ran on, the sounds of his passage through the short grass, and of his urgent breathing, obliterating all others.

The gunship suddenly shot upwards from behind the screen of trees and planted itself immovably between him and escape. He felt a terrible sense of betrayal and despair as he stared resignedly at the hovering malevolence, the flash suppressors of its twin 23mm cannon that were mounted low on the right side of the nose. He began to curse those who had sent him here; but he reserved his hatred for the helicopter.

He continued to run at it, his mind refusing to accept that he had come to the end of his dash for freedom. He felt a wild rage for this thing that had tormented him for so long. He wanted to assault it with his bare hands.

As if with utter deliberation, the Mi-24 spat its 23mm explosive shells at him for a brief half-second. Fifty rounds did what one could have. Shells meant for knocking other helicopters out of the sky lifted the running man as they tore first into his exposed chest, then into the rest of his body, turning him into a bright, glistening bloom of red that lived fleetingly. What fell back to earth did so in tiny slivers that spread themselves over a wide area, decorating the greenery with buds of scarlet.

The gunship remained where it was, as if inspecting the work it had done. Then it rose swiftly, vertically, until it had become a mere speck, before heading northwards.

On the earth below, where the splattered remains of the once running man lay, an uncanny silence descended.

There it was, anticipating his turn. Pross decelerated rapidly, forcing the other to overshoot, then he raised his tail, accelerating into the turn, again behind.

But no go. The side-flare didn't work.

The other went into a rapid, sudden climb and Pross knew that if he let that go on for too long, the rakish helicopter would get onto his tail. He decelerated once more, rotated. Ah ha. The bastard was coming down. Head-on.

Pross couldn't believe it. Another fast slash was there for the asking. The other pilot had been taken by surprise, not expecting such a fast, risky manoeuvre.

Pross did not waste the time. He got his nose down giving the Lynx all the power she would take, leapt into a fast climb, rolled over onto his back, hauled the nose up. The other pilot knew his danger and had begun his break; but he was much too late.

The sights began to pulse, marking the death knell of the other helicopter. The Lynx shuddered with what seemed like ecstasy as its twin 25 millimeter cannon pumped out their high-explosive projectiles. The narrow helicopter seemed to drift right across the sights, taking the strikes squarely amidships. It started to come apart, and began to die in the rain. It rolled away from the Lynx, headed straight down. It did not have far to go. Within the merest fraction of a second it had slammed into the wet earth, exploding in a reddish-orange ball that cooked the trees within its immediate vicinity. Pieces flew into the air to disappear in the mist of the weeping sky.

They came back to earth a long way from where they had started.

Logan felt the shock waves of the explosion transmit themselves through the sodden ground; then came the rolling sound, like a distant thunder.

She shut her eyes.

Don't let it be Pross. Don't let it be Pross. Don't . . .

She waited, expecting the worse. She had heard their angry raging up there in the unseen sky. Like giant wasps, they had snarled at each other, jockeying for the single advantage that would spell doom for the unlucky one.

Their sound had been terrifying, a strangely evil noise that had struck at the very core of her being. The sound of an attacking helicopter she felt, was one of the most frightening things that could be experienced.

Now, the loser had expired somewhere in this continuing rain.

Searle was saying: "What did I tell you? The Hellhound is a killer. Your friend Pross was stupid enough to come here. Now he'll stay. So shall we."

Logan had been about to say something quite rude to him when the Lynx came in low, rockets flailing the ground where the soldiers were.

She felt her heart sing. "So much for what you know, Searle."

A concerted rattle of small-arms fire now followed the Lynx. The soldiers had got over their surprise. She'd have to move soon. She heard a sound, rolled to look, rifle searching for the target.

Ling!

A second froze, halting the passage of time.

Ling was in the full combat uniform of a high-ranking officer of the army of the PRC. His surprise at seeing her was almost as complete as hers; but she had an edge. She had already known of his true identity, while he certainly would never have expected to see her in this place.

Even so, he was remarkably quick. His AK-47 assault rifle was already coming up at her.

She was quicker. The Beretta chattered at him. The bullets started at the groin, raked upwards to his chin, almost splitting him open. He had fired, but nothing came near her.

Ling's body seemed to collapse like a concertina. Its spine had been shot away in six places.

Logan didn't wait. That would certainly bring them.

"Come on, Searle!" She turned, shaking him.

But Searle was dead.

Pross brought the Lynx down where he thought he'd seen Logan run to with Searle. The helmet imager helped him pick out his erstwhile trap, and he shifted sideways until he was clear of it. His last attack had kept the soldier's heads down, but they'd be firing at him again. He'd collected a few hits, but nothing serious.

Something had plunked into the bottom of his armoured seat though. Too close.

He searched for Logan.

Come on, girl. You can see and hear me now. Where are you?

He spun the Lynx round. Soldiers were running up. Still far.

Come on, Sian! Come on!

And there she was, running, running. He eased the Lynx towards her. Give her less distance to cover. Watch the trees.

Come on! come on!

Soldiers. Running. No Searle. What had happened?

Put the Lynx closer. Closer! Damn the trees! Get to her! Get to her!

She was running, running, running.

The soldiers seemed to be catching up. Some had stopped, aiming. Rain in their eyes, spoiling their aim. Don't hit her. Miss, you bastards! *Miss*.

Logan stumbled, fell.

Oh God. No. No. No . . .

She was alright. She was getting up, running as strongly as ever, still carrying her rifle. Then she stopped, turned, went down on one knee all in one seeming motion, fired. The leading line of soldiers dropped.

She was running again. Some of the soldiers stayed down.

Pross grinned without humour. Bloody deadly little Logan. He kept the Lynx just off the deck, waiting for her.

Then she was grabbing at the door, yanking it open, scrambling in. Halfway in, she gasped, seemed to drop back, then she was in, closing the door after her.

Pross flung her a fast look. "*Sian!* Are you alright?" His voice was full of anxiety for her.

"I'm fine! Go, Pross! *Let's go!*"

He yanked the Lynx off, trying to beat the climb record from zero feet. Sevcral hard things spattered at them. Then they were high into the rain, racing home.

"Are you really alright?"

"Yes, yes. I'm fine." She looked towards him, smiled. "Thanks for coming back."

He looked from the driving rain and the thick clouds, to stare briefly at her. "Didn't think I'd leave you back there, did you?"

Her freckles were prominent again, and with her soaked clothes and plastered hair, she looked more waif-like than ever. He'd never known a woman who could appear to be so different in so many ways.

The green eyes looked at him, a secret expression in them. "No. I didn't think you would. I was proud of you out there."

He kept his eyes on his instruments. "Were you?"

"Yes. You're not bad yourself, Pross. Not bad."

"Thank you, ma'am."

She leaned across suddenly, kissed him quickly on the mouth. She nearly kissed the mike instead. She gave a sharp intake of breath.

"I'm trying to fly this chopper," he said, but he smiled to himself.

He didn't see her own smile as she settled back in her seat. There was a certain tiredness to it.

"What happened to Searle?"

"Ling got him," she said.

"*Ling!*"

"The same. He was there in full army rig. Brass, I think. Perhaps a general. Who knows. I got him."

She explained what had happened to Pross' astonishment.

"Poor Searle," he said after a while. "The poor sod never left China, in the end." He remembered what had happened at Southerndown and felt relief. At least he'd brought Logan back. Rees' simulated hit had not been translated into reality.

"Was the helicopter you shot down Russian?"

"Yes. One of the newest."

"So he was right."

"Looks like it."

"Pross, do you mind if I have a little snooze? I didn't sleep well last night, and all this excitement has worn me out."

"Be my guest. It's home all the way."

He brought the Lynx down smoothly, It was still raining. He had not used the Stingers, thinking he might have had use for

232

them if threatened on the way back. In the event, it had been an undisturbed flight.

He began the shut-down, said to her: "Well, Logan, the joy-ride's over. You're home." He continued the shut-down.

She didn't reply.

"I said . . ." He turned to look at her, stopped.

Her head was drooping forward.

Heart beating painfully, he reached for her. "Logan?"

Then he saw the blood.

"*Logan!*" he cried in anguish.

EPILOGUE

Winterbourne said: "That was lucky, Fowler. Very lucky indeed."

"Pross was good out there. So was Logan."

"Ah yes. How is she?"

"Doing well. The wound looked far worse than it actually was. She bled somewhat, but the damage was minimal. She'll hardly notice it."

"Nothing serious, then."

"No. Mild flesh wound. Clean." Clean, but not mild.

"Good. Don't mind telling you, Fowler. I don't like the idea of young women getting shot."

Fowler said nothing. Logan had nearly died.

"Well," Winterbourne continued, "seems the Russians are having second thoughts."

"Yes. The Hind didn't do too well."

"More importantly, neither did that . . . what did Searle call it?"

"Hellhound. He followed Nato reporting practice."

Winterbourne nodded absently. "Nasty piece of work that. One up to the old Lynx, eh?" He pursed his lips. "All the same, it was damned risky. Mad."

"We had to find out. But it never happened. That's how all parties are prepared to see it."

"Too bad about Searle."

"Yes."

Winterbourne paused. "Bit much, I thought," he said, "that Italian, Riccardi, stinging us so steeply for the use of his aircraft."

Fowler said nothing.

ONE

The bright red Porsche 928S cruised along the new by-pass south of Cardiff at well over the 70 mile-an-hour speed limit. It did so with contemptuous ease, touching a hundred. The car seemed to be playing with the road; but the faces of the two men in it held no expressions of pleasure. They were not there for fun.

A huge roundabout appeared at the end of the stretch. The Porsche turned left, heading for Barry. The limit here was 40. The Porsche ignored it, and was soon hitting the hundred again.

The hard-looking man in the passenger seat said: "What we don't need right now, is a traffic cop." He stared through the windscreen blankly, not even glancing at his companion. He'd spoken with an American accent; flat, mid-western.

The car did not slow down.

"We can always claim diplomatic immunity," the driver said with cynical humour.

"Whose Embassy do we say we belong to?"

The driver smiled, said nothing as he drifted the big Porsche expertly round another roundabout. He put his foot down. The Porsche lifted its red nose perceptibly, gave a deep-throated roar. It looked hungry as it sped on its way to Cardiff airport.

The one-roomed office was part of a group of four set a short distance behind the check-in desks. A flight of steps led up to it. Above one of the desks, the blue and white sign was lit. PROSSAIR, it announced silently; pale blue letters, white borders.

In the office, David Pross sat on the edge of his desk as he stared at his mechanic.

"There's no mistake?" he queried hopefully, regretting the question almost as soon as he'd uttered it. Terry Webb was a top-class mechanic; the best. He did not make statements lightly.

Webb said: "A hairline is a hairline. Unless you've found a way to keep a chopper in the air minus its main blades, our only choice is to send the ship to Bristol for a re-fit. Four days, maybe five. Maximum."

At thirty-three, David Pross looked ten years younger at first glance. The shock of dark curly hair held no threat of premature greying. The five-foot-ten body was solid-looking without a hint of excess weight. The face was boyish, and smiled readily; but the dark brown eyes told all. They spoke of the strains of keeping a two-ship helicopter firm flying. On the wall behind him was a large picture that gave a clue to his past life: an RAF Phantom, armed to the teeth. His face grinned at the camera from the navigator's seat.

He passed a hand through his hair, sighed. "We can't fly the bloody thing down there, so that means shipping it. Christ. A hairline crack in a main blade was all we needed."

Webb's eyes were not unduly anxious as he said: "We can stand a few days without a ship."

"What about Pete Dent? Pilots are expensive when they're sitting on the ground."

"Give him your ship. You need a break. Take some time off. See the kids and the missus. Give them a treat. They'll never believe their luck Four whole days! Probably get pissed off with you in three." Webb grinned.

A stocky, bullish man, he peered up at Pross from a deep armchair. He knew he could say what he liked to Pross.

"No wonder the air force got rid of you," Pross said. "Cheeky sod."

"I got rid of them." Webb had been a Chief Technician at St Athan, the air force station just down the road.

"The Ministry of Defence must have breathed a sigh of relief.

6

I . . ." Pross broke off his banter as the red Porsche pulled up outside the main entrance to the terminal. "Someone's loaded," he commented, staring. Webb stood up to look. "Thirty thousand quid on the hoof."

Pross glanced at him with interest. "You know what a Porsche costs?"

"Might win the pools one day. Then I could stop working for you, and buy one. Pick up all the crumpet I can find."

"You mean the wife'll let you?"

"Buy her one. Then she can pick up young men."

Pross smiled. After sixteen years of marriage, Webb was still crazy about his wife.

"Well, well," Webb was saying. "What have we here? One Chinaman, and one Yank by the looks of him. Wonder what they want? Can't imagine that lot wanting to fly from here."

They watched interestedly as the newcomers spoke to the security guard. The guard pointed to the Prossair office.

"Us?" Webb said disbelievingly.

"Us," Pross said as the men approached.

"At least they've got money. That can't be bad."

"Always so mercenary, Terry."

"It keeps the choppers flying. I'll leave you to the jet-setters. This is where humble mechanics bow out. Let's hope they want to book us for two months or so. We could make enough to buy a Porsche each."

"Piss off, Terry."

"Yes, boss."

The newcomers arrived at the door just as Webb reached it. He stood back. "Gentlemen."

They entered without a word.

Webb stared at them neutrally. "Hot, isn't it?"

They ignored him. They obviously didn't talk to the hired help.

Webb gave Pross a look that was eloquent in its delivery, went out without another word.

Pross went to his desk, sat down. He did not offer to shake hands. He did not like rude people, no matter how much money they could potentially pass his way. He studied them, while they appeared to find the photograph of the taxi-ing Phantom, canopies raised, of abiding interest.

The Chinese was small, slim, with a sharp, foxy face. His dark eyes glowed and seemed to have a life of their own. He wore expensive jeans and a white, short-sleeved cellular shirt that sported a tiny crocodile emblem. On his left wrist was a digital watch with a dark red, TV screen-shaped face. There was no read-out.

The American looked American. Marine haircut, long-sleeved short-sleeved shirt, plaid trousers.

They both smelled of money. Pross wondered what kind. He had already decided that whatever they offered, he was not going to take it. They did not look like the kind of people he would want to work for.

The Chinese said: "Great old ship, the F-4. Your pilot looks interesting." He did not look down. "Gallagher, isn't it?"

Pross looked at him cautiously. Few customers would have recognised the Phantom for what it was. Even fewer would have known it by its military designation number. Had this man been a pilot? If so, for whose air force? And how come he knew of Gallagher?

The accent had a slight American tinge, but the man's mother tongue was certainly not American. Pross had detected the traces of another accent in the voice. Having once spent several months on air force detachment to the Far East, he knew a Singapore accent when he heard one. He'd never heard of Singapore having Phantoms.

Both men looked from the photograph to Pross at the same time.

The Chinese spoke. "My name is Ling, and my colleague is . . ."

"I don't think Mr Pross really needs more names," the American said. "Does he?" He kept his hard eyes on Pross.

Ling's vulpine face gave a fleeting smile. "I suppose not."

A silence descended. The faint sounds of turboprops winding themselves up in the hot July sun penetrated it.

Pross said: "That takes care of the introductions. Now what can I do for you gentlemen?"

"We're here to offer you a job." Ling seemed to do all the talking. "There's enough money in it to buy you at least two new Jetrangers. We understand what it's like trying to keep an airline going. Expensive things, choppers."

"Prossair is not doing badly."

Ling smiled. "The line between solvency and insolvency is very, very thin in the helicopter business. All sorts of things can happen."

It had not sounded like a threat, but the elements of one nonetheless seemed to dwell in the words.

The American decided to speak. "We know all about you, Pross. You have a fine house, four-car garage. The trappings of success; outwardly. We know the house is mortgaged to keep the business going. We know you took your pilot friend out of the country illegally, in late January. You could lose your licence for that. Friends in high places decided to overlook it. It was harmless enough. They were after bigger game then; but we could arrange it so that they gave you a closer look. That's just for starters."

"You really frighten me," Pross said.

Ling's eyes danced with malign life, but it was the American who continued to speak.

"I've known guys like you. Brave until the shit begins to fly. Let's see you get angry. That's usually the next stage."

"It's no use trying to goad me," Pross said calmly, staring at the hard American. "In the first instance it's too hot, and in the second, though you might not believe it, I actually have work to do. Saturdays are not days off in this firm. You've said you came here with a job on offer. All I've heard are veiled threats, but save your breath. I don't want to hear about the job because whatever it is, we're too busy to be of service to you." He stood up. "So if you'll excuse me   "

They made no move to go. They stared at him.

Pross said: "Right. I'll leave. You can have the office." He turned to go.

"Two hundred thousand," Ling said quickly. "Pounds. Down payment."

Jesus. Outside, the turboprop-engined aircraft took off.

Pross stopped, looked at each in turn. "You've just convinced

9

me. I'd be mad to take it. For that kind of money, you could start a small war. I may be mortgaged to the hilt, but I'm not crazy. You must know all sorts of people who would jump at the chance. You've come to the wrong shop."

The American said: "There's someone in China we need to get out. He's important to us; to the West."

Pross stared at him. "As I said. A small war. China. I know I'm not crazy. I'm not so sure about you two. If you're still here when I get back, I'll have Security throw you out."

Pross was at the door when Ling said, mildly: "You were once a military flyer, Mr Pross. You've seen aircraft burn."

Pross's face hardened suddenly. He turned, went to his desk, picked up the phone

Ling said: "Don't bother calling him. We're on our way."

Pross replaced the receiver, glared at them. "I don't want to see you bastards here again. Try the CIA. You'll find them in the book."

At the door, the American turned, face like granite. "We'll be back, Pross. Believe it."

Pross watched them go, angry that they'd succeeded in making him angry. China indeed. Two hundred thousand. A small fortune More than enough to take the bank loan off the house. With more to come.

No Not a chance. He wasn't that crazy

Bastards. Threatening to burn the choppers.

He didn't want to know. He didn't play in that pool. Never had. There must be squadrons of out-of-work mercenary chopper pilots who'd jump at such a chance; that kind of money. It stank.

"So why me?" he queried aloud to himself.

He couldn't understand it. He'd never had any dealings with Intelligence departments. Who was the man they wanted out of China? A prisoner from the Vietnam war? He'd heard of groups of people trying to get downed flyers and captured soldiers out of Vietnam. Was this another of those missions? From what he'd heard, none had so far met with success.

"Bloody loonies," he said, thinking of his erstwhile visitors.

Still Two hundred grand; or more.

He sighed, found himself staring at the photograph He looked

10

at the man in the pilot's seat; the man who he knew once worked for Intelligence.

"Is it to do with you?" he asked the image. "Have they conned you into working for them again?"

He shook his head at the silent image. No. The man he knew would never have worked for such a pair of shitheads.

Two hundred grand. Whoever they wanted to bring out must be very important indeed.

He left the office to join Terry Webb on the flight line. What would Terry say when he found out that a job worth that much had been turned down?

"I can wait for my Porsche," was what he said after Pross had told him what had occurred.

Five hours later, with the afternoon sun turning the area into one of the hottest spots in Europe, the phone rang on the flight line.

Webb took the call. "We've got visitors," he called to Pross after a while. He continued to listen, nodded, hung up. He went up to Pross who was sitting in the cockpit of the ailing Jetranger. "Not the same ones. We're popular today," he added, straight-faced.

Pross climbed out, squinted in the heat that bounced off the concrete apron. "As long as no one wants me to go to China," he grumbled as he went off.

Three men were waiting with the security guard. One was tall, lanky, and looked about fifty-five or so. The others were much younger, and looked like refugees from a Guards regiment. Despite the heat, they were all in suits. The tall one wore glasses.

Pross said wearily: "I have a feeling you're not here for a trip round the bay so let's go to the office, and you can tell me your story."

The tall one spoke: "I'm Adrian Fowler, Flight Lieutenant Pross, and these gentlemen are Turnbull, and Brimms."

Pross stared briefly at Brimms whose eyes looked slightly out of true; but it could have been the heat.

"I'm no longer in the air force," he said to Fowler. He began walking towards the office. They followed.

Fowler said easily: "Habit. You know how it is."

11

In the office, Pross said: "Sit where you can." He perched on the edge of his desk, looked at each in turn. They were staring at the photograph. "Don't tell me," he went on in a tired voice. "You'd like me to go to China."

That shook them. Their eyes jerked towards him, then they looked at each other before turning to him once more.

He smiled without humour. "Surprise, surprise. Someone's already beaten you to it."

They did not like that at all.

"Who?" Fowler was visibly concerned.

Pross described his earlier visitors. They could take each other to pieces for all he cared.

Brimms got to his feet. "Excuse me," he said, and hurried out, almost at a run.

Pross stared after him. "Was it something I said? BO, perhaps?" When he returned his attention to them, Fowler and Turnbull were looking distinctly unhappy. "Do I get to know what's going on?"

Fowler gave a throat-clearing cough. "Brimms has gone to the car to pass the information you've just given us on to the . . . er . . . Department. I'll come to the point."

"It would help."

Fowler let the sarcasm pass. He pointed to the photograph. "He's in deep trouble."

Pross stared. "In *China*?"

Fowler nodded. "In China. We've got to get him out."

Pross's eyes were unfriendly. "What the hell's he doing there?"

"We . . . er . . . An operation went wrong."

"You mean you bastards conned him into working for you again? After all the shit you dropped him into before?"

"It's a long story, and it wasn't quite like that."

"It never is, is it?"

Fowler said: "Look, Pross. I don't expect you to believe me, but I never liked the way he was used. The Department hates not having him on its strength, so it sometimes resorts to subterfuge. As I've said, I never liked it. I was on the point of resigning."

"Why didn't you?"

"Kingston-Wyatt blew his brains out."

12

Pross was shocked. "The CO? Dead? I don't believe it."

"Messy business, in all sorts of ways."

"God," Pross said in a hushed voice. Kingston-Wyatt had once commanded Pross' squadron, before graduating to Intelligence duties, taking Pross' friend with him. Now, he was dead by his own hand.

"Christ," Pross began with distaste. "You people must swim in a few sewers. It would take a lot to make Kingston-Wyatt suicidal."

Fowler said: "Whatever you think of us is immaterial. The most important thing is that someone you have a high regard for is in mortal danger and he needs your help."

"Why me? There must be plenty of chopper pilots you can call on, all more skilled in this sort of business. Clandestine jobs never were my line of work."

"The reason is simple enough. He doesn't trust us."

"You could have fooled me."

Again, Fowler let the sarcasm pass. Turnbull, on the other hand, looked angry, as if Pross had no right to take such an attitude.

Pross stared at him. "Don't like my manners?"

Turnbull remained silent.

Fowler said, placatingly: "We can let him know you'll be picking him up . . ."

"How can you do that without letting the whole of China know?"

"Just take my word for it."

"The way he did? Look where it got him."

"I was not responsible for the operation. Under normal circumstances, I don't handle operatives. I have taken this on because I too have a high regard for him. I want him back in one piece."

"You look very worried, Fowler. What the hell did you people send him out there to do? Kill somebody?"

Even Turnbull looked shocked by the idea.

"Good Heavens!" Fowler said. "Of course not!"

"Then he's taking something out; something the Chinese would not like to lose. Where's he running for?"

13

"The Hong Kong border. You both know Hong Kong. You've served there . . ."

"Of course," Pross said softly. "Hong Kong. I should have known. The bloody place is hot stuff these days; hot as in potato. Falklands, here we go again. What have you lot been up to, Fowler?"

Turnbull was looking angrier by the second. Finally, the anger found release. "Look, Pross. We don't have to give you any explanations for what the Department . . ."

"Shut up, Turnbull," Fowler interrupted mildly; but it was clearly an order, instantly obeyed. To Pross, he went on: "Those men who were here before us would kill to stop him."

"Why? One was American."

"Any well-skilled person can fake an accent, look the part."

"You'll be telling me they were Russian next."

"I would not be so presumptuous. Just take it from me he is in danger from them. We never expected them to be so close."

"And where does that leave me? They've approached me. They've threatened to return, even to blow up my aircraft."

"We'll ensure that they don't."

"They don't what? Return, or blow up my choppers?"

"They'll do neither, especially if you help us."

"Is that an or else?"

"No. I don't think you'd like your friend's death on your conscience."

"If that isn't an or else," Pross said bitterly, "I don't know what is."

"I am sorry to have to put it so bluntly."

"Of course you are."

Fowler said: "We haven't got much time. We've got to pull him out by Friday next. He'll be at the rendezvous then. There'll be no second chance."

"Will I have to do a cross-border job?"

"Probably not."

"Probably? What the hell is probably? I'm a married man with kids, for God's sake! Do you think I want to spread myself all over the Chinese mainland? I can almost smell another Falklands

14

coming. Scrap merchants started that little lot, and here you are wanting me to cross the Chinese border right in the middle of what must be the diciest period in the history of the colony, to pick someone up who had no right to be there in the first place. Don't you people ever learn? Do you ever think of those who've got to go and sort your messes out? How many will die for Hong Kong if you fuck up?"

"We didn't cause the Falklands war."

"Somebody bloody well did. It didn't start by itself."

"That's unpatriotic talk, Pross," Turnbull could not stop himself from saying.

Pross stared at him. "Are you trying to give me lessons on patriotism, you wally? *Me*?" He turned to Fowler. "Where did you find him?"

Brimms came in just then. "They weren't happy," he said to Fowler.

"I hardly expected them to be. Brimms, take Turnbull with you, please. Wait in the car, or have an ice cream."

Brimms' out-of-true eyes looked at Turnbull's face, took in the situation quickly.

"Yes, sir," he said, and waited for Turnbull to join him.

"Headstrong," Fowler commented as they left.

"Stupid," Pross corrected.

Fowler gave a rueful smile. "Patriotism on one's sleeve is this season's flavour. Well? Will you help us?"

"What do I tell my wife?"

"That you're doing a survey job for an oil company up in Scotland, and that you expect to be away for at least a week, perhaps ten days."

"She'll wonder why I'm not taking a chopper."

"Your clients have a specially-adapted aircraft they want you to use."

Pross said, uncomfortably: "I don't like lying to her."

"Would you prefer to tell her the truth? How do you think she'd take it?"

"Perhaps better than we both think."

"You know I can't risk that. Besides, for the next few days, you won't be going away. You've got a crash conversion course to get

15

through. You'll be operating from St Athan. She'll think you'll be coming here every day."

"We sometimes meet for lunch. Twice a week."

"It will be a busy week. She'll understand."

"Got all the answers, have you?"

Fowler looked tired, and hot. "No, Pross. I haven't. I wouldn't be here if I had. Are you going to take the job?"

Pross turned to look at the photograph, studied it for long moments. At last, he said: "I can't very well leave him to them, can I?"

Fowler said with obvious relief: "That's what we hoped you would say."

Pross turned. "Bullshit. You knew you could put the screws on."

"I see his scepticism has rubbed off on you," Fowler commented drily.

"It's the other way round."

"We'll wipe that loan off your house, of course."

Pross stared at him. "Everyone seems to know the state of my finances. That's why I thought the American and his friend were CIA."

"You're not naïve. You know government departments know just about everything these days."

"Except about those that matter; like the Falklands invasion for instance."

Fowler said, ignoring the reference to the Falklands: "Those two were not CIA."

"Who then?"

"You'll be told in due course."

"This is beginning to sound familiar. I could almost believe I'm back in the air force." Pross passed a hand through his hair in a gesture of resignation. "Alright, Fowler. What will I have to fly?"

"The best light helicopter there is. The Lynx 3."

Pross knew all about the Westland-Aérospatiale Lynx. It was the only one in the world, as far as he knew, that could be looped and rolled without falling out of the sky. Those qualities could be used to get out of a tight spot. Fowler had played down the possibility of tight spots; an almost certain indication that there would be some.

"Not a bad little ship," he admitted. It wasn't so little, and it could be armed with a variety of weapons, including a pilot-operated cannon pod. He hoped he was not going to be given one of those. He was simply going on a pick-up, not to war. "Anyone coming with me?"

Fowler shook his head. "You'll be put in the right spot. All you'll then have to do is wait for the pick-up times."

"My wife and kids."

"What?"

"I want them looked after. I don't want those other bastards going near them."

"We'll handle that. No cause for worry." Fowler stood up. "You start tomorrow."

"It's Sunday. My wife won't believe anything happens on Sunday down here."

Fowler looked benign. "You'll have to convince her, won't you? Hard, I know. But it's got to be done. Somehow." Fowler had a lazy way of speaking that always managed to hide the steel behind the words. It had served him well throughout his long career. "Think of a man running for his life out there on the border if you find you have difficulty in coming up with a convincing reason. Concentrates the mind wonderfully. You won't be seeing me again, but I'll be keeping a close watch. Your aircraft, your home, and your family, will be well looked after until you return. You have my word."

"That means something, does it?"

"Yes," Fowler replied seriously. "It does."

Pross looked at him.

Fowler said: "Be at the gates at ten hundred tomorrow. You'll be met. The Lynx will be there. Not the one you'll be using in Hong Kong, of course; but to all intents and purposes, it might as well be. The specifications are similar." He extended his hand. "Just remember. I want him out as much as you do."

"We have different reasons." But Pross took the hand, shook it briefly.

He watched Fowler leave, before turning to look once more at the photograph. He stared at the man in the front seat of the Phantom.

"Alright, old son," he said softly. "They knew it before I did. Pross is coming."

TWO

Pross's white Jaguar XJ6 Coupé pulled up before the gates at RAF St Athan promptly at 10.00 a.m. The big car purred quietly as he waited for a man in Squadron Leader's summer gear to approach. Standing next to the unarmed service policeman, on the other side of the barrier, was an army sergeant wearing a green beret.

Pross could still remember the brief conversation he'd had with his wife at breakfast. The Pross household was always up early. The two children, a boy and a girl, made sure of it. The Dawn Patrol he called them.

"You're twitchy today," Dee had said. He'd always called her Dee; for Diane. "What's up? You didn't sleep too well last night, either. The last time I remember you being this twitchy was when you were in the air force."

She had a homing instinct that would make any self-respecting radar look sick.

"Ah it's just the cracked blade on one of the choppers," he'd explained as casually as he could. "Pete Dent's."

"I know your business twitches. This one isn't." She had powerful hazel eyes, and they'd stared at him almost unnervingly. "I suppose you'll tell me when you're ready." Radar.

He'd driven away from the little village of Craig Penllyn, near Cowbridge, with the memory of those eyes burning into him. He'd told her he was going to the airport. He hoped she would

19

not choose today to visit the Webbs, who lived a mere three miles or so away in Cowbridge itself. Terry would have gone to the airport to give credence to the story; but you never knew. Maureen Webb's radar might be as good as Dee's.

He'd told Terry, without going into detail, that he'd be working for the government. Webb knew when to keep his mouth shut. They'd decided to give Pete Dent the cover story only. No need to involve him. Dent was ex-army, and a fine chopper pilot. Not quite a partner, yet more than just an employee, he could easily handle the flying side of things. Cheryl Glyn would be her usual competent self with all the administrative work.

Feeling reasonably unworried about the business side of his life but dreading the moment of truth domestically, Pross looked up as the Squadron Leader reached him.

"Mr Pross?" the air force man queried, bending to look into the car.

Pross nodded.

"I'm Paul Sanders." He offered his hand which Pross shook. "Over there," he went on, indicating with a nod of his head the army man, "is Sergeant Rees, your instructor. Damn good jockey by all accounts. Red hot. If you'll just hang on, I'll have the SP raise the barrier."

"Thank you."

Sanders went back, spoke to the air force policeman who came forward to operate the barrier. Pross drove through, stopped. Both Sanders and Rees got in. Rees was slim, with a mournful face.

Sanders said: "S'arnt Rees, Mr Pross."

Pross twisted in his seat to offer his hand to Rees who was in the back. They shook briefly.

"Sir," Rees said. The mournful face reminded Pross of Droopy.

Pross said: "Forget the 'sir'. I'm David."

"Cado," Rees supplied after a longish pause. The voice was mournful.

Sanders said to Pross: "Drive on. I'll show you where."

Pross moved off, while the policeman stared woodenly after them.

"Cado?" he queried as he followed Sanders' directions.

There was another long pause before Rees finally said: "I was given the name Caradoc."

"Oh."

"Exactly. When I was a child I could not pronounce the full name. I shortened it to Cado. It stuck." Another pause. "I was smarter than my parents gave me credit for."

As Pross stopped at a HALT sign, a suspicion made him glance round. Rees was grinning, totally transforming his face. Pross smiled, decided he was going to like Rees.

There was a tiny smile on Sanders' face too. "Are we supposed to believe this, S'arnt Rees?"

"It's true, sir," Rees told him simply. There would be no first names between those two. Service protocol held fast.

There was silence in the car for a while until Sanders said: "Turn here and onto the pan."

The "pan" was the flightline and as he drove across the concrete, Pross could see the Lynx in full green-on-green battle-camouflage paint, parked out of the sun next to a large hangar. In the distance, he recognised a pair of Lightning F-6s.

"What are the Binbrook boys doing here?" he asked Sanders.

The Squadron Leader smiled. "Nostalgia?"

"No. I was never at Binbrook. But we practised intercepts with them."

"They come down here for their new paint jobs," Sanders said. "They're going grey." He smiled again at his little joke. "And here we are."

Pross parked the Jaguar next to the Lynx, got out. An airman approached, saluted Sanders as he too climbed out, handed him something. It was an ID card with Pross's name on it, and a clip attached.

Sanders handed the card to Pross as Rees wormed his way out of the back of the Jaguar and stretched himself. The airman departed wordlessly.

Sanders said: "Put this on. It will stop the SPs going ape if you happen to wander off." He gave another fleeting smile.

Pross clipped the card to his shirt pocket. "I can see I really was expected," he commented drily.

Sanders' face was neutral. "I know nothing about anything."

"Naturally."

Pross walked up to the Lynx, did a slow circuit of it, conscious that Sanders and Rees were giving him the full benefit of their scrutiny.

The first thing that took his eye was what he recognised as a 20mm cannon fixed beneath the nose. This was obviously a new system, as opposed to the standard pylon-mounted gun-pod.

Cannon?

He felt his stomach constrict. A *pick-up*, Fowler had said. What the hell was this?

He forced himself to continue with his inspection, the cannon inevitably drawing his eye at frequent intervals, like a rabbit mesmerised by a snake. He studied the fifteen-and-a-half metre-long aircraft, noting that the sleek lines of its nose were broken by the sensor units for target acquisition and night vision. He studied the sturdy frame, its wide-tipped main blades, its wide-spread tricycle landing gear. Twin-engined, he knew it could give him a cruise of 160 knots or so, more than 180 mph, with a max of well over 200 mph. The outboard pylons, he noticed, carried no armament; but after the shock of seeing the cannon, he would not be surprised to see all sorts of missiles suddenly grow on them as the days passed.

The doors, one on each side of the helicopter, had been removed. Pross made himself climb into the wide cockpit area. The avionics systems were unbelievable. His navigator training made him recognise how advanced they were. Gyrosyn compass, tactical air nav, Doppler, IFF, IR jamming, and of course, the acquisition and night vision monitors.

Christ. He was sitting in a fully-dedicated battlefield gunship.

He climbed out, strode over to Sanders and Rees. They looked at him warily.

"Alright," he began dangerously. "Who's going to tell me? Which war am I supposed to be going to?"

Their eyes seemed uncomfortable, as if holding a gaze was suddenly difficult. Rees appeared to be quite happy to defer to rank. He glanced at Sanders.

Sanders said: "We were merely told to give you instruction. I know nothing more."

"Fine," Pross said in a voice that clearly indicated it was anything but. "A joker came to see me yesterday. Get me to a phone, and get him on the line, or all bets are off."

Sanders looked worried. Rees looked benign. It was not his problem. Problems were for officers.

Sanders began: "Mr Pross . . ."

"You've never seen me angry, Sanders. You wouldn't like to. Don't let my happy face fool you. I'm not going to stand in this heat arguing."

Sanders gave a sigh that was eloquent. He was clearly mentally consigning to hell whoever had landed him with this job; on a Sunday too.

"Let's get back into the car please, Mr Pross," he said with a controlled calm. "Rees, you stay here with the aircraft."

Rees looked as if he'd like nothing better. Officers didn't like being told off, especially by civilians who had themselves been officers. Rees' expression said it all. It did not please Sanders who entered the car without waiting for Pross.

Pross got in behind the wheel. Sanders directed him to the station headquarters building. They made the journey in silence apart from Sanders' terse directions. Sanders led him to an office and in a remarkably short space of time, Pross found himself speaking to Fowler. He wondered whether Sanders belonged to St Athan at all. He suspected that the Squadron Leader was probably one of Fowler's men, perhaps not even a bona fide RAF officer.

Pross went immediately into the attack. "For God's sake, Fowler! A bloody *gunship*. What are you trying to con me into? I've told you before. I'm a married man with kids, not a death or glory merchant. I'm doing this because a very good friend is in trouble that your bunch got him into. So let's have it. What the bloody hell's going on?"

Pross kept his angry eyes on Sanders who had the grace to look away.

Fowler was saying in his lazy voice: "There is no need to be angry, Pross. It is precisely because you are a family man that I thought you should not go in there unarmed. If someone takes a pot-shot at you, you should be able to defend yourself."

Pross was incredulous. "*Pot-shot*? What are you talking about, Fowler? Who said anything about pot-shots? A pick-up, you said. You're setting me up for a bloody war! Which is what I will start if I swan about shooting up the Chinese countryside."

"It's just in case things go wrong," Fowler reasoned. "He's been out there for weeks now, waiting for the right time. He's been in hiding. We expect nothing to go wrong; but you know as well as I that it is sheer folly not to expect the worst in these circumstances. It may never happen, but what if it did and you could not defend yourself?"

"You never said these things yesterday," Pross accused hotly. "You lied to me, Fowler."

"I did not lie. I told you the truth."

"You lied by omission."

A sigh came down the phone. "Leave him to it if that's how you feel, Pross."

The line hummed in the silence that followed.

"Bastard!" Pross said at last and slammed the phone down. "Don't you say a fucking word!" he snarled at Sanders. He stormed out of the office.

He waited in the car until Sanders came out and got in almost diffidently.

"Mr Pross . . ." Sanders began.

"Shut up!"

Pross put the Jaguar into gear, shot off with a squeal of tyres, leaving black streaks on the baking surface of the road. He made it back to the Lynx without directions from Sanders.

He got out, entered the helicopter, taking the right-hand seat. He strapped himself in. Rees, who'd watched his angry return in amazement, climbed into the other seat somewhat cautiously as if expecting Pross to take a bite out of him.

"Alright, Cado," Pross said tightly. "Instruct me. Pretend I know nothing about choppers. Do your job."

He turned to give a hard stare at Sanders who had climbed slowly out of the Jaguar to watch and put on the helmet that had been left for him.

Rees went painstakingly through the pre-flight checks, familiarising Pross with every item of equipment. He saved the cannon firing system till last. There was even a full head-up display that would do justice to a fast-jet fighter on the hunt.

"Okay," Rees said eventually. "Let's take her up."

Pross went through the starting sequence of the twin Rolls-Royce Gem 60 turboshafts, got his clearance from the control tower, lifted the Lynx off smoothly. After the Jetranger, the power on tap felt awesome. The ship rose like an express lift.

They stayed within the airfield circuit.

Back on the ground half an hour later, Rees said: "There's not much I can teach you about handling choppers."

"There is," Pross said. "I want to know this ship inside out if I'm to fight my way out of whatever's waiting for me over there."

"All I've got is a programme to put you through. No one bothered to tell me what it's for. I think I prefer it that way."

"You would." Pross glanced out. Sanders was still standing by the Jaguar. "Let's go up again." They'd even got the helmet size right.

"It's all yours," Rees said.

Pross yanked the Lynx off the ground, tilted it over ninety degrees, headed for the Jaguar.

Sanders flung himself to the ground in panic.

Pross laughed aloud as he lifted the helicopter clear, going into a spiral climb.

"You may not like the sod," Rees said, "but you don't have to decapitate him." He was smiling, at the thought of its actually happening, it seemed.

Pross said loudly over the beat of the rotors: "Were you in the Falklands, Cado?"

"No. But I lost some mates when *Galahad* was caught with her pants down." He sounded angry. "Bastards."

"The Argentinians?"

"What do you think?"

"Doesn't sound like the Argentinians to me. What's this? Mutiny in the ranks?"

"You expect to lose people in action. But that . . . that . . ." Rees stopped, shaking his head in suppressed anger. "You wouldn't believe what some of the blokes are saying."

"Well they'd better watch who they say it to."

Rees glanced at him, eyes speculative. "Going to report me?"

Pross did not look round. "Me? I agree with you, mate."

They worked the Lynx for another half-hour before taking it down again. Sanders was still there.

He came up when Pross had shut down the engines. His look was neutral.

"How's it going?" He was talking to Rees.

"Not much I can teach him about chopper flying. I'm thinking of doing the first-stage aerobatics after lunch, and reserve the really hard stuff for Monday."

Sanders turned to Pross. "That suit you?"

Still be-helmeted, Pross stared at him. "It will have to, won't it?"

Sanders said: "Look, Mr Pross. I had nothing . . ."

"I know. I know." Pross removed the helmet. "You had nothing to do with it, and you know nothing." He put the helmet down as Sanders' lips tightened, clipped off his straps. "Tell me, Sanders. What desk do you fly, and for which spooky little department? Are you even air force?"

Sanders remained silent.

Pross glanced at Rees who was suddenly totally occupied with removing his helmet, undoing his straps, getting out of the aircraft. From the hangar mechanics were approaching the Lynx.

Sanders moved out of the way as Pross climbed out. "What's the matter, Sanders? Cat got your tongue?"

"Whatever I say," Sanders began at last, "you'll believe what you want to."

"It's a hard life."

"We've made arrangements for you in the mess," Sanders went on doggedly.

"I expected that at the very least. What about Rees?"

"He's billeted in the Sergeants' Mess. Normal procedure. You ought to know that."

Rees was talking to the mechanics and either didn't hear, or pretended not to. Pross went up to him.

"Off to lunch, Cado. See you back here when?"

"Fourteen hundred?"

Pross nodded. "Will do."

"Don't eat too heavily. We're going to throw the ship about." Rees' mournful face maintained its customary expression.

Pross didn't read much into it. He made for the Jaguar, entered. It was baking. Sanders followed him in, wordlessly. Directions to the Mess were given in a manner that indicated that Sanders wanted to stop talking as soon as he opened his mouth. The journey was made in a tenseness that was almost as palpable as the heat.

At two o'clock, Pross was back on the flight line. He arrived alone. Rees, already waiting, handed him a life-jacket which he put on.

Rees' face was transformed by a grin. "Lost your playmate?"

"He made his excuses and stayed behind," Pross said, relief in his voice.

"Not for long." Rees was looking into the distance.

Pross followed the look. An RAF staff car was just pulling onto the apron. It set off diagonally across the concrete, heading directly for the Lynx.

Pross hopped into the aircraft. "Come on, Cado! Let's see if we can get this ship off the ground before he gets here. It will be good practice." He was already strapping himself in. He grabbed his helmet just as Rees, needing no second bidding, scrambled in.

Pross connected his helmet. His hands flew as he did his checks swiftly, omitting those not vitally necessary. The main rotors were beginning to turn while Rees was still in the act of putting on his own helmet.

The engines roared into life. No warm-up needed. Pross lifted the Lynx off the deck just as the air force car came to a halt. He banked into a tight turn above the two men who had sprung out of the vehicle. Neither of them was Sanders.

He came out of the turn, took the Lynx straight up.

Rees had just finished securing his helmet. "While that was a fairly sharp lift-off, you're going to have to make your peace with the tower for not telling them."

They could hear outraged chatter on the headphones.

"You make the peace," Pross said. "If I read this little circus

27

correctly, the last thing I'll be worrying about wherever I'm supposed to be going will be air traffic clearance."

Obediently, Rees began to soothe the nerves of the irate controller in the tower.

On full tanks, they headed out to sea and were cleared for the Lundy Island area about fifty miles southwest of St Athan. From his air force days, Pross knew this to be a restricted air zone. He'd worked in it a few times, during air combat practice. It was also a refuelling zone. However, they were cleared for aerobatics up to 6000 feet.

Pross expected to find the place humming with military aircraft. But the skies were empty. No combat pairs, no refuelling. Nothing. Nothing on visuals; nothing on the radar. He was amazed. It was as if the air force had ceded the area to him.

"Someone's been working hard," he commented drily to Rees, still searching the cloudless sky. "Can't just be because it's Sunday."

Instead of an explanation, Rees pointed to the radar at the same time that Pross heard its warning tone in his helmet. He looked. A surface echo. A very small ship. A sub maybe. In the Phantom, they would have plunged down to investigate. For a brief moment, Pross felt the old hunting instinct in him.

He sensed scrutiny, glanced at Rees. The sergeant was eyeing him speculatively.

"Still there, isn't it?" Rees said. "You can still taste it."

Pross shook his head. "No. That part of me is gone for good."

"Says you."

They put the Lynx through its paces. They looped, rolled, spiralled for a good half-hour, at the end of which Pross felt a great exhilaration flowing through him. He thought of Dee waiting in Craig Penllyn, and felt guilty.

As they headed back, Rees said: "Don't know why I'm here. You don't really need me."

"I do, Cado. You taught me a few tricks today. I'm just a fast learner. I've got to be. I want to see my wife and kids again when this is all over. It's a matter of survival. Fowler is too smooth. I think the bastard expects trouble. I'm thinking of my neck. That bloody cannon under the nose gives me goose pimples. I'm supposed to be going out to help a friend, but I keep thinking I'm going to a war. It's my nasty suspicious nature. When does the firing practice feature in the programme that's been set up so nicely for me?"

Rees took some time before replying as Pross piloted the Lynx back to St Athan. At last, he said: "They're just precautions . . ."

"You can go off some people smartish; especially if they take you for a dummy. *When?*"

"The day after tomorrow," Rees finally answered, with some reluctance, "after you've done the advanced aerobatics."

"More than we've done today?"

"Yes."

Pross thought about that for some moments. "I swear to God," he said quietly, "if anything happens to me out there, I'll come back and haunt the lot of you."

The two men were still waiting when they landed. One of them was Turnbull.

Turnbull said, petulantly: "You could have waited, Pross. You saw us coming."

Pross was unrepentant. "That was the best reason for leaving."

Turnbull flushed. His face, already made rosy by the sun, took on a darker shade. It was like watching a red cloud streak across his countenance.

"You're just like that friend of yours. He's unpleasant too."

"If he's upset you, my faith in him is even stronger."

The stranger with Turnbull said: "It's no use the two of you glaring at each other on this frying-pan. Let's go somewhere cool."

Pross saw a tubby man with lank hair and a crumpled face. The lank hair was losing the battle against baldness.

"Who are you?"

"Penleith. Here to help."

"You can start by getting Fowler to keep this joker out of my hair."

"Somewhere cool. Somewhere cool," Penleith said placatingly. "We can talk there. Got some urgent news. Changes."

"Changes? What bloody changes?"

29

"Somewhere cool," Penleith insisted for a fourth time as if his life depended upon it. He headed back for the staff car.

Turnbull trooped after him, climbed in behind the wheel, waited, fuming.

Pross said to Rees: "God. Where do they find them?" He'd been standing with his helmet dangling from one hand. He placed it in the aircraft, removed his life-jacket, put that with the helmet. Rees had already removed his own gear. "Come on, Cado. Let's see the wonderful news they've brought."

"It's bound to be bad." Rees at his most mournful.

"There speaks a man of experience."

They got into the Jaguar. Pross saw Turnbull tapping impatiently at the wheel of the staff car. He took his time. Let the bastard roast.

Pross started the engine. Turnbull gave him a venomous look, and the RAF car took off with a squeal of tyres. Pross followed at a sedate pace, forcing Turnbull to slow down, knowing it would enrage Fowler's man. It was a small vengeance to take for the web they were spinning about him.

They were given a reasonably cool room in the Officers' Mess. Oddly, no one seemed to mind Rees being there. Sanders was nowhere to be seen. Pross began to wonder whether Rees was truly a sergeant. Someone had thoughtfully left tall glasses of iced fruit juice on a table.

"Met your friend once," Penleith began from behind his glass which he then proceeded to empty at one go. "Does me in, this heat," he added when he'd finished.

Pross watched him. "Where?"

"Not important. Bit of a lone wolf, that one. Good though. Must get him out. Crisis otherwise. So. Got to move things forward."

Pross was stunned. "*Forward*? I've only just started on the ship."

"Sorry. Can't be helped. Got to do in two days what you hoped to do in three. Rendezvous brought forward."

"You're crazy. Things are bad enough as they are. *I'm* crazy for going along with it."

"Think of your friend. His idea to move it forward Must be getting hairy over there."

"Why didn't Fowler know this yesterday?"

"Couldn't have. Only got it today. Message two days old."

Jesus.

Pross thought of his friend hiding God knew where, hoping the soldiers would not find him before rescue came.

"Cado?" Pross turned to Rees. "Can we do it?"

"My professional answer is no."

"But?"

"It's not a question of choice. I don't know what the operation is . . ."

"I know, Cado," Pross interrupted with mild scepticism. "So you've said. Can we do it?"

"We'll have to."

Penleith had watery eyes. They danced between Pross and Rees. "Settled, is it? Good. Sorry. But there it is. Has to be done."

Pross finished his drink, stood up. "I'm going home." He unclipped his ID card, dropped it on the table. To Rees, he said: "What time tomorrow?"

Rees said: "Because of the change of schedule, the earlier the better."

"I can be here at eight if you'd like."

Rees nodded. "I'll have everything ready."

"Fine." Pross looked at the others. "It would be nice not to see you again, but I suppose I can't bank on that."

He went out, not caring what they thought. He was not working for them. He was trying to get his best friend out of a jam. He hoped he would succeed.

He didn't dare think of what failure would bring in its wake.

There was a different policeman at the gate, but he was let through without demur. The man had obviously been fore-warned.

As the Jaguar headed homewards, Pross wondered what he would say to Dee. How to allay her suspicions without actually increasing them in the process. The feeling of exhilaration he'd experienced when tossing the Lynx about the sky began to diminish the closer he got to home. It was a great ship all the same. He was actually looking forward to taking it up again.

He got home at six. The Dawn Patrol squealed with pleasure to see him. Three and four-and-a-half, the girl was older. They had both inherited Dee's blonde hair. He carried one on each arm as he entered the house.

Oh God, he thought in a sudden spasm of fear. *What am I doing? My kids need me. My wife needs me.*

As he kissed the children, he hoped he was able to keep these thoughts from his expression, for there was Dee waiting, hazel eyes too knowing for comfort.

He kissed her as he always did when returning home, full on the lips for long seconds. The boy Euan, as he always did on such occasions, made a little strangled noise as if to say enough was enough and stretched his arms out towards his mother. She took him with a smile, while Tessa clung to her father. It was always thus.

Nothing appeared to have changed; but Dee knew it had.

Nothing was said during playtime, bathtime, storytime, and time-for-bed time. To give him extra breathing space before facing the inevitable, Pross locked himself in one of the three bathrooms for nearly forty-five minutes while he had a good soak.

That too was not unusual. It was his custom.

Dee said nothing during supper. She was equally quiet about it during the clearing of the table. Pross was beginning to find it unnerving. He was almost ready to tell.

Suddenly, she turned to him, gave him the full power of her eyes and said: "Don't. Don't tell me. I won't like to know."

He stared at her. "Dee . . ."

"Shhh." She kissed him briefly.

"But you have no idea . . ."

"That's just it. I prefer not to."

He looked at her, loving her all over again. Despite having had the two children, she looked exactly as he'd first seen her at the first Mess Ball he'd attended after his posting to the Phantom squadron. A local farmer's daughter, she'd been surrounded by eager, flash pilots all drooling over her, while he'd stood to one side feeling positively deprived with his navigator's half-wing.

Then the man who was to become the best friend he ever would have had appeared next to him.

32

"Stunner, isn't she?"

"Am I that obvious?" Pross had asked.

"Let's just say your eyes are on stalks. Come. I'll introduce you."

"You know her?"

"Of course not. But that doesn't matter."

"You can't . . ."

But it had been too late. He'd found himself propelled towards the group. She had seen them coming, and the hazel eyes had smitten him on the spot.

"I think you should meet the best navigator on the squadron," was how Pross had been introduced. "He's my navigator, so that makes him the best."

That had not been an exaggeration. Together, they'd made the most formidable pair on the squadron, consistently the top combat pair. The killer pair.

That night too, he had proposed to Diane, not believing he could have been so bold. Startled, she had said yes, and had been even more startled by the speed of her acceptance. And here she was, two children . . .

Into his thoughts, came her voice: "You're remembering the Mess Ball."

He nodded. "Let's go to bed," he said, not meaning to sleep.

"That would be nice," she said.

She had spoken casually, but her eyes burned with eager anticipation.

THREE

Monday promised to be a hot, bright day. Pross stared out of the breakfast-room window, at the splashes of sunlight that lit up the already dissolving mist that hung above a large expanse of overgrown greenery. The village playing-field. He stared at the wispy curtain melting before his very eyes beneath the onslaught of the new day's sun.

Upstairs, he could hear the Dawn Patrol and Dee in playful combat. She wanted them in the bathroom; they didn't want to go. She always won.

Nearly seven-thirty.

He always liked that part of the day, summer or winter. In summer, there was always a sense of expectancy about the life given to a new day. In winter, the day was reluctant to wake up, to get going. Each had its own elemental feel that reached for him.

He loved the village too; the haven he had come to some years ago, before Euan had been born, and long before it had become a fashionable bolthole for London's walking wounded. Now, what had once been bare, steep slopes bordering one side of the single village street, were dotted with large houses and landscaped gardens. There weren't too many, so the village still retained its character. A haven of peace.

He didn't notice the ringing of the phone until Dee's voice called: "David! Will you get the phone?"

"What? Oh!"

He put down the cup of nearly-finished coffee he'd been holding, stood up and went to the lounge extension.

He picked it up. "David Pross."

"Mr Pross," Ling's voice said. "You have made a very bad mistake." There was a long pause before the line went dead. Ling's voice had been quiet, reasonable. Somehow, that had made it sound more dangerous.

Pross replaced the receiver slowly. There was no mystery about how Ling had got his home number. It was on the Prossair brochure for all to see.

He went back to his breakfast, sat down. He had lost his appetite, and the village was no longer a haven of peace.

"David?" Dee called. "Who was it?"

"Wrong number!" he called back. He wondered if she believed him.

He made himself finish his coffee. The mist had practically vanished. It was time to leave for St Athan. He glanced at his watch. Seven-thirty exactly.

He stood up. Best to make it seem like any other Monday. He went upstairs to the bathroom where the Dawn Patrol were still carrying on their losing battle with Dee. He kissed each in turn while they tried to rope him in on their side; then he gave Dee a long kiss.

He could feel her eyes on his back as he bounded down the stairs the way he always did, every day he set off for the airport; but there was a new watchfulness in them.

He got the Jaguar out, set off for St Athan. At the gate, a different SP came forward with his ID card. He clipped it on. The barrier was raised. As he drove through, Sanders, again in Squadron Leader's uniform, came out of the guardroom, approached the car. Pross stopped. Sanders climbed in.

"I want to talk to Fowler," Pross said as he moved off.

"Certainly. I'll take you to an office."

"Good lad."

"Mr Pross, this hostility . . ."

"Who's hostile?"

Sanders seemed to take a deep breath. "I'm not responsible for what is happening. I'm only . . ."

"Obeying orders? A whole army used that excuse once."

Sanders shut up.

In the office, Sanders got hold of Fowler quickly enough, handed the phone over.

"Glad to see you're up," Pross said.

Fowler's lazy voice was unperturbed when he said: "I'm always up early. As a matter of fact, I've been here all night." He didn't say where "here" was. "The operation is hotting up. You've seen my new man."

"I've seen him. I don't like the new schedule."

"Can't be helped. Your friend called it forward. He must have had good reason."

Pross said: "I got a call from Ling this morning."

"We know."

"You *what*?"

"I told you we would cover your family. I meant complete cover. Until this business is over, your phone will be monitored."

"You've tapped my bloody phone?" Pross didn't know whether to be angry, or relieved.

"Would you rather we didn't?"

For a moment, Pross was not sure. It was reassuring to know they were aware of Ling's call.

"I suppose not," he said at last.

"That's the realistic way to look at it," Fowler said in approval.

"Just make sure you remove the tap once this thing is over."

"Of course. That goes without saying."

"I'll hold you to that, Fowler."

"You can count on me." He sounded as if he meant it. "You'll also be relieved to know that we've taken over a house that overlooks your own. We moved in on Saturday."

Pross was astonished. "You what? Whose?"

"Best if you didn't know. Be assured that your family has complete cover. We'll be watching them like hawks. No one's going to get near them."

"Fowler," Pross began quietly. "How did you get the owners to move so quickly?"

"They happened to be going on holiday . . ."

"Oh yes? Convenient." God in Heaven. They'd had all their moves planned well in advance.

"We told them it was in the national interest. We . . . er . . . helped with the holiday expenses. They were very pleased."

"I'll bet. Remind me never to buy a used car from you, Fowler." Pross hung up, turned to Sanders who'd been studiously looking out of the window. "I'd better get over to Rees. He's probably wondering where I've got to."

"He knows you're here." Sanders did not turn from the window.

"Of course. Stupid me."

Pross left Sanders in the office, went out to the Jaguar. He got in, headed for the flight line. Rees was waiting; kitted up, and ready to go. He was sweating, although the day had not yet warmed up.

The Lynx was ready too. The pylons were loaded with air-to-surface Hellfires, and air-to-air Stinger missiles. Pross had no doubt that the cannon was also loaded.

Rees said, apologetically: "This was to have been done tomorrow. We have a full day. Advanced aerobatics to include defensive and attack manoeuvres; firing practice, and fast landing and lift-off exercises, all this by day, and by night."

"By *night*?"

"As I said. A full day." The mournful face was still apologetic. "You're doing it in full combat rig. Park the car nearer the hangar. There's some kit waiting for you in there. I'll do the checks while you're getting ready. Okay?"

Pross stared at the Lynx's armament. It looked lethal squatting there, waiting to go.

He nodded thoughtfully. "Fine. See you when I've done."

As he changed his clothes for full flying gear, Pross found himself thinking about how each new day brought fresh upgrading of this allegedly simple pick-up. It was as if, knowing the full hairiness of the operation and having already secured his acceptance, they were too scared to give him the details except in small doses.

He put on his life-jacket. Outside, the Lynx started up. It

appeared to sound more aggressive, as if raring to mix it with an antagonist.

He picked up his helmet. What, he wondered, was really waiting for him in Hong Kong? He could always quit, even now; but he knew he wouldn't. He couldn't. Of course they'd known that. They'd played him like a fish, and hooked him.

He left the hangar, went up to the Lynx, stooped to avoid the whirling blades, ran at a crouch, climbed in. Rees was strapped in, helmet on. Pross settled himself into the seat, did up his straps. He put on his helmet.

"What am I supposed to be doing?" he said loudly against the noise of the helicopter. "Taking on the whole Chinese air force?" He made it sound like a joke.

Rees' mournful countenance did not alter. "Take her up," was what he said. "Today, you're really going to find out if you can fly this thing."

Pross gave him a questioning glance, but took the Lynx up smoothly. The added weight of the weaponry caused him no problems.

Rees' voice came on the headphones: "How does she feel with the extra weight?"

They were again heading out to sea, this time at little more than two hundred feet.

"She feels okay," Pross replied, and went into a climbing spiral to two thousand feet.

The Lynx behaved impeccably.

They again headed for the Lundy Island area. The target radar was on and fifteen minutes later, the contact warning sounded in Pross' headphones. He glanced at Rees who appeared totally occupied with the radar.

"Let's have a visual," Rees said.

Pross took the Lynx into a shallow climb to get above the target which seemed to be moving quite slowly. A light aircraft? A Sunday civilian who had strayed into the zone?

The target suddenly changed course, seemed to be diving.

Pross followed, lost height swiftly in a spiral. Now, he was below the target, and gaining. The target changed course again, rose.

What was going on?

He increased speed, maintaining height, but still following the target's course.

Then he saw the speck, barely visible in the empty sky. It dropped perpendicularly, turning tightly at the same time. The rotors gave it away. He caught a brief, side-on view before it disappeared beneath.

Another Lynx.

So that was their game.

"Take him," Rees commanded. "Cannon."

Pross activated the head-up display, tilted the Lynx, hauled after the target. He switched the cannon to simulated fire.

The target Lynx rolled, showed its belly for a brief fraction of a second, looking from above like a strange fish from the depths of the grey sea; then it was gone. The radar had lost it too.

Pross rolled onto his back, half-looped, dropped like a stone. The radar locked on again just as he saw the target. It was going straight up. In fleeting seconds, he would pass it going down. There would be the barest flash of time. He went into hover just before he reached the bottom of the half-loop, tightening it as he did so. There was a time-lag before the new mode came into effect and the Lynx continued to descend, though decelerating rapidly.

He heard a grunt of what he took to be satisfaction come from Rees.

The target Lynx, in the brief moments available to it, obeyed the laws of physics and rose like an express lift. Pross commenced the firing sequence just before it entered the illuminations of the display. The sights pulsed three times, then the Lynx disappeared upwards.

"Bingo!" Rees crowed into his mike. "A kill! That was bloody great, David. Your little trick caught him with his knickers down. Was he surprised!"

"Cado!" came over the headphones. "Who taught you that trick? It's not one of yours, you sod!"

"That would be telling!"

"Drinks on me."

"Bribery will get you nowhere."

Without looking, Pross knew Rees was grinning.

"Spoilsport!" came the rejoinder before transmission was ended.

Rees said: "Well done. Well bloody done, David. David?"

Pross was deep in thought, flying by instinct as he took the Lynx out of hover and gained height. He had felt the same sense of elation that once came to him in the old days whenever they'd had a successful "kill" in the Phantom. He did not like the feeling. Neither did he like the growing certainty that he would have to fight another chopper – or choppers – during the course of the pick-up. What choppers did the Chinese fly? One thing was certain: they would not be Lynxes.

"What's next?" he asked Rees. The combat exercise had taken ten minutes from the time of visual contact.

"Simulated missile firing. Track him. This might be harder. He'll be out for revenge and will be trying for a kill. You must get him before he gets into optimum firing position. Imagine it's a live one coming at you, because that's exactly what it will be over there if the worst happens."

As Pross resumed the hunt, he found himself thinking of Dee and the children back in Craig Penllyn. He owed it to them to ensure that he survived.

Rees said: "You're doing marvellously, David. Bloody magic."

"It worked against another Lynx. I don't think they have Lynxes in China; unless we've been selling them some. American Phantoms scored well against other Phantoms. Then they got a shock in Vietnam. I intend to come back alive, Cado. What am I going up against?"

There was an uncomfortable silence. Then: "We don't know."

"Great."

Rees seemed to retreat into himself and lapsed into silence.

Pross continued to hunt for his adversary. To be predictable in air combat, he knew only too well, was a certain way of committing suicide. He would be unpredictable now in this exercise, as he would have to be when he found himself in the New Territories.

Soon, his radar warned that he was being hunted. He went into a sudden, sideways descent, hovered, reversed course at the

40

hover, continued in a forward descent. The warning died. They'd lost him.

He kept going, heading for zero. The Lynx skimmed the water. Pross kept it there. Let them come looking.

He sensed Rees looking at him, but Rees kept silent.

Then the target radar found the other Lynx. Pross smiled to himself. So they had come down too. They were holding steady. He had seconds before they would wake up.

He chose the launch moment well, making sure the computer would not introduce sun interference to nullify the kill. Lock-on came. He "fired" two missiles, waited. Fifteen seconds. Anything could spoil.

"Bang, you're dead!" Rees chortled.

"Oh shit!" came disgustedly over the air.

Rees laughed. "Let's go home, David. I think you've earned a break. You must have been shit-hot on the Phantom. Haven't forgotten much, have you?"

Pross was reluctant to return. He wanted to move on to the next phase while his blood was still up. They had been out for just over an hour, and he calculated that the combat exercises had used up at least another hour's worth of fuel. The Lynx had an endurance of three and a half hours on cruise; not enough to enable them to do more exercises and return to base with a reserve. A check of his fuel state proved his calculations correct.

Bowing to the inevitable, he headed back towards St Athan.

He sensed Rees looking at him. "You alright?" Rees asked.

"I'm fine. Will I be doing live firing?"

"Well . . . er . . . no." Rees was apologetic. "What with the cuts and all, stocks are precious."

"Cannon's loaded, isn't it?"

"Yes. But that's to give you a feel of the handling with full stores."

"It still won't have the same feel as the Lynx they'll give me over there."

"No. But it will help."

"I think I should give the bloody cannon a try, *and* let off a missile. I've only got the computer's word that these things work."

"I'm not authorised . . ."

"You're going to have to get the authorisation. There was a Chiefy who used to work on our ship. He was in Malaya when it used to be called Malaya, as a green airman. Somebody put him on guard duty on a train from Singapore to Kuala Lumpur. He was given an old .303 with five bloody rounds of ammunition – not loaded – to help guard a slow train making its way through guerrilla infested territory. CTs they used to call them, he said. Communist Terrorists. *Five* bloody rounds, Cado. One burst from a submachine gun and he'd have been done for. Imagine trying to load a sodding .303 with all that shit coming your way, knowing that even if you'd succeeded in getting your precious five rounds in and firing them off, that would have been your lot. You'd then have had to stay there and wait for it.

"What I'm trying to tell you, Cado, is that there is no way I'm going to continue with this until I've had a feel of the cannon, and satisfy myself that the bloody missiles *will* work if I have to use them. I've seen missiles do more crazy things than you'd believe, including shooting down the host aircraft. We're not going to be shot down by our own missile, are we, Cado?"

"The system's very reliable . . ."

"Not until *I've* tested it, it isn't. This ship stays on the deck until you get the authorisation for live firings. Or rather, it goes where the hell it likes, only without me."

"We'd have to set up the practice range . . ." Rees began in protest.

"Do it."

"But the time!"

"Do it, Cado. Tell them now. Save time." Pross' tone brooked no argument.

Rees began transmitting to St Athan.

"Homebase from Foxglove."

"Homebase," came St Athan immediately.

"Foxglove for Sanders. Range facilities required. Urgent."

"Understood."

Rees cut transmission.

"That will make Sanders happy," Pross said.

"It won't."

42

"Too bad. He's not paid to be happy."

Sanders was waiting when they set down. "What's all this about wanting the range?" he asked barely seconds after the rotors had ceased turning. He had run up to the aircraft, face like stone.

Helmet still on, Pross glared at him. "No range practice, no go."

Sanders said: "The other Lynx has come in and gone on its way. You scored twice, a kill each time. That's very good. Exceptional, in fact. Surely you're satisfied?"

"When it's my neck on the line, Sanders, I'm never satisfied." Pross removed his helmet, aware of Rees doing a shut-down of the equipment. "Will the range be ready?" He stared hard at Sanders.

"Yes." Grudgingly. "I've had to ask them to put off a Tornado shoot. 9 Squadron will want my guts. Have you any idea how long they've been waiting for a slot?"

Pross was unrepentant. "I knew them before they had Tornadoes. They'll let you off with a mere boiling in oil."

Sanders didn't smile. "I see no humour in this situation, Pross."

Pross climbed out, forcing Sanders to move back. "I want a pee." He walked towards the hanger without a backward glance.

"I'll have everything ready and a full fuel load!" Rees called after him.

Pross brought the Lynx down in a heart-stopping spiral, went into hover, darted sideways, shot forwards, rolled onto his back, fired, rolled upright while the sound of the bark of the cannon was still in his ears. It had been beautifully executed, each manoeuvre flowing smoothly into the next. When he had fired, the Lynx had been inverted fifty feet above the water, vibrating to the recoil.

Rees said, in a voice that tried hard to be calm: "I didn't think our main blades would clear." He cleared his throat. "Good shooting."

It had been. The target, stretched between two poles mounted upon non-anchored buoys, had been neatly perforated in the centre. The movement of the sea had not made it easy, for the buoys shifted this way and that, continuously altering the target's aspect.

Some distance away, the recovery launch rolled gently in the mild swell, engines at idle.

"For a few seconds," came a voice on the launch in their headphones "we thought we'd have to come and pick up what was left of you."

"Sorry," Pross said to the voice. "No custom today."

"We live in hope."

"Morbid sods," Pross said as he cut transmission; but he grinned.

The target was quickly replaced, and a missile shoot was made from three miles, in forward motion, and practically skimming the sea. It hit the target, its tiny practice warhead exploding on impact.

They thanked the launch, left the range area. Thirty-eight miles away to their left was the west coast of Wales. They headed back inland, for the next phase of the exercise.

Rees said: "I know a good home for a Lynx pilot."

"If that's an offer, forget it. This is a once-only job. I've acquired a taste for the comfortable family life and my little Jetrangers. Besides, I've grown out of uniform. No offence meant, Cado. But that's how it is, and how it's going to stay."

"I was only joking, anyway," Rees said mournfully.

Pross smiled to himself as he altered heading and took the Lynx south towards Brawdy where another change of course would take them towards the Gower peninsular.

Southerndown, a popular little beach, lies four miles or so south-east of Porthcawl. Access to it by road is from the north only, a narrow stretch barely wide enough for two cars in some places. Usually, anyone unfortunate enough to be driving up the steep slope while another car was coming down would be forced to spend agonising moments trying not to scratch the paintwork. This did not deter the hundreds who flocked to the place each weekend, and much of the week too. On this Monday, Southerndown was conspicuous in the total lack of

44

traffic. A police car at the top effectively blocked the sideroad that led to it.

One of the patrolmen was repeatedly telling those he and his colleague turned away that it was a temporary measure only.

Further enquiries invariably got the reply that the road was being checked for safety reasons. Most didn't believe it and privately thought the police were meddling again, as usual. Those who wanted to wait were told to move on. Others, who claimed to have seen a helicopter stooging around and off-loading men with rifles, were politely but firmly told to mind their own business.

Pross knew Southerndown well, having taken his family there on several occasions. One striking feature of the place was that it was bounded north and south by two ramparts of high ground that ended in spectacular cliffs, falling perpendicularly to the staggered shelves of slate far below. To the south, the cliff curved outwards, sloping towards the sea. In this curve, part of the cliff had crumbled, forming a dangerous-looking rockfall that rose thirty feet from the beach. When the beach was crowded, the more adventurous children liked to test their climbing skills upon it. No one so far, had been killed by it.

When they were about a mile away, Rees said: "There are soldiers positioned about the place, and they're all using laser simulators on their rifles. You've got to get in and collect your pick-up, and get out again, without setting off the laser receivers on your body. I'm not going to tell you what to do. How you do it is your own business."

The receiver harnesses that had been fixed to their flying gear at St Athan had twelve micro-processor controlled detectors that would be activated if the laser shots scored. The detectors were so placed that a direct hit would cause them to give off a loud, continuous note which would be sounded by a loudspeaker specially attached to the instrument panel. A long note meant a fatal shot; a brief note, a near miss. There were six detectors along the front, four on the helmet, and one on each arm.

"After you've done this pick-up," Rees was saying, "we'll do it again, at night."

"Thanks for nothing."

Unperturbed, Rees went on: "Your man is somewhere in those trees."

The trees in question were an isolated clump some distance inland, on a rising slope behind the southern rampart. They were quite unmistakable. That part of the clump which faced the sea had been bleached a dirty white and stripped bare of foliage. The petrified trees were permanently bent away from the memory of the vicious sea winds that had come at them during bad weather. They gave the clump a strangely crippled look; the look of half-life.

Pross fixed the position of the trees in his mind, but did not go closer inland. Instead, he did a fast run across the tiny bay, staying close to the water.

There were no noises from the laser detectors. Either no one had taken a shot at them, or a number of misses had been scored.

He activated the mast sensor, a globular affair mounted above the main rotor. This would give him vision while keeping the ship hidden behind a screen of trees or tall bushes.

It would have to be fast; straight in and out. No hanging about. That was the theory. The chances were it would not happen like that out east; but every aspect had to be covered, or attempted.

He swung the Lynx round the headland, kept going. He curved inland, tilting the aircraft onto its side, rolled level, climbed to get over the high ground, and began hill- and tree-hopping. He was not sure, but Rees appeared to be gripping his hands tightly.

Pross brought the Lynx to a sudden hover behind a screen of trees. No laser warnings sounded, and nothing appeared on the sensors. No vehicles, no soldiers.

Still Pross waited. His pick-up zone was two tree-clumps away, about a mile or so.

Pross remained there for over ten minutes, the crucial timespan by which remaining at the hover would normally begin to deteriorate with most pilots. Pross held position until fifteen minutes had passed.

Still nothing showing on the display units.

He settled the Lynx to the ground, but kept the Rolls-Royce Gems going. The engines were relatively quiet, but he was not happy about the amount of time he had already spent in the area.

He decided that for the real thing it would either have to be a fast dash in and out, or a quiet let-down, with engines off after landing, and a wait. But that would carry enormous risks.

Laser detectors had also been placed at various points on the aircraft, some where a hit would disable or destroy it, others where it would suffer minor damage but still be able to fly, and still others in areas where hits would be of little consequence. A display unit showing an image of the Lynx would record hits with pulses that would remain on-screen; green for inconsequential hits, blue for minor damage, pink for heavy but not crippling damage, and red for disabling hits.

Pross said: "I've been sitting here too bloody long, Cado."

The longer he stayed the less he liked it. Yet, some instinct told him not to move.

The defensive radar was quiet. Everything was quiet.

Rees said nothing, keeping a studious eye on the radars and monitors.

Pross decided to take the Lynx up cautiously until the main rotor sensor just peeped above the treeline.

And there it was on the monitor. An image, coming up fast. Another helicopter.

Pross "armed" a Stinger for simulated fire, waited. Rees was again looking at him. He ignored the Sergeant, kept his eyes on the image. The Stinger locked-on.

Now!

He took the Lynx up so suddenly Rees said something like "Oof!" Pross fired, dropped down again, sent the aircraft hurtling just above the ground, behind the screen of trees.

Rees said, with some satisfaction: "That was a hit! You would have blown him out of the sky."

Pross said nothing, concentrating on keeping his blades off the deck and out of the trees. As he hurtled from cover, pulses began to show on the damage display unit. So far they were all green. They were now taking ground fire.

He kept the Lynx low and fast, jinking at unexpected intervals to throw the soldiers' aim. Still only green hits, and no ominous long notes to indicate a body hit.

"*Jesus Christ!*" Rees shouted suddenly in horror.

Pross had tilted the Lynx for a brief second. It was a toss-up as to which the blades would hit: the ground, or the tops of the trees. They hit neither.

Pross said: "What are you worried about, Cado? You're still alive, aren't you?"

He had known precisely what he was doing. There had been no real danger; but to anyone else it would have looked suicidal. He smiled to himself, enjoying his mad dash.

Cover. Another screen of trees, but hits were still registering. Blue ones now. Some of the bastards were hiding in the trees. Out, out, out!

He took the Lynx high and suddenly. It leapt skywards as if shot from a catapult. The hits ceased to register. He flung it sideways. The Lynx seemed to skid across the sky. Now he was dropping inverted, directly above the target clump of trees. Now he was the right way up, skidding sideways again, still dropping.

To someone watching from the ground, the Lynx must have appeared demented. It dropped behind the trees.

Pross halted his descent abruptly. Momentum carried the Lynx the rest of the way, full hover making it a gentle touchdown. Hits were registering once more; an increase of blue ones.

Rees, his voice still shaky from the experience of what he felt had been a near-crash said: "They didn't know he was hiding in there, but they'll be up and running for us now."

A pink hit. The first. Rotor sensor gone. That would have severely cut his target acquisition capabilities from cover had this been a real combat.

Pross was beginning to feel impatient.

Come on, *come on*, whoever you are.

"We've been here thirty seconds," Rees intoned.

Pross did not glance at him. A man had broken cover. The newcomer wore the full laser harness, with its individual loudspeaker, a small unit, attached to his back. Pross wondered who he was, but could not as yet see because of the combat helmet the man wore. The man sprinted towards the Lynx.

It was important that the attackers should not score any hits on him. That would add complications that could wipe the whole operation. The man was carrying a rifle that had a laser sight attached.

Blue and green hits were registering on the helicopter. Perhaps they were still too far away and could not as yet see their target properly.

The man suddenly paused, went down on one knee, brought up his rifle and seemed to lay down a burst of fire. The hits on the Lynx stopped abruptly.

Hmm, Pross thought as the man was up and running again. Would the pick-up in the East be armed?

"He got a few," Rees said unnecessarily.

The man reached the Lynx, looked at Pross, who recognised the black-smeared face.

Sanders.

"Gets around, doesn't he?" Pross remarked drily as Sanders rushed to the main door in the side, tugged it open on its slide rails, tumbled in. Pross was already on the move before Sanders had fully slid the door shut.

"Welcome aboard," Rees mourned.

"Well done, Pross," Sanders said as he squatted, braced himself against a former near Rees' armoured seat.

Pross gave a brief nod of his head, putting all his attention on the job of getting out. A green hit registered.

He held the Lynx fast along the ground, shot for the high rampart to his left. Lots of blue hits.

There was a sudden shrieking tone, and Pross thought he had been hit.

"Good thing I'm not going with you," Rees said at his most mournful. "I've just been killed. Somebody down there's a good shot."

Sanders pulled out a strange-looking handgun, pointed it at Rees, squeezed the trigger. The noise stopped.

The Lynx had reached the edge of the cliff. Pross appeared to heave it over. The Lynx plunged down. All hits stopped as the helicopter dived out of view.

Rees stared disbelievingly, certain they were about to smash themselves to oblivion on the deserted beach. It didn't happen.

49

Instead, the Lynx skimmed away mere feet from the beckoning, rock-strewn sands.

Something tumbled at the peripheral vision of Pross' left eye.

"Someone just fell," he said sharply.

"What?" From Rees. "Are you sure?"

"Positive." Pross was already bringing the Lynx round, heading back for the cliff face.

Rees was saying into his mike to whoever had been monitoring the exercise on the ground: "Casualty, casualty! The exercise has ended. I repeat. The exercise has ended. Someone has fallen off the cliff. We're investigating."

Pross brought the helicopter as close as he dared to the rockfall. This was where, he was certain, he had seen the sudden, tumbling movement. He held the Lynx at the hover, peered down. Nothing. He glanced up, as if to give himself a reference point. Several figures had appeared at the top, all carrying rifles. They too appeared to be searching for something below.

Pross cautiously jockeyed the chopper.

Rees said, a strange excitement in his normally deadpan voice: "Someone's pointing."

Then Pross, who had been again searching the rocks below, said calmly: "I see him." He wished he'd been mistaken. "It's going to be tricky to get him off. That fall looks unstable. What was he doing there, anyway?"

"Probably hoping for a surprise shot," Sanders suggested. "Might have succeeded too, if he hadn't fallen. Shows initiative."

"Not if he's lying dead, it doesn't. I'll get as close as I can. One of you will have to try and get to him."

"I'll do it," Sanders offered immediately.

Pross had expected him to.

"Fine," Pross said, and began gingerly to manoeuvre the Lynx closer, hoping the vibrations of the blades would not bring more rocks down upon them. It would not do to be totalled by a rockfall.

Sanders was at the door. He slid it open.

"Can you see him?" Pross called.

"Yes! A little closer and I'll be able to reach that slab of rock quite easily."

Pross edged closer still. Rees seemed to be squirming.

"What's up, Cado?"

Rees was peering upwards. "I'm worried about our blades digging us into the cliff. Must be just inches to spare by now." His voice sounded quite calm.

The Lynx suddenly felt a shade lighter.

Rees, peering backwards and down, said: "He's off . . . *Sweet tit*! No . . . he's alright. I thought he was about to join that poor sod down there for a minute."

Pross shifted the chopper away from the cliff face, turned to point it nose-on. He could see Sanders scrambling gingerly, but with discernible swiftness down the rockfall towards the stricken soldier. The soldier appeared to be lying quite still, in an uncomfortable-looking posture.

Sanders reached him, began to inspect him, touching him only briefly. Presently, Sanders straightened, looked up at the helicopter, drew his fingers across his throat.

"Well that tells us," Rees said. "Poor sod."

Pross felt sick. He could see soldiers running across the beach towards their fallen comrade.

Rees saw them too. "They'll take care of him," he said quietly. "The other Lynx will take him back. Let's go. Sanders can hitch a ride."

Pross took the Lynx high. All elation had gone. A man had just died; and the real mission had not even yet started. He had an uncomfortable feeling that many more, too many, were to die before it would be over. His gut feeling was that he wanted no more of it; but he would feel worse, he knew, if he did not go. His sense of guilt would become an intolerable burden. Fowler had programmed him well.

Rees said: "You had nothing to do with what happened to that man. It was his fault for picking that position. Soldiers die in training all the time. What about those who die on the Brecons?"

"That supposed to make me feel better?"

"You're not supposed to feel bad, either. You had nothing to do with his death . . ."

"He was there because *I* was."

"He was a *soldier*. He knew the risks. Just as you knew the risks when you used to climb into a Phantom. You're taking a risk now." Rees smacked the instrument panel. "This thing could fall out of the sky without warning. Yet you're here. You fly your choppers every day. It's all a matter of accepting risks. You did very well today. You should be pleased."

"One missile shot at a target," Pross said, "and a brief cannon blast at another target, inert, and unable to bite back. The rest was computer games. It's never the same in real combat. We had perfect conditions today; not even a wind to speak of. A weak cross-wind can change a good shoot into an embarrassing miss, especially if your target can shoot back. No, Cado. The computer had a good day. Not me."

"What about the flying? Did the computer do that? And what about the laser units? You received no body hits. They were pouring everything at us. Had they been using real ammo, you would have made it alright. Not even a wound."

"And you would have been dead."

"That's why no one is going on the pick-up with you."

The rest of the flight to St Athan was made with total silence between them.

FOUR

Soon after they'd landed, Pross phoned home.

"Will you be back soon?" Dee asked.

"No. I'll be a bit late tonight. Is everything alright?"

"Shouldn't it be?" She could always throw him with tactics like that, and when he hadn't fallen into the trap, went on: "Perhaps I should be asking you. You sound depressed."

He tried not to think of the unfortunate soldier falling to his death off the cliff face.

"It's been a tiring day, that's all. I'll be alright."

"Would you like to come home for a bit? I could fix something . . ."

"No, Dee. Thanks all the same. I'd rather get it all over with then come straight home. I'll have a bite in the . . . er . . . snack bar." He'd nearly said Mess.

"How late will you be?"

"Not sure, but I'll try not to be too long."

"We'll be alright. Don't worry."

Now why had she said that? You never knew with Dee.

"Fine," he said, and hung up.

They never blew kisses at each other on the phone. Too tacky, she'd once said.

At nine-thirty that evening, he walked across the darkened flight line with Rees. Faint traces of the departed sun still hung in the gloom of the sky, but too weak to overwhelm the brightness of the stars.

53

"You alright?" Rees queried as they reached the Lynx.

"I'm fine," Pross assured him. "I've had a good rest."

Pross knew that was not what Rees had really meant, but by tacit agreement, it seemed, neither mentioned the accident at Southerndown.

They climbed into the aircraft. The last phase of his crash course, flying with the night vision system in operation, would be carried out at Southerndown. People lived in the little valley between the ramparts of high ground. This meant that the exercise would have to be as brief as was practically possible.

Inwardly, Pross was glad of this. He wanted to go home.

At the front of the house overlooking the Pross home, Turnbull looked through his binocular nightscope and stiffened. Someone was at the door, pressing the bell-button. Turnbull knew it was none of his colleagues. He rose slightly from his position on one knee, in order to see better.

He continued to rise, but now it had turned into an agonising stretch as his body reacted to something at once hot and cold that had plunged into it, delivering a paralysing, searing pain that tore the breath out of him. The scope fell from his frantic hands as he tried to reach behind him, to get at the dreadful thing that was twisting and turning, butchering the vital organs within him. His mouth opened to scream, but there was no energy left to propel the air out of his lungs.

No matter how hard he tried, the invading thing remained out of his reach, though it continued to ravage his insides, spilling his lifeblood within him. At last, the hot-cold thing departed. Turnbull felt an overwhelming sense of relief as he died. The entire incident had taken fractions of a second. To Turnbull, it had felt like a hundred years.

Inside the house, Turnbull's two colleagues were sitting at a table playing chess. They looked up as a shadow fell across them. They did so casually, expecting Turnbull. They barely had time to register their horrified surprise before the silenced automatic coughed at them. One took the first nine millimetre round in his open mouth. It kept going, taking the back of his head with it. The other, with incredibly fast reflexes obeying urgent

54

commands, had flung himself backwards off his chair, clawing at his own automatic. Fast though he was, he was still too late. The complete surprise had stolen irrevocably any advantage his speed might have given him. The second 9mm bullet took him in the left ear, nailing him, it seemed, to the floor. His assassin left as quietly as he had entered.

Out on the single, quiet village street, the fourth and last member of Turnbull's team walked towards the Pross home, coming from the northern end of the village. He had no intention of going in. His instructions were that no evidence of the reasons for his presence must be noted by the Pross family. His patrol was a casual by-pass to check that all was still well.

A tall hedge hid the front of the house from him. He was so preoccupied with the thought of reaching the large gate so he could see better, that he did not notice the figure that came out of the bushes behind him. Fatal knowledge came to him when something cold and unbelievably sharp plunged deep and upwards into his back. His fleeing thoughts were filled with outrage that anyone had sought to violate his body in such a manner. He was dragged unceremoniously away; but he was too dead to care.

Pross came in low from inland, to the rear of the waiting soldiers. The integrated helmet and sighting system gave him a thermal image display of the area, enabling him to fly the helicopter with a feeling of confidence that was almost equal to a daytime flight. In addition, his altitude, speed and heading were also displayed on the image, allowing him to receive his most vital information without the need to take his eyes off the terrain. One slip and it was goodbye to his family, and instant cremation.

Rees, keeping an eye on the damage display unit, said; "So far so good. No hits. You're doing well."

"Do they have nightscopes down there?"

"Quite likely."

"Then hold on to the praise. We're not out of the woods yet . . . if you'll pardon the expression."

Rees made a noise that could have been a snicker.

"Is that other Lynx going to be around?" Pross queried.

"Possibly."

"You're a great help."

"I'm not here to make it easy for you," Rees said good-naturedly.

"No. Really."

"You're getting sharp with me again, David," Rees said with mournful reproach.

"I'm tired and I want to go home."

"I thought you said you were okay."

"That was back at St Athan. Ah!" Pross had been holding the Lynx at the hover between a low hill and a quite extensive copse when a tail rotor appeared briefly within the thermal image. "Did it show on the monitor?" he asked Rees, to see if the mast-mounted sensor had also picked it up.

"No," Rees answered.

"Are you being the neutral, or is that the truth?"

"The truth. Nothing on the screen."

"Somebody was careless," Pross said with satisfaction.

He now knew exactly where the other Lynx was hiding. They were obviously lying in wait, hoping to catch him off-guard. Was that what would happen on the border?

He cautiously eased the chopper forward, a few feet above the deck, keeping in cover, yet not losing his reference to where the target waited. He was well aware that the other Lynx might have moved to a new position, but it had not left its own clump of woods.

"Are they carrying similar equipment?" he asked Rees.

"Possibly. Assume they are. They're supposed to be hostile, remember? Take nothing for granted."

Pross never did, but he made no comment, keeping his eye on the target's hiding place. As yet, no hits were registering on his own Lynx. Suddenly, he went backwards, rose swiftly, pointed the nose down as he swept over the group of trees. There beneath him, was the other Lynx, moving slowly, thinking it was still hidden.

"Cannon, I think," Pross said as he took the Lynx down again.

The head-up display was on, the target acquired. Pross brought the chopper right down until he was in a perfect line astern, with the target Lynx nice and fat in the sights; not as fat as a broadside

56

target, but it would have to do. They appeared oblivious to his presence behind them. They had fleeting seconds to find out.

Pross "fired". The sights glowed, pulsed.

"Bang! You're dead!" Rees howled with unrestrained glee into his mike.

"Oh bugger!" someone snarled in disgust, and the other Lynx suddenly leapt for the sky to disappear in a hurry.

Almost immediately, laser hits began to appear on the monitor. Plenty of greens, but an unhealthy number of blues, some too close to the tail rotor for comfort.

Pross took the Lynx out of there quickly.

"Where is he hiding this time?" he asked.

"Where we've just come from."

"*What*? Why didn't you tell me before? Besides, it's bloody hot down there now. They'll be waiting."

"Yes," Rees said unhelpfully.

"Bugger!" Pross said in annoyance, echoing the sentiments of the pilot of his erstwhile target. "Smoke," he went on. "I'll need smoke dispensers and rockets for the real thing." The smoke would hide, and the rockets would be good for suppression of ground fire. He'd saturate the place if need be.

But that would advertise his presence even more over there, making him a marker beacon for reinforcements; though if things deteriorated to that level, pyrotechnics and noise would be the least of his problems. He'd be fighting for survival.

"I'll try a feint," he said now to Rees, and took the Lynx high and away from the area.

The laser hits petered out, stopped altogether. He went out to sea, dropped almost to surface level, came back in, heading for the cliffs. He sensed, rather than saw Rees brace himself for the crash he was sure was about to happen.

Smiling to himself, Pross brought the chopper up steeply until it appeared to pop above the top of the cliff. Nothing came at them as he took the Lynx on a nap-of-the-earth skim down the slope from the cliff edge. They had been taken by surprise.

He gained a little height, winged over, headed for a clump of woods well away from where Rees had said their man was hiding. Still no ground "fire" came at them. The surprise was still holding, and the sudden change of course would have thrown off the aim of anyone who might have been sufficiently alert. No one, Pross was certain, would have been near the edge; not after what had happened earlier in the day.

He hovered for a brief moment above the copse he had selected, before settling to the ground. He kept the rotors turning at high revs so that anyone listening would interpret it correctly as being the sound of a helicopter about to take off in a hurry.

He waited. Any moment now, they'd be running up to close in on him from their many hiding places.

Rees watched him for long moments, but said nothing.

Presently, green hits began to appear on the monitor. They were shooting through the trees, and were not seeing their target properly; but that state of affairs would not last for much longer. When he felt he'd held the Lynx on the ground long enough to get the bulk of the soldiers heading towards his hiding place, he lifted the machine off the deck until it had risen above the wood, banked it hard over, levelled off, pivoted, dived for the ground once more, skimmed towards the spot where Rees had said the man was waiting. The Lynx never stayed on the same course or in the same attitude for more than fleeting seconds. The success of these manoeuvres was proved by the fact that they collected only a few green hits. Pross used all the cover he could find.

Rees was strangely silent as the ghostly landscape rotated and pivoted about the ship. Pross could hear him breathing shallowly.

"What's up, Cado?" Pross began lightly, his voice belying the workload that sort of flying was putting upon him. "I thought this was what you wanted of me."

"You're . . . you're doing . . . great," Rees said in a barely-audible voice as the Lynx seemed to drift perilously close to a hungry-looking cluster of branches.

Then they were down in the designated area, rotors at just below hover speed, waiting for their man to come running.

They saw him break cover, heading for the Lynx. No hits registered.

Pross said: "My little trick must have drawn them off."

"Perhaps," Rees said, sounding unsure. He seemed to have got his normal, mournful voice back. "Hold on," he added softly.

"What's up?" Pross held himself ready for a rapid lift-off.

"I'm not sure. I thought . . ." Rees stopped, clipped off the nightscope from its position near his doorway, put it to his eyes. "Shit!"

"What?" Pross glanced at him.

"Two bloody soldiers, rising behind him. Shit, shit. They left a couple, just in case. Come on, lad," Rees urged the running man. "Come on! Oh balls!"

The running man had thrown up his arms theatrically, falling to the ground. He rolled onto his back, causing the laser detectors on his body to be switched off, and played dead.

The Lynx rose like a startled dragonfly as Pross took it straight up.

"Thinks he's in a bloody film," Rees continued sourly. "Why the bloody hell didn't he check to see he wasn't covered? He should have taken those two out before he began his run. Bloody idiot."

Pross wondered if Rees was talking about Sanders. Whoever had played the part down there, his "death" had left a dry taste in Pross' mouth. It felt like a bad omen.

"The person I'm going to pick up may not be armed," he said to Rees.

Presently, a voice said in the headphones: "Sorry we got your man." The apology was made with gleeful satisfaction.

"Piss off," Rees muttered to himself as he replaced the nightscope he'd still been holding on to. "Let's go home, David. That's our lot."

Pross took the Lynx high, pulled over in a hard left bank, watched the lights of Wales reach above the cockpit. He levelled off, headed for St Athan.

He felt strangely defeated. Would he have taken off with such alacrity if the situation had been the real one? Would he have left his friend, dying with AK bullets in him on an unknown patch of the Chinese People's Republic?

There was only one way he would ever find out.

On the other side of the world, it was just coming up to six in the morning and a shrouding mist, brought by the heavy night

59

rain, hung ethereally across the deep green hills. An ageing RAF Wessex, carrying ten troops on an anti-illegal immigrant exercise clattered in and out of the mist, its tadpole-like shape giving the impression of some monstrous creature darting through the underwater soup of a primeval lake.

The Wessex was not aware of the other creature following it. This one, more sleek, more predatory, looked very much the hunter. From a good mile's distance, it shadowed its prey, flitting swiftly between the curtains of mist, using them and the hills as cover.

Oblivious to this, the Wessex from Shek Kong continued with its flight in the Closed Area and turned north towards the border. It had no intention of straying. Just before it reached the Sha Tau Kok river it turned right, continued along the border, heading east.

The predatory shape followed, still undetected, in the mists.

The Wessex followed the border faithfully, never once straying. Eventually, it came to a body of open water, the Sha Tau Kok Hoi, known to its crew and its passengers as the Stirling Straits.

The Wessex went low, veered north, intending to curve right and southwards on a course that would take it across the scattered islands lying to the northeast of the New Territories. It was looking for small boats, and was forced even lower by the continuing, though thinning mist.

It never made it.

Neither the crew nor the passengers had any warning when out of the wispy curtains the Aphid missile took them broadside on.

The Wessex exploded in a ball of orange fire that seared the mist into invisibility. Pieces of the aircraft and its occupants spread themselves over a wide area before disappearing beneath the uncaring waters.

The Wessex never had the time to get a message off.

The unmarked Mi-24 Hind gunship disappeared into the mists that still existed a mile away, as secretively as it had come.

In the straits the waters had already settled; and the sudden disappearance of the Wessex would eventually baffle those whose job it was to enquire into why it had happened.

Pross drove the Jaguar with some urgency towards Craig Penllyn, though he could find no reason why. He knew it was not just because he wanted to get home to see his family. It was more than that. There was an edginess he could not understand. It was unaccountably very, very important that he got home as quickly as possible.

After they'd landed, Sanders had come up to the Lynx. A soldier had apparently been detailed to play the part of the pick-up. Sanders had apologised for the man's apparent laxity.

It hadn't made Pross feel any better. He felt that the soldier's actions had been more in keeping with someone running for his life in an implacably hostile environment; and as he'd said to Rees, there was no certainty that the fugitive would be armed.

Pross had left St Athan with a handshake from Rees. The Sergeant had said that Pross was a Lynx ace and that he'd fly with him anytime, provided he could keep his heart from leaping into his mouth from time to time; but he'd grinned as he had said it.

Sanders had said that Fowler would soon be in touch with further instructions. They'd shaken hands with the barest civility.

Pross drove through Llanblethian, approaching the B4270 which would take him to Cowbridge. Soon, he'd be home. To hell with Fowler.

He arrived at the wide gate feeling a great sense of relief. The lights in the lounge were on, and all was quiet. He wished Dee had not waited up for him, but felt pleased all the same.

He drove directly into the open garage, turned off the Jaguar's engine gratefully. He got out, stretched, walked to the front door.

Dee was waiting.

His sense of relief almost making him weak at the knees, he gave her a hug that was so tight it drew a muted squeal of protest from her. He kissed her the way he had done on that very first night: with a tenderness that belied the strength of his embrace.

She put her hands against his shoulders to hold him off. "We're being rude," she said.

"Rude?" He stood in the lighted doorway, still holding on to her, trying to make sense of what she had said. "What do you mean, rude?"

"We've got a visitor."

"What visitor?"

Pross felt a surge of irritation. Bloody Fowler. Why did he have to come to the house?

Dee said in a whisper: "Don't look so annoyed. Is that the way to greet an old friend?"

Friend? Fowler was no friend.

"He's not my friend," Pross said in a low grumble.

"He knows you. He said you were old friends from Singapore."

Pross thought his heart was about to jump straight out of his chest; thumping loudly enough for Dee to hear, he was certain.

Ling.

It had to be. Oh Christ oh Christ. Ling had been here all evening with Dee and oh God the *children*.

Pross now felt his legs actually tremble. Dee was looking at him anxiously.

"David?" she began worriedly, her voice still low. "What's the matter? You look as if you've seen a ghost."

He took her by the shoulders, forcing himself to remain calm, to keep his hands from gripping her; to try and hide the terror that was eating away at him.

"The children," he said, fighting the tremor that was about to betray him. "Where are they?"

She couldn't understand. Her eyes said so. "Where they usually are." The eyes searched his face. "That's a silly question, David. What's . . ."

"Go and look. Go and look!"

She stood looking back at him for long moments, the hazel eyes trying to fathom what he was trying not to tell her; then as if something had been communicated to her, she turned abruptly, and ran up the stairs.

He closed his eyes briefly, not daring to think about what she would find, body tensed for the ear-shattering scream he was dreading to hear.

It didn't come.

"We have not harmed the children."

Pross jumped. Ling stood to one side, at the entrance to the lounge.

"Do come in, Mr Pross," Ling went on in a soft voice that carried unspeakable menace within it. "You can't be a stranger in your own home." The foxy face took on a brighter mien as Dee could be heard returning. "David!" he said brightly and loudly. "You old rat. You never told me you had such a charming wife. Diane has been a wonderful hostess while you were out making your hard-earned money." The luminous eyes held no smile, and were quite deadly.

Feeling trapped and looking it, Pross tried to act out the charade for Dee's benefit. He tried to speak, failed, tried again.

By the time Dee had reached them, he was able to say with reasonable control: "And who'd expect to see *you* in Wales?"

"I like surprising people," Ling answered shamelessly. "You know me."

Dee, hazel eyes more confused than ever, said: "Well, now that you two have got together, I'm off." She smiled at Ling. "Do excuse me, but the children tend to wake up long before I'm ready to, *and* they do that every day. No days of rest for mothers, I'm afraid."

Ling smiled. "Ah! Children. Little terrors, but what would we do without them?" He continued to smile at Dee, but the luminous eyes held Pross briefly in a malignant glance. He held out his hand to Dee. "Thank you for being such a charming hostess. David is a lucky man."

"Keep saying that!" she joked, gave Pross a quick kiss. "I know you two will probably get drunk now talking over old times. You must tell me what he got up to in Singapore," she added to Ling.

"Ah! I could tell you such stories!"

Pross listened to the banter, wanting to throttle Ling on the spot.

"You're quite welcome to stay the night," Dee went on to Ling as Pross cringed inwardly with the horror of it. "There's plenty of room."

"I would not like to put you to so much trouble . . ."

63

"It's no trouble. The time has not yet come when an old friend of David's . . ."

"Forgive me for interrupting," Ling said politely. "But what I really meant was that I have already made prior arrangements. Besides, I have a business colleague waiting." Ling was reason personified.

"Well that settles it then. I'll leave you two old campaigners to reminisce. Goodnight."

"Goodnight, Diane."

"'Night, love," said Pross, feeling violated. "See you later."

She left them with a smile.

They watched her climb the stairs, each with a smile on his face; each with thoughts that were totally hostile to the other.

Ling said, still looking up: "Shall we return to the lounge?" The voice was cold. He looked down at last, fixing Pross with a baleful stare.

Pross said: "Why not?"

He'd been trying not to think of it, but reality forced itself upon him. How had Ling made it so easily into his home? Where were Fowler's men? Where was the so-called cover?

"I can see the shock coming into your face now," Ling said calmly as they sat down. "You hid it well from your wife after the initial surprise."

"I'm astonished she let you in. She's not always so trusting with strangers. She's normally quite astute."

Ling smiled without humour. "I can be very charming, and helpless, when I need to be. Those are two of the strongest weapons in my armoury."

Dear God. They could have done anything to her.

Pross could not restrain a shiver.

Ling smiled again. "As you can see, we have done them no harm. The object of the exercise was to show you how easily we *can* do harm."

"People are supposed to be guarding this house."

"Ah yes. Fowler's men." Ling sighed. "Pity."

"Pity?" Pross knew what was coming next, wished he didn't.

"Yes," Ling said. "We had to kill all four of them. Pity." He made it sound as if he'd just run over a hedgehog. "We had to let you know, you see. We had to make sure you realise what you're up against. We had to make you understand that Fowler cannot possibly give you the cover he claims he is able to."

The luminous eyes burned into Pross. "You might as well go to Hong Kong for him, but you'll be working for us. You'll be met there. I know we can count on you. We shall not touch your family . . . unless you step out of line. They will be quite safe here. Forget Fowler's protection. It is non-existent. In a way, he has done us a favour. He has trained you, for us." The foxy countenance broke into another smile. It held no more friendliness than the previous two. "Should you be entertaining the idea of moving your family, my advice to you is don't. We shall take that as a hostile act which could endanger their safety. Are we understood?"

Pross said nothing. Only his eyes spoke the hatred he felt for the man sitting so cockily in his home.

Ling nodded slowly. "We are understood." He got up briskly. "I think I shall go now. I am quite sleepy. Don't bother to see me out."

Pross had made no move and did not look up as Ling went out. He heard the front door shut quietly. Presently, he heard the sound of a powerful motor. They must have parked the red Porsche further down the road so as not to give him warning.

He sat where he was, staring blankly at nothing, trying to come to terms with the fact that his family, his very home, was totally vulnerable to Ling and his crowd. His home had been invaded with the same ease that would be one day employed by the People's Republic of China to re-take Hong Kong. A walkover. He couldn't even count on Fowler.

"Christ," he muttered. "What do I do now?"

And who was Ling? An agent of the Republic? Of the Kuomintang in Taiwan, perhaps? CIA? KGB?

Jesus Jesus Jesus.

Pross looked up suddenly, startled. Dee had entered the room. Her eyes told him she knew everything. She came to him, kneeled on the floor between his legs, threw her arms about him. She was trembling.

"Oh David!" she said in a shaky voice. "I came back down.

I heard it all! The children. Oh God I'm frightened for the children."

He held on to her tightly. "Dee you shouldn't have taken such a risk. He might have seen you!"

"I hid in the lavatory. He didn't know it was there."

"What made you come back?"

"I didn't believe him."

Radar.

Pross shut his eyes. She'd spent all that time with Ling, knowing. The thought sent a bolt of fear through him. Suppose Ling had suspected? He might have thought Dee would call the police and God only knew what reaction that might have provoked.

Pross held on to his wife even more tightly. He had to protect her and the kids. For the moment, the only way to do so was to go along with Ling and to trust the man's word. Pross would sooner trust a wounded viper; but he had little choice.

Dee settled her head against his chest. "Will you tell me now?"

He felt guilty. "I didn't want to worry you . . ." he began.

"I know," she said quietly. "I know. You didn't really think I believed you about the airport, do you? I understand you too well."

Despite himself, he found that he could smile at her words. "What about your offer of hospitality?"

"Oh that." She seemed to have regained some of the bravado she'd used on Ling. "I knew he wouldn't have accepted, being what he is."

"You were taking a hell of a chance," he said to her seriously. "Ling is the sort of person even someone you wouldn't like to meet on a dark night would be wary of."

There was silence for a moment. A car drove along the village street, slowly; too slowly.

Dee gripped Pross with tense hands, her entire body taut, waiting for something dreadful to happen.

The car's engine faded. It did not return: Dee relaxed.

Pross knew it was Ling or Ling's men. They were reminding him he was well and truly on a new hook.

After a while, Dee said: "I want you to tell me about it. I want to know everything. I want to know what we're up against."

So he told her, from the very beginning. She listened in complete silence. She remained silent when he was finished.

"Now," she said at last, "I'm frightened for you."

He looked down at her. "Do you understand that even if Ling had not come on the scene, I could not have left him to the Chinese on the other side of the border?"

"I would not have expected you to." The hazel eyes were quite clear about that. "He's your best friend. *Our* best friend. But Ling is involved, and that makes it even worse. My God!" she said with sudden anger. "These people are so useless." He knew she was thinking of Fowler's mob. "I know it's horrible that those men were killed out there tonight, and I'm trying not to let it sit on my mind or I'd go crazy; but if they'd done their job long before now, they wouldn't have had to drag you into their mess. Oh David. I hate them, I *hate them*! I hate them for coming into our lives." The hazel eyes filmed over.

He held her head to his chest, stroked the back of her neck.

"It always comes, it seems," he said, almost to himself, "no matter where you are, or what you do. Our own little war has come to us. It's the nature of the beast. We are condemned beings." He paused. "All of us on this mad planet; and we seem unable to do anything about it. And that's all the philosophy you're going to get from me tonight," he finished, attempting to cheer her up.

He felt her face move, knew she had smiled a little.

"When will you be leaving?" she asked after a while.

"God knows. I've got to wait on Fowler. He probably doesn't even realise his men are dead."

"Will you tell him about Ling?"

"He'll know who did the killing . . . when he eventually finds out what happened. But I won't tell him Ling came here. God knows who Ling really is. He speaks English with an American accent, but I can detect the Singapore intonations; or maybe it's even Hong Kong. But that means nothing. As Fowler said, anyone skilled enough can fake an accent, so Ling could belong to any one of a number of intelligence groups. It's supposed to be very hard to tell these days, especially out there." Ling, he decided, was probably Taiwanese.

"I wonder what happened, what really happened, I mean; why they were forced to come to you."

"An unholy cock-up, that's what. Where that puts Ling's man, I couldn't even begin to guess. Maybe they want Ling's man dead. They told me the mission had not been an assassination . . ."

"He wouldn't agree to do that, would he?"

Pross knew she was talking about his ex-Phantom pilot friend.

"Of course he wouldn't," he assured her with more certainty than he felt. He knew his friend had killed during the course of his undercover activities. But a deliberate hit? He would not like to bet on it either way.

"What if it's the other way round?" Dee asked, bringing up the unwanted. "What if Ling wants Gordon Gallagher dead, so that *his* man can get out? And now he's got you. He'll use you so that he can kill . . ."

Pross put a hand gently over her mouth. "Shush. We don't know. Let's not torture ourselves about it. Let's concentrate on living through this nightmare and make sure that the kids are safe. I'll take everything else as it comes."

He couldn't tell her how really scared he was. He had a feeling she already knew.

The doorbell rang at precisely 2.05 a.m. Pross was sure of it because he was staring at the clock on his bedside table when it happened. He had been unable to sleep and had dozed fitfully. Ten minutes before, he had woken up in disgust, irritably wondering what to do next, and had switched on the bedside lamp. Dee had turned over sleepily, asked him if he were alright, rolled over again, and had gone out in seconds.

Now, she was sitting bolt upright. "They'll wake the children!" she hissed angrily. It was typical that she should first be angry before being scared. The fear came soon enough. Her eyes stared at Pross. "What do they want now?"

Pross was already climbing out of bed, putting on a short dressing-gown.

Dee said, the fear quite naked in her voice. "You can't go down!"

"If it's Ling," he said, "he's not going to kill me." Yet, he didn't add. "He needs me. If it's Fowler's people . . . well, they're supposed to be on our side aren't they?"

"Oh David. Do be careful." She watched him anxiously. "If I hear anything strange, I'm going to get the chidren."

He stared at her, realising what that would mean. "Alright. If anything funny happens, lock yourself in here with them and call the police."

They might just get to her in time before the door was broken down; assuming the telephone would not have been put out of order first.

He left her, those disturbing, frightening thoughts weighing on his mind. He went down the stairs, strangely without fear for himself. The quiet terror he felt was for his family; for Dee, and for the Dawn Patrol upstairs.

He went to the door, turned on the porch light before opening it. Penleith blinked at him. There was no one else.

"Sorry about the unsocial hour, Pross. Unavoidable. Disaster. Unmitigated. May I?" Pross stood to one side to let him in. "Thanks."

Pross shut the door after a quick peer into the darkness beyond the light. He wondered where Ling's men were. Had they observed Penleith?

He led Penleith into the darkened lounge, turned on a light.

Penleith said as they sat down: "Got a drink, old son? Need it. God. How I need it. Vodka. Neat, if you please."

Pross stood up again to get the drink, handed it to Penleith. The man looked haggard. Pross could well understand why. He sat down again, waited.

"Disaster," Penleith repeated. "Men covering you all dead. Butchered. Bastards. Still. No worry for you. More men. Clean sweep made of village. Nothing. Bastards." Penleith downed his drink in one long gulp. "Butchered. Barbarians."

He was so agitated, Pross almost felt sorry for him; but he reminded himself that these people's trade involved killing if the need arose.

So did mine, once, he thought grimly.

But flying Phantoms was different. If you tried hard enough, you could always persuade yourself it was so and hoped you'd never have to find out the truth.

Pross pointed a finger at the glass. "Would you like another?"

Penleith shook his head. "Thank you. No. One's enough. Just needed a stiffener. Been in this long enough not to be shaken. Four at one go. Rough. Never. Before. Rough." He drew a deep breath, let it out in a sharp rush as if holding it caused unbearable pain. "So. So, Pross. Next move. Got to get you over. Fast."

"How fast?" Pross waited, dreading that Penleith would say now.

Penleith stood up abruptly. "Six o'clock. Get some sleep." He was already moving out of the lounge.

Pross had no choice but to follow.

Penleith was talking on the move. "Came to tell you. More secure than phone."

"But you're tapping me, for God's sake. Surely you can make that secure too?"

"Awkward. Being tapped too. Us."

"Jesus." They were at the door.

Penleith gave what passed for a sheepish smile. It fled almost as soon as it had appeared. "Very complex these days. Tappers being tapped by tappers who are themselves being tapped." Penleith looked as if the unaccustomed length of the sentence had worn him out. "But there it is. Can't be helped. Computers handle it. Going mad. Computers. So. Six o'clock, Pross. Be ready. Goodnight."

He was out the door before Pross could reply. Pross shut the door, locked it, turned off the porch light. He went to the lounge, turned off that light. He decided to leave Penleith's used glass where it was and made his way slowly back up the stairs.

In the bedroom, Dee was wide awake, waiting for him.

"Penleith," he said to her before she had said anything.

"So when do you leave?" No beating about the bush.

"Six."

Her eyes widened, troubled. "This *morning*?"

He nodded.

She put her fist to her mouth, bit on it, closed her eyes. She did not open them as he took off the dressing-gown, dropped it to

70

the floor. She kept them closed as he climbed back into bed. They were still closed when he reached out for her to hold her close to him.

She took her fist away from her mouth to put her arms about him.

"I won't be silly about this," she said. The steadiness with which she tried to speak was betrayed by the slight tremor which sneaked into her voice. "After all, flying Phantoms had its own risks, and you fly those Jetrangers practically every day. You've searched for rock climbers in bad weather, and picked people up from the sea off Barry in gale-force winds. You take risks every day. I . . . I know that. So . . . so I won't be silly. I won't." She was holding tightly on to him, belying every word she had spoken.

"It will be a simple thing," he said gently. "A simple pick-up."

She raised her head to look at him. The hazel eyes could not be fooled.

"Tell me anything you like, but never that. I know it won't be simple. Two years as a service wife was enough to teach me that lesson." He looked so guilty, she kissed him. "I understand why you said it. Thank you. But there was no need." She leaned against him once more. "What else did Penleith say?"

"They've got more men watching the house, and they've also done a sweep of the village."

Dee gave a snort of scepticism that spoke eloquently of her confidence in the capabilities of Fowler's people.

"You and the children will be safe," Pross said.

"As long as you do what Ling wants."

"As long as he *thinks* I'm doing what he wants. I don't as yet know how I'm going to handle it. I'll just have to see what comes up; but I'll take no chances with your lives."

"You can't let him get away with it, David. You can't."

"Dee, as long as it's a choice between the safety of you and the kids and doing what Ling wants, there isn't a choice. Ling gets what he wants. I'm not going to gamble with your lives."

"But David . . . what about . . ."

"I'll try to save him somehow, Dee," Pross interrupted quietly, wondering how he was going to work that little miracle. "I won't leave him behind.

71

She was giving him the full power of her eyes again. "You must promise me, David. You can't let him down. Promise!"

"I promise," he said. He smiled at her. "Besides, how can I let down the man who went through all those flash pilots to get me to you?"

For a brief moment, the worry left her eyes, and she smiled back as she remembered. "You were so nervous! Not at all like the best navigator in the squadron."

"Ah well. We top people do need a little modesty now and then."

"Oh, David. I love you."

"You'd better," he said, and kissed her long, with a great passion.

Their subsequent love-making had all the tender eagerness of the very first time. She screamed towards the end of it.

"Oh God," she said in wide-eyed dismay. "I've woken the children."

"Don't be daft," he said as he started on her again. "They'd sleep through the H-bomb. Come to think of it, most people will."

"David!" She giggled almost hysterically at the unreal quality of the situation. "What a thing to say at a moment like this."

He wanted to keep her mind off what the new day might bring. If this helped, it was worth it. He wondered if this were the last time he would be making love to her.

FIVE

At six o'clock sharp, the unmarked white Rover 3500S pulled up in front of the Pross front door. Pross watched its distorted image through one of the frosted-glass panels in the door. He kissed Dee, went up, opened it. Unbelievably, the Dawn Patrol were still asleep. He had never known that to happen before. He tried to persuade himself there was nothing particularly meaningful about that. It didn't help.

Penleith was the only person in the car. He did not get out.

Pross turned to Dee. "I'll be back before you know it." He'd kissed the kids before coming down. Even that had not woken them. "Look after yourselves."

She nodded, saying nothing, eyes wide, almost staring. He went up to her, kissed her briefly on the lips.

"Bye, love."

He went out without looking back. He carried only a small, flat suitcase with him. It carried all he felt he'd need. He wore a casual, lightweight suit, and looked like a successful executive leaving on a business trip.

He opened the passenger door of the Rover, put the suitcase in the back, climbed in. Penleith nodded at him as he shut the door. The car was moving even as he clipped on his seatbelt. As the Rover turned to nose its way back out, he glanced towards the door; but Dee had already shut it. He knew she'd be looking through a window.

Penleith took the village street at speed, heading north towards the M4.

Penleith said: "Not to worry. They'll be alright. Positive."

Pross refrained from saying what he thought about that.

"Same mistake won't happen twice," Penleith went on, as if to convince Pross. "Count on it. Not again. Definite."

Pross was not listening to Penleith. He was wondering where Ling's men were. Had they seen him leave with Penleith? He tried to put away from his mind the thought of Dee and the kids back in the house, totally vulnerable, despite what Penleith was trying to say. Ling had proved quite conclusively that Fowler's people were wide open to being taken.

He shut his eyes for long moments as Penleith hurled the Rover round the narrow country bends with abandon. His family was being held hostage in his own home, with no kidnappers in sight. It was a very neat piece of press-ganging.

They reached the M4, miraculously without hitting anything. Penleith headed east, took the Rover up to a hundred. Some miles later, they passed a motorway patrol car at nearly forty miles an hour over the speed limit. The police car ignored their blatant infringement.

Pross said: "They've been warned, have they?"

"Yes. All cars have been told to look out. Leave us alone."

"I feel important."

Penleith glanced at him as if to test the words for sincerity. "You are." It was quite seriously said.

Pross glanced behind. There was some traffic, but no one seemed to be keeping up with them. Penleith interpreted the glance for what it was.

"No tail. Been seen to. Anyone doing our speed stopped. Sharpish. Ling won't get a second chance."

Says you, Pross thought grimly as Penleith kept the speed up.

They crossed the Severn Bridge in silence. Every now and then Pross would glance out of the rear window. Penleith might think all was secure but Pross would never forget the ease with which Ling had invaded his house. He fought back the thoughts that kept trying to make him imagine Ling going back to the house and leaving some unknown goon in there with Dee . . .

74

Pross drove the malevolent thoughts out of his mind. Any more of this and he'd be telling Penleith to take him back; which was the very thing he could not do. Either way, he was trapped.

The Rover continued along the M4, cruising at about a hundred and ten now.

"Going to Lyneham," Penleith said.

Pross was well familiar with the RAF's air transport headquarters in Wiltshire. He'd used it during his service days.

"RAF plane," Penleith continued. "Take you. Be in Hong Kong sometime tomorrow. Secure."

Pross did not share Penleith's feeling of confidence, but he said nothing. Every so often, his glance would take in the traffic behind the Rover. There was still nothing attempting to catch up. Everything they passed receded swiftly in the distance.

Just after Junction 18, Pross saw what looked like a Ford of some kind parked on the hard shoulder. Its bonnet was up.

As the Rover flashed past, he felt a twinge of sympathy for whoever the unfortunate person was. He glanced back to be greeted by the receding view of a pair of male buttocks whose upper body seemed to have disappeared into the maw of the engine bay.

"Poor sod," he said as he looked front again. "What a place to break down."

He could not have seen another man lying prone, hidden by the bulk of the car, and the high-powered Steyr sniper's rifle aimed at the Rover; but he would appreciate the man's astonishing accuracy.

The Rover slowed with a suddenness that took Penleith completely by surprise; but remarkably, the car retained some stability even at its high speed as Penleith strove to control it. All Pross could think of was that someone would come along at any moment and go straight into them as they lurched across the three lanes and back again.

Imagine dying in a bloody car crash, he thought angrily as the road ahead weaved, a suddenly maddened ribbon of asphalt.

He felt no fear, that having long given way to a sense of outraged futility. Couldn't Fowler's people even put decent tyres on their cars.

Penleith at last regained control and the Rover limped onto the hard shoulder.

"Wretched pool cars!" Penleith said as they stopped. He took a deep breath, let it out slowly in his relief. He unclipped his belt, climbed out.

Pross joined him to inspect the shreds of the near-side rear tyre. Penleith, he felt, had done a good job in getting the speeding Rover to a safe stop.

Penleith was staring at the wreckage with a lively hatred. He looked at Pross. "Spoke too soon. Now we're on the hard shoulder." He stared at the offending tyre for a brief moment before hurrying back inside. "Wretched pool cars!" he said again as he picked up the radiophone.

Pross looked into the car. "That was a very good piece of driving."

"Better not to have happened." Then Penleith was barking his short, jerky sentences into the phone, much of which concerned the mechanical efficiency of the car pool engineers. None of it was complimentary.

Pross let Penleith vent his spleen on the people at the other end. He stared as a phalanx of cars, all closely bunched in all lanes, roared past, all doing seventy at least. They might have been keeping to the speed limit, but he was glad not to be among them. If one of them suffered the Rover's sudden loss of a tyre, the carnage would be appalling. So much for speed limits.

He watched the disaster area continue on its way looking for somewhere to have its accident until it had shrunk into the distance. He poked his head back into the car. Penleith appeared to have finished bawling at his colleagues. He looked at Pross, eyes angry.

"Wait, they said. Idiots! What else can we do?" Penleith sighed. "Sometimes."

That was when the car rushed up, pulled to a halt across the Rover's nose. Pross straightened up, startled; then he felt horror as he recognised the car that had been stopped on the hard shoulder with its bonnet raised. The horror was compounded as he recognised Ling, hurrying towards the Rover, pistol in hand.

Ling went straight up to Penleith who was fatally too slow to appreciate the danger. A look of utter despair came upon Penleith's face as he looked into the snout of the 9mm Steyr 18-shot GB automatic that Ling was pointing two-handed at him.

Ling fired, five times. Pross jumped with the shock of it. Penleith's face disintegrated all over the interior of the Rover. Pross found himself moving frantically back for fear of getting blood and splintered bone all over him.

Ling came round the car to face Pross. The foxy countenance smiled briefly.

"Do not worry, Mr Pross. I'm not here to kill you. This is just a reminder, to let you know we're still very much in control."

"My wife . . ." Pross began.

"I have given my word. She will not be touched. Your children will not be harmed. No one will go near your family. We are not barbarians, Mr Pross."

Ling smiled again, and was walking back towards the nondescript car before Pross appeared to have realised it. In seconds, the car was moving swiftly away.

Pross stared into the Rover, but made no move to go closer. The thing in there had once been a living man. It had happened so quickly; mere seconds, it had seemed. He could still hear the sounds of the shots; five rapid barks that had cut across his mind. And now Penleith no longer had a face.

Pross was still staring at the car when a police car pulled up. One of the men came across to him. The other went to the Rover.

"*Jesus!*" he yelled when he saw what was in it, and ran over to the verge to vomit.

The one who had approached Pross went across to look, whitened, swallowed, but held on to the contents of his stomach. He turned back back to Pross, the purposeful look in his eye contrasting sharply with the wanness of his visage. His colleague was still retching into the grass verge. Cars were beginning to slow down, their passengers gawping.

"Now, sir . . ." the policeman began.

The arrival of another police car interrupted him. This was not a patrol car, but a plain blue one with a single light on the roof.

The men in it were not in uniform. They climbed out quickly, almost before the car had stopped.

One came straight across to Pross, showed the policeman a card. "Alright. We'll take over. Stop those vultures from poking their noses in. Send them on their way."

"Yes, sir," the policeman said, with evident relief.

"Take a look at your mate too. Looks like he needs some help." It was said kindly.

The policeman went off to see to his colleague. The new arrivals were all over the Rover. One exclaimed: "Shit!"

The man said to Pross: "Mr Pross, is it? Or are you Penleith?"

"Penleith's in there," Pross said in a voice devoid of emotion.

The man glanced back. "Nasty business. Saw who was responsible?"

Pross didn't know who these people were. He fell back on the infallible rule of when in doubt, don't.

"No," he replied. "It happened too quickly. Anyway, they wore masks." Besides, there was no telling how Ling would react.

"They?"

"There were two of them." No harm in that.

"I see."

Another man came up. "Tyre was shot off. High-powered job."

The one who happened to be in charge nodded. He had tiny blue eyes. They remained fastened upon Pross. He was a roundish man: round face, round stomach. Small feet. Pross didn't like big men with small feet.

The man who had come up went away again.

The round man said: "I'm Meaker, Mr Pross. Anti-Terrorist Squad. We were told to cover you."

Pross' eyes were lifeless. "Nice job you did."

Meaker's eyes grew smaller. The impossible had happened. "That was uncalled for, Mr Pross."

"Try telling that to Penleith."

"We were told to keep well back."

You lot couldn't handle Ling with his hands tied behind his back, Pross thought sourly. *While you were hanging behind, he was ahead of you.*

He merely stared at Meaker, and said nothing.

Meaker said: "It would help if you could give us some idea . . . the car they used, the clothes they were wearing . . ."

"It all happened very quickly. I was too busy trying not to get shot."

"You were obviously successful." Nastily delivered.

"Equally obviously, they didn't want me. They knew who they were after."

Meaker pursed his lips. They were round too, and made him look like a small-eyed guppy sucking sweets.

"I hate mysterious murders on motorways, Pross." No mister now.

"So do I, Meaker." Two could play that game. "Especially when I happen to be around when the guns are going off."

"No blood."

"What?"

"No blood on you. None at all."

"We both got out of the car after Penleith had managed to stop it. Then he went back in to radio for assistance. I was looking at the wheel when those people turned up. I took one look at the gun and ducked. As I said, they were after Penleith. Anyway," Pross went on with a touch of irritability, "you're not here to question me. Shouldn't you be taking over from Penleith and getting me to where I'm supposed to be going?"

Meaker's round lips pursed themselves again. "Not me. I'm just a simple policeman on a minding job."

"I'm supposed to stay here?"

The little eyes were unblinking. "Another car will be here presently. In the meantime, my job is to see that you're still in one piece when it does get here."

Pross refrained from saying what he thought about Meaker's ability to keep anyone in one piece if Ling wanted it otherwise.

"Then why the questions? Beyond your brief, isn't it?"

"Nothing's beyond my brief, Pross. A crime's been committed. Police and crime go together."

"In what order?"

Meaker's anger was halted by the arrival of another white Rover.

You'd think they would change the type of car, Pross thought wearily.

The men who got out of the Rover were patently Fowler's men. Brimms, with the out-of-true eyes, was with them. He was the only one familiar to Pross.

Brimms wasted no time. "Right, Mr Pross. Let's go."

"There's a suitcase in the back," Meaker said.

"Mine," Pross said. There was blood and bone all over it. "Leave it. I'll get some other stuff." His passport and wallet were on him. Fowler's people could replace the items in the suitcase. It was the least they could do.

Pross was hurried to the new Rover which set off as if launched from a carrier flight-deck. He didn't have the heart to tell them there was no need for speed. No more attacks would be made; for the time being.

"We're no longer going to Lyneham," Brimms said.

"Oh?"

"We were never going to Lyneham."

"Oh."

"It was a feint."

"Good news for Penleith."

"He knew."

"Make him feel better, will it?"

Brimms' out-of-true eyes turned on Pross. "I don't particularly like you Pross, or your fancy jet-jockey pal over there. I don't know why they keep wanting him on strength."

"Could it be because he's good? Better than the lot of you, perhaps?"

The eyes glared in two directions at once before they returned to zero on Pross. "Your friend has already cost the department five good people, Pross. *Five*."

"I can count."

"Don't get funny with me, Pross. Left to me, I'd send you right back to that sleepy little Welsh village. Amateurs are a pain in the arse in this business. They cause ground clutter."

"I've got news for you, Brimms. Left to me, I'd go back there so fast I'd take your breath away. So you see, on this one thing at least, we're in total agreement."

80

Silence, broken only by the smooth roar of the Rover's engine, descended upon the car. There were four people in it. Pross and Brimms were in the back. The front seats were occupied by two solid-looking men who Pross was certain had been recruited from the police, or perhaps from one of the heavier army mobs.

Bodyguards? Pross thought uncertainly.

During his little chat with Brimms, not a single expression had appeared upon their features.

The Rover swept off the M4 at junction 17, and took the A429 to Cirencester where the A419 took it west into the Cotswolds. Long before Stroud, it left the A419 and, using a series of B-category roads, headed south, though still continuing westwards. Eventually, it pulled into the long drive of a quite imposing, small Georgian manor.

Pross climbed out of the Rover when it had stopped before the bayed front of the building. Pross stretched himself, studied the house. It was two-storeyed, with a huge bay window on the upper floor, supported by four massive columns.

Pross looked about him. The grounds were extensive, and well-kept. From where he stood, the ground sloped gently for some distance before being traversed by a small stream. The beauty of the Cotswolds was all around him.

"Lovely, isn't it?"

Pross turned. Fowler was standing by the columns. He looked as if he belonged there.

"Yours?" Pross asked.

"The Department's. People sometimes come here to rest."

As if it had been waiting for Fowler's appearance, the Rover took off for another part of the property, spitting gravel from its rear wheels. Brimms and the other two went with it.

Pross nodded, looked at him; waiting.

"I'm sorry you had to see what happened to Penleith," Fowler said. His thin-cheeked face took on a sudden careworn expression, as if the mere mention of Penleith's death had aged him further. "He's a great loss to us. One of our best. You may have thought him bumbling, but that was his best asset. It put people off-guard. Penleith could merge himself into the scenery with quite amazing skill. He had a sharp mind, and was exceptionally good with guns. He lived in Greece once, for a whole year, waiting for someone we'd had our eye on to come into the open. He ran a taverna, and had everyone believing he was Greek. When the target eventually showed – a KGB man also masquerading as a Greek – Penleith took him. It was so neatly done that Penleith continued to run the taverna for another six months in complete safety. The owners were sorry to see him leave. He'd made them handsome profits. They gave him a fat bonus and a lot of free brandy."

Fowler smiled abruptly. "Not the kind of obituary you'll read anywhere. Do come in. Can't have you standing out here all day, can we?" He stood aside for Pross to enter, and as Pross did so, added: "I've had some breakfast prepared, seeing you've not had time for a proper one."

As Fowler led the way to the breakfast room, Pross could not help wondering how Fowler managed to take the decimation of his forces with such apparent equanimity. Perhaps that was how it was in the Intelligence fraternity. These were the kind of people his friend had worked with; a breed in their own right.

The table was set for two. Fowler joined him. It was a table laid out for what promised to be a quite substantial meal.

"The condemned man," Pross commented drily.

Fowler was unfolding a napkin, monogrammed. "What? Oh I see. The hearty breakfast. Well, you needn't worry about that. Nothing's going to happen to you."

"I wish people wouldn't keep telling me that. It merely increases the certainty that something will."

Fowler paused in his exercises with the napkin. "Your version of sod's law?"

"Bitter experience."

Fowler looked benignly at Pross. The spectacles completed the illusion. "Do eat."

"I don't think I can. Not after seeing how Penleith . . ."

"If things had happened the other way round, be assured Penleith would not have chucked a good breakfast."

Pross looked shocked. "That's a callous thing to say."

Fowler was unperturbed. "Not at all. It does not make sense to starve yourself over something you can do nothing about. Your

82

fast will not bring Penleith back to life." He raised a hand briefly to stay an interruption from Pross. "Let us suppose that when you flew Phantoms you walked away from a crash . . ."

"I did."

Fowler permitted himself a brief smile. "I know. From your records, it appears that it did not hamper your making off with the top navigator's award. There was also a quite serious accident on your squadron. Both members of the crew lost. You kept flying."

"I couldn't eat properly for days afterwards," Pross said, "and I can't eat now."

Fowler gave in gracefully. "At least have some coffee. It's very good. Even a doctor, I would think, would recommend that you have one."

Pross said: "I'll have the coffee."

"Good. You will excuse me while I eat, won't you?"

"Of course."

Fowler poured Pross the coffee, then filled his own bowl with a mixture of cereals. As he poured the milk carefully over it, Pross found it hard to resist the association with a TV commercial. He drank his coffee slowly, while Fowler ate. The coffee was indeed good.

Fowler did not speak again until he had finished his cereals. He dabbed at his lips, placed the napkin on the table, leaned back in his chair.

"How do you feel?"

"A little better," Pross admitted.

"Good. Brimms will have told you," Fowler continued, "that we had no intention of using Lyneham. We wanted to draw the opposition. The results, unfortunately, were not quite what we expected. You would have been taken to Lyneham, then out again. Different car, but same model, down to the colour. The idea was to get them to follow a flock of white Rovers. Confuse them. Penleith would have brought you here himself. Ling, however, appears to be ahead of the game. Meaker says you did not see their faces."

"I'm afraid not," Pross lied. He wondered whether Fowler believed him.

"Oh well. Can't be helped. Not that it matters. It can only have been Ling, or people working for him."

"Who is Ling exactly, and who is the American? When I last asked you, you said they were not Russian . . ."

"I said I would not presume to call them Russian. Ling – let us call him that, though it is most certainly not his real name – is a new one on us. We have never heard of him before."

"You have my description of him. Why not have him picked up?" It was the last thing Pross wanted.

"Easier said than done. We need to know more about him. He may be the tip of a very large iceberg, and pulling him in will not remove the threat. He is picking our men off, but he wants you preserved; for the time being. He wants to blow our operation . . ."

"He wants someone out. That is what he said when he came to the airport."

"He might as well have said he wanted to fly a kite to the moon. It would be just as believable. He wants our operation. He wants your friend."

"Why?"

"To kill him, of course."

Hearing Fowler confirm what Dee had suggested filled Pross with a sense of despair. The deeper he got into Fowler's operation, the stickier it became.

"But why kill him? What is it about this affair that makes him so important that a group of people are trying their best to make sure he does not get out?"

"I'm afraid I cannot tell you at this stage. It is more than you need to know."

Pross said, angrily: "Don't give me that eyewash. I'm not in the air force anymore. I am here, because you have used emotional blackmail to force me to bail you out of some . . . *thing*, some mission you started which then blew up in your face. You're sending me in blind . . ."

"I'm sending you in to carry out a simple pick-up because you are the only one he will meet. We want him out and yes, it was an important operation. More than that, I repeat, you have no need to know for the moment."

"And Ling? What about him?"

"If I knew that answer to that one, we would have neutralised him by now."

Pross did not believe a word of it. Fowler had as much chance of neutralising Ling as pigs had of doing a slow roll fifty feet above the deck.

"When do I leave?" he asked Fowler.

"Tonight. A chopper will take you to Heathrow. Ling, or whatever his name is, will know nothing of it. You'll be in Hong Kong long before he suspects it. The mission will have been successfully completed while he's still looking for you here."

Says you.

"What about this house? How secure is it?"

"Very. This is a family house," Fowler went on, straightfaced. "Nothing untoward happens here. There are no fences, searchlights and what-have-you to draw undue attention to it. It is hidden in the best possible way: in plain sight."

"It really is your house, isn't it? Why did you hand it over to the Department?"

Fowler said: "It is a rather large place for a man without a family."

Those words gave Pross such an insight into Fowler's make-up that he paused in what he had been about to say. A beautiful house, marvellous grounds, and no one with whom to share it. He wondered if Fowler had ever had a wife, but did not ask. Such a question would have been out of place, and too personal.

Fowler smiled. "Yes. There was someone. Once."

Pross looked at him, surprised, sheepish. "I didn't . . ."

"I know. You didn't ask. But the thought was there. I don't mind. It was a long time ago. Berlin . . . of the Airlift days; but that's another story." Fowler drew a firm veil over whatever had taken place in that beleaguered city all those years ago. "Please do not worry about your own family. We shan't make the same mistake twice."

But the stable door had been shut much too late. Besides, Pross wondered grimly, how do you cover a sniper?

Ling still held all the cards. It was depressing.

Pross said: "I'll need new things. I couldn't take the suitcase out of the car. Not with Penleith's brains all over it."

"Of course. Understandable. Make a list. I'm sure we can pick up whatever you need in Nailsworth, or Stroud if necessary. We foot the bill, of course." Fowler's eyes seemed amused; but it could have been the spectacles.

"Of course." Pross drank some more of his coffee. He'd practically drained the cup.

Fowler indicated the pot. "Help yourself if you feel like it."

Pross did. As he poured a young woman, dressed casually in blouse and skirt, entered with a plate of bacon and eggs. She put it down, took Fowler's unwanted cereal bowl away. Fowler thanked her.

She paused, looked at Pross. "Will you not be wanting breakfast, sir?" Her accent was Northern Irish, much gentler than Pross would have expected.

He shook his head. "Thank you. No."

She smiled at him, left.

Fowler said: "We call her Sian, and when she's not making excellent meals in partnership with our other cook, a man who considers himself better than any London chef, she drives some of our . . . er . . . visitors around. She's met your friend. She's an excellent shot. All the staff are. May need to defend themselves one day. Sian can take your eye out at fifty paces with a 9mm auto faster than you could blink. I've seen her do it."

"Where? Across the water?"

"No," Fowler said, and did not expand on that.

"Is all this supposed to make me feel safe?"

"That depends. She'll be flying to Hong Kong with you."

Pross stared at him. "I thought no one was travelling with me."

"No one's going on the pick-up with you. Getting to Hong Kong's a different story altogether. You may need someone with Sian's skill. Less obvious, I feel, if you're accompanied by a woman. Even in this day and age, people still find it hard to credit a woman with shooting skills. In our trade, that's an asset . . . depending, of course, upon who you're up against." Fowler tucked into his bacon and eggs.

86

Ling, Pross knew, would not think twice about taking the young woman out, if she got in his way.

Fowler paused long enough to say: "You're looking anxious again."

"In my shoes, you would be."

"It would probably give you a feeling of greater confidence if you did a little gun practice yourself."

"No way," Pross said firmly. "The less I've got to do with those things, the better."

"Strange sentiments from a man who once flew one of the most lethal pieces of weaponry ever devised; but I do have some sympathy. I hate the damn things myself."

They didn't speak again until Fowler had finished his meal. The aroma had tempted Pross, but not strongly enough to make him call for a plate. He thought that perhaps later he would be able to forget Penleith's shattered face long enough to get some food down.

SIX

She called herself Mary Chi, but that was only to Europeans who were either too ignorant or too lazy to pronounce her real name, Chi Mui Li, properly. She had long since tired of trying to tell them how to say it. After all, she pronounced their names properly, giving them the respect that should always be given. She expected the same respect in return. It was only natural.

She felt no real sense of hostility, only a slight measure of sadness. It was a continuing thing between the West and the Orient. She wondered whether it would ever change. Such things had occupied her mind greatly in recent weeks, ever since she had met the photographer from England who had told her he'd come to take glossy pictures of the New Territories. They had gone to a party where an air force man in a bid to impress her, had claimed to know him, saying he was a Phantom pilot. The air force man had pestered her at every opportunity when her escort's back was turned. She grimaced with displeasure, remembering.

Then the photographer had returned to England. She had missed him for a while, philosophically accepting she would never see him again. Unbelievably, he had returned to Hong Kong; but he had not been exactly pleased to see her again. She'd got the impression that Hong Kong was the last place he'd wanted to be; then had come the strange news that he'd gone across the border, and was still there. That was what the men had said. They had also known he had been in the air force.

Mary Chi sighed, and wondered what she'd got herself into.

She had an interesting history. Hong Kong born, her father's people had fled to the colony during the 1911 uprising that had ended the rule of the Qing dynasty. Cantonese from Guangzhou, they had vague ties in Changsha, the very source of the great revolution.

Her mother's people had come much later, during the war between the erstwhile allies, the Communist Party and the Kuomintang. Her mother's family, she'd been told, had their roots in the far northwest region of Xinjiang; border people who claimed descent from Alexander the Great's army. She'd always smiled at that, though there was one factor about her she could not deny. A recessive gene, ploughing through the centuries, sometimes made her smile waver into a thoughtful expression.

Mary Chi had startling blue eyes.

Throughout her young life, she'd had to cope with the reactions this had produced. Her mother had seen it as vindication of her own belief in her Greek ancestry. Mary secretly thought it was more probably Russian, considering how close the high, majestically beautiful mountain regions were to the northern giant. Who knew what mixes had taken place down the years? Border areas were the same everywhere. China itself was a vast mix of groupings. A Kazak did not look like an Uygur, but both were Chinese nationals, and shared the northwest regions.

At twenty-four, she held an executive post with a vigorously-expanding electronics firm. She had planned her life well. It was under her control, and she knew where she was going.

She was of good height, about five-foot-seven, again due, her mother always insisted, to that far-flung Greek blood. Her body did not have the slender, willowy shape that many Westerners had come to see in the Chinese woman as confirmation of the stereotyping that dwelt in their minds.

There was, instead, a greater fulness to her body that gave her a devastating feline grace. Her hair was a gleaming blue-black, and her features were a delicate blend of her exotic ancestry. She was a thing of beauty, at once vulnerable, yet strong. She wore light-reactive spectacles; but they were totally unnecessary. Her eyes were perfect. The glasses were both for defence, and offence.

She had long since discovered that the best way to avoid unwanted comments about her eyes was to hide them. Behind glasses, eyes tended to lose significance for most people. As offensive weapons in business, they were highly potent. Many was the deal she had clinched by the mere removal of her fake glasses.

She glanced at her watch. Nine o'clock. Time to be going home. There was a knock on her door.

"Yes?" she called in English. Probably Tommy Ho, she thought. He usually worked as late as she, and was always trying to take her out. Apart from the fact it was strictly against her policy to go out with colleagues, Tommy was not her type, much as she liked him. He was good to talk to, but that was it.

The man who pushed open the door to her office was not Tommy Ho. It was a man she'd hoped never to see again. He was followed by the other who had accompanied him the last time. Both were Chinese.

She was furious. "What are you doing here?" She used English.

He answered her in Fujian, instead of the more widespread Cantonese. "I didn't realise we needed your permission." It was cockily said.

"I don't understand what you're saying," she lied. Her mother had taught her.

"We don't need your permission," he said, this time switching to English. His accent was pure public school. He glanced at his silent partner. "Do we?"

The partner remained silent, gave Mary Chi a continuing stony look.

She looked from one to the other, trying not to seem afraid. She kept her glasses on.

"I'm very busy," she said, "as you can well see. I have plenty to do before tomorrow."

The man smiled. "A go-ahead little capitalist."

"Did you come here to give me a political lecture?"

"No. I leave such things to the Comrades in Beijing. Political lectures bore me. But don't tell them that."

She didn't smile.

"Have you further thoughts on our last conversation?"

he asked. The smile was still there, but the voice had grown cold.

"I understood nothing of what you said to me."

He sighed. "Miss Chi. You are very settled here, are you not? Executive position, gained because of a good education – in Europe, no less – and a comfortable bourgeois background. You live in a flat that possesses a certain degree of luxury, and you drive a BMW. As I've said very settled. It would be quite terrible to lose all that."

"You cannot threaten me. I am Hong Kong born."

"Hong Kong is *China*! Never forget it. You exist by the grace of the People's Republic. We can erase you at any time. Your family's background is well-known to us." He suddenly reached forward to remove her glasses. The blue eyes stared up at him, unafraid. "Very pretty," he commented. "For a Russian."

He put the glasses down, walked out. His partner followed him.

Mary Chi stared at the glasses before picking them up and slowly putting them back on. She was not sure whether she should feel fear. Two days before, this roly-poly man with the chubby, baby-like face and his sharp voice had come into her life.

She had been about to get into her car when he'd swaggered up to her, telling her he'd had urgent news for her. Thinking it had been something to do with her mother – her father having died a year ago in a boating accident off High Island – she had waited for him to continue. Then had come all sorts of questions about the photographer. She had professed ignorance. It was obvious they had not believed her. What could they possibly want of her?

She collected some papers she wanted to work on later, put them carefully into her briefcase. She shut the case.

How had they got into the building? She had a feeling she should be frightened of them; but for some reason, fear had not yet come to her. She knew why. She was too well insulated. The two men were beings on the extreme periphery of her life. How could they affect her? She would have been more frightened of a bona fide Hong Kong criminal.

She wondered whether she should contact the police. How could agents of the People's Republic operate so freely?

91

The question was answered in her mind almost immediately. Of course they could, and with the greatest of ease. She was being naïve.

She picked up the briefcase, turned off the lights, left the office. As she took the lift down, she again wondered what she should do, decided to go and see the one person she really trusted: her mother.

As she left the building, she thought the security man looked guilty, but wasn't sure. Had he been bribed to let them in? She'd never be able to accuse him.

She went out to her car, a new BMW 323i. She found herself becoming tense as she approached it, almost expecting to be accosted by the two men. But no one stopped her. Droplets of water touched her face. Rain.

She climbed in, started the car. She would drive to Kowloon to talk with her mother. Perhaps she would then know how best to handle this problem. Tiny splashes on the windscreen sparkled in the night.

She drove to Wan Chai to take the cross-harbour tunnel to the mainland. She took it easy, allowing herself time to think. To anyone watching, she seemed a rather studious executive type, occupied with the problems of business. She beat the rain to her mother's house.

Her mother greeted her with reserve, apparently unsure how to cope with this daughter who had turned out to be anything but traditional Chinese. Tea was made, which was taken formally.

"This is unexpected, Mui Li," her mother began, in Cantonese. "I am always pleased to see you, but so late after your work tells me you have great cares. Is it the work?"

Mui Li shook her head. She had taken off her glasses. She never hid her eyes from her mother.

"I have been approached by two men. Twice, in two days. They are Comrades."

Her mother made a sharp sound that was very close to one of pain.

Mui Li stared at the older woman. "Mother? Are you ill?"

"No. No." The voice was almost a whisper. "The Comrades. I had hoped . . ." The words tailed off.

Mui Li said: "What do you mean? Do you know these people?"

She could not believe it. What had those two men to do with her mother who'd never made a political statement in her life?

"What did they want to know?" her mother asked at last. There was a very real fear in her voice now.

Mui Li was greatly puzzled. Why was her mother looking so frightened? What had she hoped for?

With these thoughts tumbling through her mind, Mui Li said uncertainly: "They wanted to know about my friend from England."

It was now her mother's turn to look puzzled. "The one from the air force?"

"He is no longer with the air force. But the men . . . the Comrades said he had gone over the border. They wanted to know why. They seem to think I should have this information."

Her mother was looking frightened again. "You have told them he was with the air force?"

"They already knew. I said nothing. I *know* nothing."

"That is at least good. Perhaps they will leave you alone." There was little hope in the older woman's voice. She clearly expected the worst.

Mui Li said: "You must tell me why you are frightened. It is not only to do with me, is it?" The startling blue eyes that had unnerved so many were now fixed upon her mother.

The older woman looked away, anguish upon her face. Mui Li became alarmed.

"Mother! What is it? You must tell me! Are you in danger from them?"

The mother, Ching-Li, took a long time replying, seeming to wrestle with something within her before trusting herself to speak.

At last, she said: "My daughter, I had hoped the day would never come when I would have to say this to you." She looked away from Mui Li as she spoke, unlike her daughter's almost disrespectful habit of staring directly into the eyes. "Before my parents came across, we lived over the border in Guangdong. Some of the family were Kuomintang, others not. My parents were, so we left, in 1949. I was twelve years old, by the Western calendar. I had already taken some political instruction, unknown to my parents, and did not share their ideology. However, I obeyed them, and came across.

"For many years, I maintained contact. I was told that I must remain here, and that one day I would be needed, when Hong Kong was again restored to its rightful place within the Republic. And then, I met your father."

Mui Li listened to all this in growing wonder. She could hardly believe she was listening to a woman who was the epitome of one whose husband had been immensely successful in a capitalist society. She remained silent, her blue eyes wide, waiting for her mother to continue.

"The attraction," Ching-Li went on, "was powerful and immediate. We met during the Dragon Boat. I found him very exciting to talk to. But he was a Kuo, though not the kind on Taiwan. He believed in Sun Yat-sen's ideals and we spent many hours discussing them. It was not long before I began to agree with him. I agreed that the original Kuo had admirable principles before it became corrupt. Of course we argued. It would have been unnatural otherwise; but in the end, my love for him led to my neglect of the Comrades over the border. I kept less and less in contact until at last, all contact ended. They did not try to force me to recommence, and I was greatly relieved.

"Your father and I were married and he went on to prosper in his business which took him both to the Republic and to Taiwan. When you were born, we were made very happy. I saw your blue eyes and knew my ancestors had smiled upon us. I was determined that you would be given the best chances." Here, Ching-Li permitted herself a rueful smile. "You have exceeded even my expectations. I was also determined that you would not be lost to the Republic." Another rueful smile. "I had changed." Ching-Li looked about her. "I had also grown to like this. The romance in the child had given over to the appreciation of reality, without turning from the customs of our people."

Mui Li knew this was a side-swipe at her own independent life-style, but chose not to interrupt her mother, knowing instinctively that more startling revelations were to come.

"I did not know," Ching-Li continued, "that your father also did small services for the Kuo on Taiwan . . ."

Mui Li could not contain herself, and committed the unpardonable breach of cutting across her mother's words. "*What?*"

Ching-Li appeared to ignore this apparent disrespect. "It was nothing very dangerous, nothing complex; but they were still services. The Kuo wanted impressions about the eventual take-over of the Territories, and how that would affect Taiwan. Your father was well-respected by both sides as a businessman. It was felt that those in the Republic would feel at ease with him and talk freely in general conversation. Then last year, it all changed. He began to seem worried. I do not know why, but I believe the Kuo asked him to do something that became dangerous. He never told me about it. That is why I am so sure. It was too dangerous for him to tell me who was closer to him, even in business, than his own colleagues. He would discuss every plan with me before putting it to the company; but of this one thing, he would not speak." Ching-Li paused, as if for breath.

Mui Li said, as if afraid of what she would hear in return: "Mother, did they kill my father?"

The older woman did not reply for some time during which Mui Li's troubled eyes searched her mother's face, the finely-shaped features that had a blend of Samarkand and the Pamirs within them struggling to remain composed.

Ching-Li finally looked at her daughter. "I have no proof of this but equally, I do not believe his death to have been an accident. Someone killed him; either the Kuo, because he would not do as they asked and therefore knew too much, or the Comrades, because they caught him."

Mui Li closed her eyes. They felt hot, but she was determined not to cry. She'd had a very special love for her father. He'd been so unlike other Chinese fathers – if the comments of her various friends had been anything to go by – he had been more of a friend than anything else. It was her mother to whom she'd normally extended the traditional codes of behaviour; but now it seemed she'd known neither her mother, nor her father, at all.

The Marine Police had found his speedboat drifting in Rocky Harbour between Kau Sai Chau and High Island. No one could explain how it had got there. The weather had been perfect that day. His body had never been found. The most favoured theory had been that he'd somehow fallen overboard, hit his head on a convenient rock, and had drifted unconscious out into the South China Sea; to be eaten by the fishes.

She felt the trickle of tears, wiped them impatiently. *Oh, father.*

Ching-Li saw her daughter's tears and reached foward to wipe them gently away.

"I wish," she said, "that I could have spared you this distress. You were very special to him."

Outside, some of the 870 millimetres of rain that would deluge the colony over the next five weeks, began to pour.

Ching-Li said: "You must stay tonight. I do not want you driving back in this. Will you stay?"

She nodded. She had not felt like going home anyway.

"Your room is as you left it," her mother said. "Nothing has been disturbed."

Even after two years.

The rain continued to fall, its all-enveloping roar seeming to shut them completely off from the outside world. Mui Li always liked to listen to the rain from a cosy shelter. As a child, she used to hide under a sheet and pretend there was no one else around; only she, and the rain. It would seem to become one with her, the rushing sounds matching those of her blood through her veins and arteries. The rain made her feel safe.

The phone rang.

Daughter and mother looked at each other, wondering who it could possibly be. Ching-Li left her seat to pick up the instrument. She caught it in the middle of the fifth ring.

"We would not have stopped ringing, Comrade," the voice said in Cantonese.

Ching-Li flinched. Her face, an older image of her daughter's, but without the blue eyes, suddenly looked far older than her years. Mui Li was instantly on her feet. She went across to her mother.

"Please allow your very beautiful daughter to speak," the voice continued in Ching-Li's ear. The phone trembled in her hand as she passed it wordlessly to Mui Li.

Mui Li stared questioningly at her mother as she took the receiver. "Yes?" she began hesitantly. Involuntarily, she had spoken in English.

"Even the capitalist tongue comes to you instinctively," the voice said, still in Cantonese. "Be at the main entrance of your place of work at midday tomorrow. You will be met. There are things to discuss with you. Do not keep us waiting." The line went dead.

Outside, the rain continued to hurl itself at the earth. Mui Li put the phone slowly down. They had followed her. She closed her eyes briefly, felt herself tremble as her mother put a comforting hand to her shoulder.

She listened to the rain. Safe, she had thought.

The helicopter rose swiftly into the darkness, a strange, thrumming insect of the night. Pross looked down at the receding shape of Fowler's manor, a darker silhouette etched out from the surrounding landscape by the few lights showing within the grounds.

The helicopter winged over, and view of the building was lost. He made himself relax. He was not a good chopper passenger. There were very few people he liked being piloted by, especially in helicopters. He suffered the airlines, because there was little else for it; and when he'd been on fast-jets, he'd been comfortable with only one pilot. Now, he was off to try and pull that very man out of what looked like the kind of situation they would have both run away from; if they'd had the choice.

Would either of them come out of it alive? he wondered.

"Of course you will."

Pross looked at Sian Logan, his fellow passenger. He had not realised he'd spoken his thoughts.

He said, sheepishly: "Thinking aloud."

She seemed to smile in the subdued light within the machine, touched his shoulder briefly. "Don't be embarrassed. It would have been very strange if you had not thought it. It's the same thing that kept you alive when you were on Phantoms. Deep down inside, you know that."

She was dressed to look like the wife of an executive, even down to engagement and wedding rings. The change in her appearance had surprised Pross. She had metamorphosed from being an almost invisible person about Fowler's home, to a woman of quite startling attractiveness. He had noticed she had pale green eyes, and a constellation of freckles that curved from the corner of one eye, down the cheek and across to the bridge of the strong nose, over to the other cheek and back to the corner of the other eye. It was an unusual pattern that gave her an oddly elfin look. Yet she was not a small woman, but was tall, and strong-looking. Her tanned, bare legs were a source of constant wonder to the male personnel, he'd been told.

But they all knew, as well as he did, just how deadly she was. No one took liberties with her. He knew that within her innocuous handbag she carried a short-barrelled revolver of blued steel; a powerful, man-stopping .357 Ruger magnum. Fowler had assured him she could use that cannon with breath-taking accuracy; yet he found it hard to equate the elegant, soft-spoken woman sitting next to him with such destructive power.

He knew his own prejudices were responsible for this. Sian Logan was no Dee; but given a different set of circumstances, could Dee have become as deadly with a gun, and Logan the warm, caring mother and wife? But Logan was warm too, and probably would one day be just as loving a wife and mother if she chose to be; if she lived long enough.

He looked down at the darkened earth, punctuated by flares of light, galaxies that spread out from the massive concentration of other absorbed galaxies that was London. One day, he thought, it would be possible to fly from Edinburgh to London without once seeing a patch of darkness. One massive city, flaring continuously into the night that would flee before it. From 40,000 feet, the whole country would look like a glowing jewel in the blackness of the ocean.

The small helicopter, one similar to the Prossair Jetrangers, landed unobtrusively inside the Heathrow perimeter. A car was waiting. As they climbed out of the machine, Pross noticed

Logan opening her handbag. The light was poor, so he wasn't sure.

She must have seen his look, for she said: "You never know. Can't be too careful."

The Jetranger's whipping noise at idle changed to full rotor-induced *thrumm* as it lifted off and disappeared into the dark of the sky. They were alone with the car. No one had come out of it.

Pross stood, slightly irresolute, the new case with new clothes that Fowler's people had got him in one hand, and Logan's own case in the other.

She said, quietly: "We wait till they move."

"Ling couldn't have known about this surely." Pross suddenly felt very naked. "Even if he did, why would he want to kill me here? He could have before, and he chose not to." He found he was whispering.

"Always assume a hostile to be hostile," she said. "Was that not how you worked with your Phantom? If Ling's people are in that car, the fact that they have not yet shot at us means they want something else. Me. Alive."

He didn't like the way she'd said that.

"I'd be another bargaining counter," she explained.

"Do they know who you are?"

"Probably not. But they'd play safe. For all they know, I may be just someone sent with you to play the part, while your real minder is hidden among the passengers. Then again, I may not be."

"We can't stand here forever." Barest seconds had passed. "We've got a plane to catch."

"They should have come out to us by now," she said calmly, but there was a hint of tenseness in her voice. "*Drop!*" she hissed suddenly, pushing him down.

He needed no encouragement. They both hugged the ground. He knew without looking as he tried to flatten himself into the rough earth near the peritrack, that she'd pulled out the magnum and was pointing it at the car.

Nothing happened.

Not again, he thought wearily. *Ling couldn't have found this out.*

Still nothing.

"I'll have to go and look," Logan said.

"What? You don't know what's waiting for you. Besides, I can't let you do that."

He heard what he thought was a sigh.

"Let's not get silly about this, Pross," she said in a low voice in her soft Irish accent. "You were an excellent Weapons Systems man on Phantoms. Oh yes. I know your record. You know how to handle a chopper, and from reports we've had, you can make a gunship do cartwheels. This, is *my* job, and I know how to do it. So let's forget all about your letting me do anything. I'm a big girl now, and I really can take care of myself. Do please stay here while I go and check what's going on. Don't try and follow me. You'll only get in the way."

So saying, she slipped off her shoes and vanished in the gloom, leaving a chastened Pross behind.

"That will teach me to open my big mouth," he said to himself.

Now and then, he thought he could see a swiftly moving form, but he wasn't sure. Logan was wearing a sleeveless, pale-grey, lightweight dress that made her practically invisible. He turned his head slowly. All about him, the airport glowed with countless multi-coloured points of light; but where he lay was in shadow. He strained to hear her, over the continuing noise of aircraft movements.

He tried to orientate himself, wondering which part of the airport this was. He could see the cluster of the terminal buildings in the distance. A major road ran beyond the perimeter to his right. The A4, he decided. There was also a line of buildings ahead and to the right. He knew Heathrow well enough. Apart from knowing it from the air and from air force photographs, he'd used it often enough. He was at the eastern end of the airport. Runway 1 was a little to his left. Shouldn't the place be crawling with security patrols?

He tensed. A shape was coming up to him. Logan.

She dropped silently next to him. "Bad news," she whispered. He knew it with a sense of foreboding, before she went on: "Two of them. Dead. Shit!" she added exasperatedly.

He said nothing, allowing her the silence to think out the next move. Besides, there was a hard knot in his stomach. He still could not believe that Ling had somehow managed to get ahead of Fowler yet again. So where were Ling's men now? Watching from seclusion? Christ. They could be anywhere.

"You don't mind my swearing?" A strange question from Logan.

It surprised him. "No. Should I?"

"You never know with some men."

"You ought to hear Dee when she gets going."

"Ah yes. Your wife."

"Yes."

"If she were here, I'd tell her not to worry. I'll get you out of this."

He was suddenly worried for her. It was an unenviable responsibility. "Don't get killed trying."

He thought he heard a stifled laugh. "Worried about me, Pross?"

"Yes . . . and," he added quickly, "not just because you're a woman. Eight people have died since this began . . ."

"They didn't die because of you."

"Because of whom then?"

"Not of whom. Of what. A fucked-up mission." She went on, almost defiantly: "Does Dee . . . your wife . . . use such words?"

"Worse."

"I don't believe you."

"I'll prove it to you. You'll have to meet her."

There was a definite chuckle. "You've got faith, Pross." He saw her pick some things up, put them in her bag.

Her low-heeled shoes.

She said: "Can you manage alright with our bags?"

"Yes. They're not heavy."

"Right then. We'd better get moving. If they're out there waiting, they're prepared to hang about. So it's our move. We're not touching the car, just in case."

They stood up slowly, cautiously. Nothing happened.

"Your feet," Pross said as they began to walk.

They did not hurry. Logan was totally alert. She walked with the magnum pointing downwards from her left hand.

"What about my feet?"

"You could step on anything; broken glass, rusty nails . . ."

"Even dogshit." He could almost hear the smile in her voice. "Anyway, if the airport people have done their job, no dogs should have got in. Don't worry about my feet. They can take care of themselves."

They continued to walk, and nothing continued to happen.

Pross said, after a while: "That accent's not Belfast, is it?"

"No," she said, and did not expand.

They walked on. Suddenly, she pushed him vigorously so that he went stumbling forward.

"*Down!*" she screamed. "And don't get up! Just stay down there out of my way!"

Several things were happening at once and vaguely, as he pressed himself to the ground for the second time that night, he was aware of the sudden roar of an engine; the startling blaze of lights; the silhouetted figure of Logan bringing up her magnum two-handedly.

Christ, he thought. *I can't leave her to handle this on her own.*

As if aware of the thoughts in his mind, she bawled: "*Stay down!*"

He would never forget the stark picture of Logan standing pinned by the lights of the fast-approaching vehicle, looking dreadfully vulnerable; one fragile, soft, human body pitted against a hurtling mass of metal.

Then the magnum roared three times, with incredible rapidity. The lights went out. The magnum tore the night with a second burst of three, then Logan dropped.

At first, he thought she'd been hit; but the vehicle was yawing crazily away from her. The further it went, the wilder its swings became until it suddenly teetered on two wheels before turning completely over and over. It hit the concrete in a shower of sparks that sprayed brief beams of lights in every direction. Then it exploded in a bright ball of orange that seemed to rocket upwards on a tail of fire that stretched like an umbilical cord as the ball got smaller. It got thinner and thinner, then snapped. The ball vanished. Flames continued to lick about the wreck.

What had seemed to take an immeasurable length of time had lasted for fleeting seconds, Pross realised. Although Logan had seemed pinned in the lights forever, she had in fact been far too quick for whoever had been in the vehicle. They had not had the time to fire at her. She had not hesitated, and had struck with the speed of an attacking snake.

Pross said: "How did you know? It could have been an airport security patrol."

"Couldn't have been." She seemed to be breathing deeply. "They were warned to keep away from the area."

"Just in case?"

"Just in case."

Pross looked to where the vehicle continued to burn. "Well, that will bring them running."

She gave a little cough. "We needed a lift anyway." She coughed again.

Pross didn't like the sound of it. Was she wounded, after all? Had they fired, and he'd not heard because of the noise? They might well have used silencers.

Logan coughed again.

"Logan! Are you okay?" He reached out to touch her.

She did not move away. "I'm alright. I just did something quite silly. I've swallowed some dust. Did it when I dropped."

He moved his hand quickly, not wanting her to get the wrong idea.

He heard her say: "It's alright, Pross. I won't bite." There was definite laughter in her voice.

He smiled to himself, said: "You were bloody amazing."

She was looking towards the wreck. "I wasn't bad, was I?"

"Not bad at all." He would remember it forever.

He began to get up. Without looking, she put out a hand to stay him.

"Not yet," she said. Then she seemed to be fumbling with something on her body as she leaned on one side, back to him.

The available airport lighting, aided by the fire of the burning vehicle enabled him to see her quite clearly, but he could not see what she was doing. Presently, he heard the clicking of bullets going into the chamber of the magnum. She was re-loading.

"Where did you get bullets from?" he asked, astonished.

"My knickers," she answered, almost giggled. "My upper

thighs," she went on more seriously. "I've got garters that carry six bullets each; but keep it a secret."

"Bloody amazon," he said. "You don't expect more of them, do you? Nobody got out of that."

She was holding the gun ready. "You never know. If you'd just been in a fight in your Phantom, would you relax before you'd made it back to base?"

"No," he admitted.

"Well then. Ah. Here come the cavalry."

He looked. In the distance, three separate sets of winking blue lights were converging on the area. One set streaked towards the wreck. Pross could make out the shapes of fire-engines. The other two sets, made up of smaller shapes, came towards them, headlamps blazing.

Logan stayed down until the newcomers were practically upon them; then she said: "Might as well let them see us. We wouldn't like to be run down."

They stood.

The headlamps dipped violently under sudden braking, and the cars fanned out, surrounding them. There were six in all. Men piled out, some in uniform.

"Logan!" It was Brimms. He rushed up to them. "What the bloody hell happened?" He was obviously senior to her.

Logan said calmly: "Ambush. Challon and Jennings are dead. We left the car alone. Go and look."

Brimms looked stunned. Pross couldn't see the out-of-true eyes properly. The men from the cars had spread out.

Brimms said: "But we got the all-clear from Challon. He confirmed your landing, and the departure of the chopper. He even said Jennings had left the car to meet you."

"It certainly wasn't Challon who spoke to you. He was dead by then."

"But his voice! I recognised his voice."

"Somebody is good with accents. That's all I can say, sir. It would be even easier over the radio."

Brimms looked unhappy, Pross thought; but Fowler's man nodded, reluctantly accepting what Logan had said.

Brimms said: "Your flight's been held back. Obstruction on

104

the runway." He looked towards the wreck, and Pross thought he had a grim smile on his face. He turned back to look at Pross. "The dead appear to follow you, Mr Pross." Then he was again talking to Logan. "A car will take you directly to the plane. All documents are on the back seat." He seemed to be peering down. "Your shoes. Where are your shoes Logan?"

"Pross has them; in my bag." She was quite unperturbed.

"Put them on when you get in the car."

"Yes, sir." She was looking at Pross who got the distinct impression that the unseen green eyes were looking at him in conspiratorial exasperation.

Brimms pointed to a car. "That one will take you to the aircraft."

They began walking towards it.

"Oh Logan."

They paused, looked back.

Brimms said: "Nice work, Logan."

"Thank you, sir." Her voice said thanks for nothing; but Brimms either didn't note it, or didn't care. "I think, sir," she went on, "you ought to tell Mr Fowler we're leaking very badly."

She turned and walked on to the car. Pross followed, leaving Brimms staring after them.

In the car, she put the gun away, but left her shoes in her bag. The documents were there. She put them into it. "Sod him," she said.

Pross said nothing until the car drew up by the waiting aircraft. She put her shoes on then. The aircraft was not British Airways.

He said, as they went up the steps: "Your favourite person, is he? Brimms?"

They were allowed to keep their luggage in the cabin. No one searched them, and the places they were shown to had no one close by.

It was not until they were strapped into their seats that she commented upon what he had said.

"Brimms is of the old school of thought. There are two places for women: in the kitchen, or on their backs."

"You call that thinking?"

She smiled suddenly, patted his hand. "You're alright, Pross." The aircraft began to taxi. "Italy, here we come."

"Italy? I thought it was Hong Kong."

"It still is. We're breaking the journey. It's all been arranged. But once we're in Italy, I'm going to change things."

Pross stared at her. "Christ. Fowler . . ."

"Sod Fowler. Sod Brimms. We're leaking at the seams. Every move we've made has been matched. My job is to get you to Hong Kong. I'll do it my own way."

Pross wasn't sure he liked the idea of trying to make it to Hong Kong without the cover of Fowler's organisation, despite the fact their security seemed to have more holes than a sieve. Dead people all over the place and Ling apparently knowing everything in advance was not a recipe for confidence. At the same time, Fowler's organisation went through bureaucracy like a hot knife through butter. With the best will in the world, Logan would not come near.

The aircraft reached its hold position at the end of the runway, then it began its take-off run. Soon, it was rearing its nose into the sky in the classic high-angle Heathrow take-off.

Pross said, as the plane gained height: "Won't that be leaving us a bit naked?" The warning lights went off, and he undid his seat-belt.

She said: "What do you think we were back on the ground if not naked? We were ambushed where we shouldn't have been."

"So how are you going to do it? They didn't search us for guns when we came aboard. Presumably that was because Fowler had fixed it. If we move from under his umbrella, that's one little service you'll lose. I don't fancy an Italian jail. You can say goodbye to Hong Kong if that happens."

She gave him a secretive smile. "I'll work something out."

He hoped so. If getting to Hong Kong carried such mayhem in its wake, what was the actual mission going to be like? He could not understand why Ling was attacking Fowler's people with such continuing ferocity. He could understand the first terrifying warning; but these attacks seemed almost wanton.

Unless there were other reasons that he could not even begin to guess at. It could be Ling's way of letting him know he was on the firing line should he decide to risk warning Fowler; keeping

106

him on his toes, no matter how many people had to die to make the point.

Or it could mean there were others in the game.

He found himself shivering. What if tonight's ambush had been meant for him too? What if this other group, if indeed there was one, did not want him in Hong Kong at all?

Logan was looking at him: "You look like a man with indigestion. Don't tell me you've worked it out." Her eyes raked the cabin, seemed to satisfy themselves there was no one hostile about.

"Another group?" he suggested, voicing his fears and hoping he was wrong.

"It's possible." She sounded very calm.

"Doesn't it worry you?"

"A lot of good that would do."

It had been so different, he remembered, in the Phantom. You knew your risks. You were at risk every time you climbed into it. An aircraft could fall out of the sky at any time; but you accepted that. It was all part of being strapped into a machine that only stayed up because there was some kind of propulsion unit to keep it moving so that it wouldn't go where it really wanted to; which was down. It had all sorts of devious ways of killing you but, he felt, none of that was as frightening as the present situation. In the Phantom, you had control. You could work within known parameters. You could modify your actions according to the factors that presented themselves. It was different, he insisted in his mind, and far more dangerous to attempt to deal with the vast spectrum of unknowns within which he had reluctantly found himself. He couldn't understand how Logan could be so calm about it.

He said to her: "I don't envy you."

The green eyes stared at him. "And I don't envy you. You'd never get me into that metal-bound excuse for a dragonfly to throw it about the sky the way they say you do. If that isn't crazy, I don't know what is."

He smiled to himself, as he relaxed in his seat. It was all a matter of degree. He told himself he shouldn't be feeling relaxed. He was a long way from Hong Kong, and an even longer way from the time he would be getting out and heading back to his home in Wales; and Dee, and the kids. There were all kinds of people willing to kill to get him there, to prevent him from getting there and quite probably, to prevent him from getting out again, if he did make it.

Wales was a lifetime away. He closed his eyes.

He heard Logan rummaging in her bag. She kept it close to her for quick access to her weapon. He heard her get something out, tear it open. An envelope.

"Ah ha!" she said softly.

The satisfaction in her voice made him open his eyes to look at her. She was passing him something, green eyes triumphant. He looked at it.

A white sheet of paper. The envelope it had come from was still held in her other hand. He took the paper from her. There was a brief scrawl upon it.

"'In case of leaks'," he read, "'use initiative'." He returned the paper. "Fowler?" There had been no signature.

She nodded as she reclaimed the note. "It's his writing. I know it well enough. He doesn't have to sign it."

"Where did you find it?"

"With the documents. The envelope was sealed. His personal seal. If I hadn't recognised the writing, I would still have known. He's cut out everybody. No one knows he's given me full authority to make it to Hong Kong in my own way. He's even cut out Brimms, who's more or less his second-in-command when monitoring a field job." She sounded awed. "He's really stuck his neck out."

"He must have faith in you, or he wouldn't have done it."

"You're not going to believe this."

"Try me."

"It's more frightening knowing he's given his backing."

Pross said: "You mean you'd have felt better, less frightened going off on your own?"

"Failing on your own is not as bad as failing when someone like Fowler says he thinks you can make it."

"You'll make it."

"Is that what you believe, or are you just saying that to bolster your confidence, and mine?"

The freckles seemed very prominent beneath the green eyes. It shook him to suddenly realise how very young she looked.

"How old are you, Logan?"

"Twenty-three." She'd answered without hesitation.

Good Christ.

A smile played about her lips. "I seemed to have shocked you, Pross. At last. My swearing doesn't, but *this*. Ah! I'm old," she went on, "in the game of killing. Boys of seventeen, younger, in one or two cases, went to the Falklands. In Beirut, they start at twelve. There are those who will tell you even younger than that." She looked away. "No, Pross. I'm old at the game." It was reflectively said.

"Have you killed many people?"

The aircraft engines whispered into the night as she took her time. Then she turned to him again, eyes seeming to widen at him.

"It's almost like asking how many lovers I've had. It's a personal thing."

"I didn't . . ."

She silenced him with a brief finger on his lips, smiled sadly, almost self-consciously: "Not many. Too many." She would not say more, and turned away again.

She looked younger than ever; and for the moment, the continuation of his life rested solely within her hands. It was a daunting thought upon which to take a nap, but he decided there was little point in his sitting bolt upright waiting for disaster. He reclined the seat a fraction, closed his eyes once more.

He knew Logan was looking at him.

SEVEN

Fowler received the news with a mixture of grimness, satisfaction, and anxiety. The grimness was a reaction to the fact that even the airport rendezvous had not been secure; the satisfaction, that Logan had proved herself to be as proficient as he'd always thought her to be; and the anxiety was for her safety. He knew she would do all she could to get Pross to Hong Kong on time, even at the risk of her own life.

He stared at the phone that had brought the scrambled call from Brimms, hating it.

Pross came awake as the cadence of the jets changed subtly. His experience told him the let-down was about to begin. The aircraft lowered itself vertically for a few feet as the flaps came down. He fastened his seat-belt, looked to his left. Logan was staring at him, and he appeared to have caught her unawares, for she blinked quickly once, as if her thoughts had been elsewhere. Her belt was fastened.

"Did you have a good nap?" She smiled at him, as if she'd found that amusing.

He nodded. "You?"

"No." The green eyes were as alert as ever. "Got a job to do."

The jets were spooling back, the gear began to clunk down. The aircraft banked, steepening into the circuit. In his mind,

Pross was going through all the pre-landing procedures. He told himself the pilots knew what they were doing.

The gear locked down. The aircraft straightened, began the run-in.

She said: "When we land, we'll be met. We'll be taken to a hotel, suitably anonymous. We'll leave it as soon as I've made certain no one's aware of it."

"Won't that upset Fowler's people over here?"

He'd hoped that Fowler's blessing to use in-the-field initiative had meant using on-site personnel without recourse to England. It now appeared that Logan was quite determined to work on her own without department back-up. She obviously did not trust the overseas staff either.

She said, almost teasingly: "You're looking as if you've got another dose of indigestion."

The aircraft was sinking for the runway. More flaps. Down, down, down. Flare out, touch-down. Relief. She was rolling. Nothing was going to get her back up. Nose down, thrust-reversers, velocity bleeding off to taxi speed.

Logan was looking at him quizzically. "Were they that bad?" She'd hardly noticed the landing.

"They were very good. Nice touch-down. Feather job."

"You hate being flown by anybody else."

"With one notable exception."

"The man in China."

"The man in China."

"He must have been good."

"The best."

The plane trundled its way to the terminal, stopped. A man was waiting for them at the customs desk. The customs officer did not check them in.

"Good flight?" the man said to Logan as they walked away. They seemed to know each other. The man didn't introduce himself.

"Yes," Logan answered. "We went to sleep." She didn't introduce Pross.

He took them out of the terminal to a waiting 2.5 litre Alfa Romeo saloon. Another man was in the driving seat. He was not

111

introduced. Logan and Pross climbed into the back, keeping their luggage with them. The man who had met them got in next to the driver. The Alfa shot off almost before he had closed the door properly. It headed at high speed for Rome. No one spoke.

By the time they'd made it to the hotel after an excursion through a maze of sidestreets, no one had broken the silence. It was the most unreal drive Pross could remember ever having experienced.

They climbed out. The main entrance of the hotel was right on the street. The man in the passenger seat got out.

He said to Logan: "You're expected. We'll be back in the morning to pick you up for the onward flight."

He was perhaps late twenties, Pross thought, and looked like one of those people you saw on television playing university graduates of the thirties; the kind of people who travelled to the Continent for the adventure promised by the seductively dangerous times of the Europe of that period. Even the haircut looked the part. The clothes, however, were of the eighties, and Italian.

Logan said: "Alright."

He gave a tight smile, got back into the car. The Alfa squealed round a corner and was gone.

"They call him the model," Logan said drily.

"Who does?"

"Everybody on our team. Probably the opposition too." She didn't define "opposition". "It's because he likes to dress trendily."

"Dangerous for him. It makes him more noticeable."

"On the contrary. He fits in well with the crowd he's supposed to be monitoring."

She did not explain further, but had been surveying the narrow street with its high buildings casually as she spoke.

"Let's go in," she said, apparently satisfied.

They were given a double room.

Pross said: "I'll doss down on the floor."

"There won't be time. We're not staying." Her eyes held something unfathomable as they looked at him.

112

They did not unpack. Logan went to the one armchair, curled up in it.

Jack Wisyczyk was arguably the best aircraft mechanic at Shek Kong; which was why he was given a very special job to do. Wisyczyk was also a Senior Aircraftsman, when by rights, his skills should have made him a sergeant; at least. There were reasons why he was not. For a start, he'd already been there, his hold upon that exalted rank having lasted a breath-taking three months. Those who knew him well, a very few, had been astonished at the length of time. They would have bet on three days.

Wisyczyk had a fatal flaw: he hated everything, and everyone, save for his beloved aircraft. He hated first of all and far above everything, all officers of every description, particularly civilians who were once officers. He hated soldiers, sailors and airmen, including himself. He hated rain, wind, and sunshine. He hated the night; and he hated Hong Kong with a vengeance. He hated those who had sent him there.

Wisyczyk opened his eyes, stared at the day that greeted him through his barrack-room window, and hated it.

"Fakking hell!" were the first words he uttered to the rain-fresh day. He climbed out of bed. "Fakking hell!" he repeated, and hunted for a cigarette in one of the pockets of his bushjacket. He searched each one without success. "Fakking hell!" he said for a third time and went off for a wash.

It was a great way to start the day.

Short and stubby-looking, Wisyczyk was born in the East End of London nearly thirty years before, to an English mother and a Polish father. He had developed a pattern of speech that people swore needed its own dictionary, and walked with a fast little sideways gait that had broken the hearts of drill instructors and parade commanders alike.

The smart NCO or officer was the one who knew enough to direct his energies towards keeping Wisyczyk off a parade ground at all costs. Non-commissioned officers and officers of similar intelligence also tended to look the other way at Wisyczyk's frequent, though minor breaches of discipline, insubordination being one of them.

There was a story going round that an unfortunate pilot, new to the Wessex, had once brought the big helicopter down a little heavily, thereby bending a wheel strut. Wisyczyk had waited for the pilot to climb down from the cockpit, and had berated him in front of those standing near the aircraft. The performance would have earned an ovation, had not the others around been rather more conscious of retaining their ranks. The pilot had later said he had found the subsequent inquiry over the damage to the aircraft infinitely preferable, despite the fact that he had been quizzed by officers senior to himself.

There was another story that all new pilots to the squadron were forewarned about the fearsome little Wisyczyk. Both these stories, however, could have been pure fabrication. There was no denying, nonetheless, that as far as things aeronautical went, Wisyczyk was a near genius; not bad going for someone who had hated school with such complete thoroughness, he had deprived all educational institutions of his singular presence from the age of fourteen.

There were many who expressed the opinion that if there were any justice in the world, Wisyczyk would be the commander of a maintenance base. Those champions of justice also believed in fairy stories.

Wisyczyk walked across the flight line, hating the coating of water left upon it by the night rains. Breakfast had been hateful as usual. But he was coming alive now. Love was beginning to flow into his heart as he approached the hangar where his sleek new pride and joy waited.

Somewhere in the corner of his mind, he still harboured a grudge against those who had lost the Wessex that had disappeared near Starling Inlet. It was one he had worked upon, and considered it a personal affront. Until the remains of the aircraft were found, faulty servicing could be considered a contributory factor. It mattered little to him that everyone knew his reputation and that besides, the responsibility was not his, but the crew chief's. Whatever had happened, he knew, it had not been caused by faulty servicing. He suspected pilot error, this theory not being helped by his generally low opinion of all pilots. His wild guess was no wilder than those being aired by people of far greater rank.

He entered the hangar, and a sigh of pure pleasure escaped him as he stared at the gleaming shape of the Lynx 3. It was so new the national markings had not yet been painted on.

"Fakking beautiful," he murmured as he went up to it. He stroked it as he would a beloved pet.

It stood there upon its tricycle gear, sleek, armed and dangerous. Beneath the wide, flattened nose, was a pair of 20mm cannon, mounted side by side, and the outboard pylons carried rocket pods and missiles.

He had been working on it ever since it had arrived, crated, over a week before. His one regret was that other people worked on it too: engine men, avionics whizz-kids, armourers, painters. But it was still his baby. Everyone knew that he could make anything go up, and stay there till required to return.

The crew chief responsible for the aircraft's maintenance was already there.

"Well, Jack," he greeted him. "In a day or so, we'll see if this piece off shit will fly."

"It will fakking well fakking fly," Wisyczyk said confidently. "I worked on it. Got a fakking fag, Chief?"

"You know we don't smoke in here, Jack," the crew chief said with some patience. The ritual was the same every day.

"Fakking hell. Yeah. I forgot." Wisyczyk spoke absently, as if his quest for a cigarette barely merited more than half a second's effort. He had eyes only for the Lynx.

The crew chief said: "Don't you ever buy your own fags, Jack?"

Wisyczyk was poking about beneath the helicopter. "'Course I do. But I always seem to fakking run out by morning." Sounds of patting came from the aircraft. "Oh you fakking beauty. What do you think she's for, Chief?"

"We don't need to know, Jack my son. We don't need to know."

"All I care is that the fakking joker who takes her up doesn't fakking bend her."

"Or himself, Jack. Or himself."

115

"That's his fakking lookout. All I want is my fakking ship back, in one fakking piece." More patting. "Who are you going to take on, eh, my lovely? Who are your lovely guns for?"

"Jack."

"What."

"That's two sentences I've heard from you without your swear word. Found religion in the Lynx?"

"Fakking fak off, Chief."

The crew chief grinned.

Mary Chi climbed into her BMW, looked back at her mother. Already, she had become the high-powered executive once more. The girl who loved the rain had been left behind. The rain was no longer something that made her feel safe. It had not protected her from the telephone.

She put on her glasses. The blue eyes were hidden from the world. The smells of the new day drying itself after the night's heavy rain came at her through her lowered window. The sounds of Kowloon cranking up for business were all around her.

She started the car, waved to her mother, moved off to join the early traffic to the tunnel. She was halfway across, when traffic came to a halt. She raised her window to keep out the fumes, waited patiently and tried not to think of the millions of cubic metres of sea above her head.

Ten minutes later, she was still in the same spot. People were blowing horns, they too becoming apprehensive about the weight of the water above them. She found she was trying hard to prevent herself from looking up at the roof of the car. A man, she saw, was coming down the line of cars, keeping to the inside.

A policeman in plainclothes? She suddenly felt her heart beat furiously as she recognised him. It was the roly-poly man from the night before.

She locked the car doors. They were going to kill her, right here in this tunnel with all the noise of the car horns and all that water above her head. No one would hear the shots because of the noise. Her legs trembled a little. She kept her glasses on. She would not let him see her fear. She wanted to scream. Perhaps she should get out and run. But where to?

116

To another car! That was it. They . . .

The man reached her and as if knowing what was in her mind, came round remarkably swiftly to the driver's door. He knocked on the window, politely.

She stared straight ahead. He would have to shoot her through the glass, then everyone would see. Already, people were turning round to look. In her mirror, she could see the interest on the faces of the people in the car behind.

The man was reaching into his pocket. A pistol? She could not believe this was happening to her. Why wasn't she screaming for the world to hear? No one would hear her; not with all this noise. But they would see. They would see the man, and he would be caught; and she would still be dead, just like her father.

The man was tapping something against the window. She looked, knowing it could not be a gun; not with all those people looking.

It was a police ID.

So that was how they were going to do it. They had trapped her. All the people looking would have interpreted his actions wrongly. Police matter. No one would interfere. The man could do whatever he wanted. How had he come by the ID?

Legs shaking again, she lowered the window. The cacophony assaulted her..The man lowered his head as he put the card away.

"I just wanted to see if you were in good health," he said, and smiled. He had spoken in English.

He walked away, leaving her gaping, and trembling quite violently. She didn't care what the other people thought now.

Very soon after, it seemed, the traffic began to move. She arrived at her office still shaking. She didn't think it possible that they could have engineered the tunnel blockage; but she knew she could now expect anything of them. They had killed her father. They were showing her how easy it would be for them to dispose of her if she did not do as they asked.

They could get into her office, they could shadow her at will, they could get hold of police IDs, and they could make her father disappear. They could do anything they wanted. Why did they need her? What could she possibly do for them?

She sat at her desk. Her briefcase lay upon it. She had not done any work, and could not bring herself to open the case. She stared at it.

There was a brief knock on her door, and Tommy Ho entered.

"Mary," he said to her in English. "You're looking quite ill. Are you alright?"

She looked up at him, eyes hiding behind the glasses. "I'm alright, Tommy. A little tired. That's all."

"Too many parties." It was said jokingly, but there was also a tinge of mild reproof.

He had never liked the idea of her seeing the photographer from England.

"Your father would not have approved," he had said, sounding almost like a schoolmaster. "He was very tolerant with you, but he would not have liked this."

That had been the only time she could remember being thoroughly angry with him.

"What I do with my private life," she had snapped at him, "is entirely my own business. Never forget it."

He had been contrite, and she had felt sorry for him; but she had never forgotten. She was certain he had not either.

"I wish I could blame it on a party," she now said with some feeling.

"Troubles with the family?"

She seized upon it. "Yes." Trouble that concerned the family, so she was not lying to him.

He misunderstood, just as she knew he would.

"Your mother," he said with some concern.

She nodded.

He sighed. "It is only a year since it happened. I suppose there are times when she finds it difficult."

Glad of this wrong tack which was so close to the truth, she decided to be less remote with him.

"I spent the night there. We talked for a long time."

"Ah. So that's why you're so tired." He glanced at the un-opened briefcase. "Did you finish?"

"No. I . . ."

"I'll do it."

"No, Tommy. I can't allow that. It's my responsibility. You know how . . ."

"I know how you feel about doing your own work. Yes. But this is different. You have had a hard year. I know it has not been easy. I would also like to make up for trying to interfere." She knew he was talking about the photographer. "This is my way. Let me help."

She could not refuse without making him feel worse. It would have been very unkind of her.

"Alright, Tommy," she agreed at last. "Most of the difficult parts are finished so you won't have that to plough through. Are you sure you can spare the time?"

"I have some light reports I can pass to James Wu. It's no problem."

She pulled the briefcase towards her, opened it, took the relevant papers out.

She passed them on. "Tommy, I hate doing this."

"Don't worry about it," he said as he took them from her. He glanced quickly through them, looked at her. "Most of it's done. You've hardly left anything. I feel cheated." He smiled. "Workaholic."

She gave him a weak one in return. She felt as if she were using him. "Thanks."

"For what? There's no work here; just diversion. It will all be ready for the afternoon meeting. We could have lunch together, if you feel like it."

"I'm sorry, Tommy. I'm already engaged."

His face fell. He tried to disguise it, but was not successful. "A thought. That was all."

He went out, looking wounded.

Though she felt he had no right to be, she knew she would have had lunch with him, because she liked talking with him; provided he stayed off anything that could be construed as personal. She had not liked refusing him, and being unable to say why.

That was the moment when she began to hate the roly-poly man who had so unceremoniously barged his way into her life.

She removed her glasses. The vivid blue eyes now held a stubborn fire within them.

EIGHT

There was suddenly a lot of movement throughout the hotel.

"Tourists returning from the Rome nightlife," Logan said wryly.

Whoever they were, they were very loud.

Logan stood up. She had taken off her shoes, now she stepped back into them. Pross looked at her enquiringly.

"The best time," she said. "I'm going out for a minute to make a call."

He glanced at the hotel phone, knew why she was going to make the call outside. She took her bag, with the gun in it. He watched her go, hoping she'd be alright.

She came back nearly half an hour later, while he was slowly going up the wall with anxiety.

She saw the look on his face, smiled. "Were you worried about me, or about being left here?"

"Both," he answered truthfully. "I had visions of you being shot down in a Roman street, and me being quizzed by the Carabinieri or whatever they call themselves."

"You've been watching too many high-brow Italian movies on the box."

He gave her a tired smile. "Well? What do we have?"

"We'll be picked up in half an hour. Sorry I took so long, but I wanted a public phone well away from here, and I also had to check that no one followed me."

"You don't have to explain."

"No. But I feel better telling you." Then as if thinking the conversation was becoming too personal, she added: "Just making sure you don't think you're being deserted." She smiled again, this time a trifle self-consciously.

Pross said: "These people you called. Friends?"

"A very good friend. Someone I met at university. We used to take holidays together. Once, we were swimming in the south of France, off Hyères. She got cramp when we were quite a way out. I brought her back. Her family seem to think they owe me something, for life." She gave a little self-deprecating shrug.

"What can they do?"

"Oh they've got all sorts of contacts." She was being deliberately vague.

"Does the Department know about them?"

"They'll be on my vetting sheets, but I doubt if anyone will pay much attention to it. At least, not until it will be too late to matter. There's nothing overtly political, nor is there an Intelligence link to them. No one will expect me to go to them for help."

"What about the contacts though?"

"Unless someone has been very scrupulous and run a check, which I doubt . . ." Her expression was not kind to the vetting people. ". . . there is no reason to suppose anything is known about them. Mark you, I'm glad of it." She grinned suddenly, looking quite mischievous.

"You're crazy," he said. There was affection in his voice.

She stopped grinning almost as suddenly, looking uncharacteristically unsure of herself. She turned away, busied herself with her bag. The magnum came out. She took it apart with a skill that won a look of admiration from Pross. She put it together again, re-loaded it swiftly.

Pross said: "You look as if you could do that on a dark, wet night, with a blindfold."

"I can," she said simply. "I've done it." She took aim at a wall.

"I should have known."

She gave him a quick smile, put the gun away.

"It looks like a fine weapon, but what made you choose a cannon like that?"

"Not a woman's weapon, you mean?"

"I didn't say that. After what happened at Heathrow, I'm bloody glad you did."

"Do you know much about guns?"

"Not unless they're attached to aircraft. Mind you, we were given sidearm training, but I couldn't hit a barn door at two feet. Slight exaggeration, but not all that much. But my pilot . . . ah . . . now there's a gun expert. He's good; bloody good."

"So I've heard. Fowler rates him very highly. I think he really likes him, whatever you may feel."

"Fowler dumped him in China. I'd hate to be hated by your boss if that's what he does to people he likes."

"Fowler didn't do it."

"So I keep hearing."

Logan looked at her watch, dark-faced, with no markings upon it. She squeezed a tiny button. The time showed briefly. The body of the watch, like its strap, was all matt, and close to flesh colour. It would not give off reflections either in daylight, or artificial lighting; a factor which under certain conditions could prove the difference between life and death.

"Time to go," she said.

Pross stood up with her, picked up his case. "Logan."

"Umm?" She looked at him.

"That aircraft we came on was civilian. I thought they didn't fly across Europe at night from Heathrow."

"The Department has a contract with a private carrier." Which was all she was going to say.

"But the passengers . . ."

"What passengers?"

"Ask a silly question."

They were about to leave when she said: "Just a minute. Take my bag." She hurried across the room, pulled the sheets unceremoniously off the bed, then went to the shower. Pross heard her turn it on.

"Right," she said as she returned. "You take our stuff out while I talk to the man at the desk." She glanced back at the wrecked bed, smiled.

They left the keys in the room. The bed looked as if a wrestling match had taken place upon it. He made no comment as he followed her out. They did not shut the door, but left it slightly ajar.

They went cautiously down the two floors to the small lobby. Pross waited while Logan walked up to the night porter. She had rumpled her short, reddish-brown hair so that she looked as if she had just come through a bout or two. The night porter was in his fifties, and benign. He had no chance against Logan. She engaged him in conversation while Pross sneaked out.

He waited in the empty street, feeling glaringly exposed. There was some street-lighting, but there were more shadows. He half expected to see squads of Ling's men leap out of them. He looked up and down the narrow street. Nothing moved. Somewhere in the night, he heard the squeal of tyres and the shrill cadences of police sirens. He hoped they were not coming his way. If the police found him carrying Logan's bag with her massive cannon in it, they'd lift him before you could say *prego*.

Come on Logan.

She came out with a huge smile on the freckled face, took her bag from him, commenced walking. As he walked by her side, Pross felt like a refugee, looking for somewhere to spend the night.

It was three in the morning.

She said: "The car's waiting. I told her not to come to the hotel, just in case." She glanced round suddenly.

"Something?" he queried. They had not paused.

"Nothing," she said. "No one's seen us."

"Plenty of places for a watcher to hide."

"They'll be here nearer dawn, if there are going to be any. No one else knows Fowler's given me permission to run independently. They, whoever they are, won't come before dawn. Traditional hour, you see." She sounded as if she found that amusing. "I like to be unconventional."

They turned left at a corner. There was a sudden rush of sound as a police car shrieked past, sirens blaring, lights blazing. It didn't stop, for which Pross was profoundly grateful. They would have, he felt, had they not been in such a hurry.

The new street was wider, but that was about all it meant to Pross. He did not know Rome.

They crossed the street, continued walking. Every now and then, Logan would look casually about her. She apparently saw nothing to alarm her. Pross could not dispel the feeling of being accompanied by a wild creature on the prowl.

Up ahead was a line of parked cars. One of them suddenly came to life, its tail lights coming on like beacons, its indefinable shape low and gleaming.

Pross felt his steps slow involuntarily.

Logan did not pause. "It's our car," she said.

The car was a big Ferrari 400i. Pross did not know it as such; merely that it was the sleekest, most powerful-looking Ferrari he had ever seen. Logan seemed to know the right people.

"Someone's got a private oil well," he murmured.

Logan opened the wide passenger door. "In you get. Hurry!"

He complied. She kept her bag as she climbed into the front, shut the door.

She said: "This is Grazziella, whom I've told you about."

Pross caught the flashed smile of a pretty face in the gloom of the car, then the Ferrari gave a roar from its four tail-pipes as it pulled out from its parking space to hurtle down the street. The force of its acceleration pinned him to the seat. Logan, he noted, had not given his name; neither had she told him what she'd said to the nightman at the hotel.

Grazziella seemed dwarfed by the size of the car, but she handled it like a Mini.

Pross settled himself in the back by positioning himself sideways.

"Go to sleep if you want," Logan's voice said from the front. "It's going to be a long drive. We're leaving Rome."

Pross said nothing, fascinated by the way Grazziella carved her way through the streets of the ancient city. Soon, they were on the orbital road, heading in which direction he could not guess; then she turned off it, going right. Pross saw a sign flash past. *Pescara*. They were on the autostrada.

The Ferrari seemed to pick up speed just when Pross thought it was already getting ready for take-off. He peered over Grazziella's shoulder at the big circular dials of the speedometer and the tachometer. The speedometer, calibrated in kilometres, was marked beyond three hundred. Pross thought the needle was creeping perilously close to it, but he knew his mind was exaggerating.

Even so.

He closed his eyes, lay back and prayed they hit nothing.

He would remember that drive forever. Grazziella used the Ferrari like an extension of herself. She seemed to be at one with it. It went where she pointed it, and seemed eager to do what she asked of it; which was to try and break every autostrada speed record in the book.

Or so it seemed to Pross.

From time to time, he would peer out, only to be greeted by the blur of the passing landscape as the new day lightened. Once, he looked out, and swore in his mind they were skirting the edge of a precipice. Up front, Logan and Grazziella chatted like the reunited students they were. Logan didn't seem to mind the suicidal speed.

Once, he glanced out of the back window and thought that he could see on the rapidly streaming belt of road, a tiny speck, marked by the pinpoints of its lights. He wondered about it briefly, decided it was most unlikely that anyone would be following them. No one could keep up with the Ferrari, anyway; not with Grazziella at the wheel.

He looked at her, which was a serious mistake at that particular moment. She had become quite animated in her conversation with Logan, and took a hand off the wheel to wave it about, emphasising a point about someone she had met at a party. It was a funny episode, and she laughed, taking *both* hands off the wheel for what seemed to Pross' nervous eyes like interminable minutes.

Logan glanced round. "Are you alright?"

He had not thought he had voiced his nervousness. Caught out, he said: "I thought I saw something."

The green eyes were serious. "Far in the distance? I saw it too. It's still there, but it may be nothing."

Shocked that his hurried face-saver had crystallised into reality, he turned round to check. Far behind them, the pinpoints of light followed.

126

He turned back to Logan. "But I saw them long ago. I thought we'd have lost them by now." What could possibly be keeping up with this Ferrari?

"Someone else driving fast," Logan said. "This is Italy. Everyone's a racing driver." She glanced at Grazziella, who laughed. "Whoever it is is not catching up, assuming it's anyone interested in us. We're probably gaining slowly."

It was the wrong thing to say. Grazziella promptly took that as a cue for more speed. After a while, the pinpoints of light disappeared. Perhaps they hadn't been following after all and were, as Logan had said, merely some people wanting an early morning burn-up.

By five-thirty, they were by-passing Pescara and heading north along the Autostrada Adriatica towards Ancona. The day promised to be bright, dry, and hot. Grazziella, still sparkling, chatting away to Logan, dropping a gear when baulked and roaring away to overtake, then keeping her foot down as much as possible, urged the Ferrari on.

With the light of the new day, Pross could see her properly. She was very blonde, he saw, and quite slim. Her long delicate fingers seemed to caress rather than hold the wheel, and the car appeared to thrive beneath such control. Her finely-chiselled features spoke of the breeding of old Northern families, and her blonde hair glistened in the morning light.

Pross glanced at Logan. By comparison, being a more solid-looking woman, she appeared clumsy, unfinished. Yet, that was an illusion; for Logan could, when she wished it, become quite elegant. Pross, looking at them, decided it was not every day one was driven at high speed in the epitome of glamorous cars, in the company of two such women. He smiled to himself. A far cry from gunships

"What's the smile for?" Logan was looking at him.

"At my age, I shouldn't be surprised by anything life can produce. But I have to admit it. I'll always be." Except when flying, he didn't add. Then, anything could happen, and should be anticipated. He would have to anticipate in Hong Kong. That was what this little jaunt was all about. That was where the ride in the fast, glamorous car would eventually lead.

"Now you're looking thoughtful."

"Plenty to think about. What did you say to that night porter? Are you going to tell me now? I'm still wondering how you got out unseen."

Her smile was full of mischief. "I told him we would be having a shower, so could whoever brought our coffee up please walk right in. He took one look at me, put two and two together, and came up with seven. It never entered his head to think that I could have used the phone to order. I'll bet anything he took the coffee up himself. When he sees the bed, he'll be dying to look in the shower."

"And see that we're gone. Bang goes our lead."

"He won't look. He'll smirk at the bed, and leave."

He hoped she was right. "What about our friends in the Alfa?"

She consulted her watch. "In about half an hour, perhaps three-quarters, they'll know."

"And then?"

The green eyes were still. "The shit hits the fan. Whoever's leaking will panic."

"And we'll be truly on our own." With everybody trying to find them.

She glanced at Grazziella who seemed to be in the process of overtaking right under the wheels of the biggest truck Pross had ever seen.

"Not quite," she said.

The truck was overtaken safely. Pross stifled his sigh of relief.

"Good, isn't she?" Logan said mischievously. The eyes were sparkling now with wicked humour. "When we were at Cambridge, she once frightened a poor soul so much he was actually sick; sick as in vomit."

He could believe it.

"What was that car, Grazzi?"

"Oh . . . ah . . . the Aston . . . nonono . . . it was the Mercedes 350. Yes. The Mercedes."

She couldn't even remember her cars.

The were both laughing, remembering the poor wretch who'd been given the Grazziella treatment. Pross was seeing Logan in a new light, as she giggled uncontrollably at the memory.

"Stop making me laugh!" Grazziella howled. "We're doing two hundred and ten!" She giggled.

Logan glanced at Pross. The green eyes seemed to be saying something to him. It took him a few moments to understand; then he began to understand Logan's game. Grazziella, Pross realised, had no idea of the true nature of Logan's work. So what excuse had Logan used for their night-time flit?

He glanced at the speedometer. They really were doing two hundred and ten kilometres an hour. No. Two hundred and thirty. Jesus.

Grazziella kept her foot down. The Ferrari pranced along the autostrada.

Pross tried to relax in his seat, pretended to be asleep. In truth his mind was alert to every sound the car made, persuading itself that the hurtling machinery was not a mere few inches from the road surface. At the front, Grazziella and Logan kept up their cheerful banter as they recalled other episodes in their past lives.

The Ferrari stopped once for petrol, left the autostrada for Porto Civitanova, from where Grazziella headed inland. The road began to climb, in places quite steeply. Half an hour later, they arrived at their destination. They had covered over 430 kilometres, and the time was still just barely past 6.30.

Pross climbed stiffly out of the car, and stared about him in wonder. Grazziella's home looked like a small Renaissance palace, but that was not what held his attention. They had arrived within the walls of a small city that appeared to be suspended in mid-air. Positioned high above two deep valleys among wild-looking mountains, the place looked magical in the light and mists of the early morning.

Pross, aware that Grazziella was looking at him with some amusement, said: "Where is this place?"

"You think it is beautiful?" Her voice, darkly rich, had that semi-strangled quality that made some Italian women sound so sensuous.

"It's magic," he almost whispered, and meant it.

Logan said: "Don't start her off. She'll give you the full history if you give her half the chance."

"This place reeks of history," Pross said. "Well, Grazziella? Where are we?"

"Macerata," she answered, which meant nothing to him. She smiled at him. "But I promise not to give you all the history. This is an old city, some say it was once Roman. We cannot see from here, but down there in the valley of the Potenza river is a ruin of Helvia Ricina, the first Roman city in this area. We call this the Marche, and the Adriatic is where we turned off to come here. Not far." She paused, glanced at Logan. "That was short, wasn't it?"

Logan said to Pross: "You're lucky. I got the full treatment when I first came here. She calls it her Renaissance painting."

A short man, oozing reverence, had come out of the mini-palace and approached the car. He spoke in rapid Italian to Grazziella, who turned to Logan.

But Logan spoke first. "Tell him it's alright. We'll carry our luggage."

Grazziella passed the message on. The man, fiftyish, Pross thought, nearly bowed, went back inside looking slightly hurt.

She said with a smile: "He is a little offended, I think."

Pross said: "Because we didn't let him carry our stuff?" Amazing.

"It's his duty," she said simply.

Quite.

They followed her into the building, walked across a marbled hall. As if to give credence to Grazziella's story about the Roman descent of the city, a small mosaic was set into the floor. Pross dared not ask if it were genuine. The place felt empty.

She said: "Would you like to have some coffee? Or would you prefer to sleep for a short while?"

Logan said quickly: "Sleep please, Grazzi. Coffee later. You must be shattered. It was good of you to come."

Pross said: "You came all the way to Rome?"

"Oh no. I was already in Rome. It was a great surprise to hear from Sian, at that time of the night." Grazziella's face lit up with a conspiratorial smile. "But how could I refuse? Such an exciting thing! I hear nothing from her, and suddenly, she is married!"

Pross glanced at Logan as they trooped up a marble staircase. "Exciting?" he said to Grazziella.

The blonde head turned briefly to look at him. "Oh yes. When Sian told me you were trying to get away from her ex-boyfriend who is very jealous and has sent men to kill you, how could I not help my good friend? I understand about jealous men."

I'll bet, Pross thought and glared at Logan who looked pointedly away to ask Grazziella to call someone called Giorgio.

At the top of the winding staircase, Grazziella led them along a corridor laid with a richly-patterned carpet. Pross did not know much about oriental carpets, but this one, he could see, would probably buy a good slice of his home. Along the walls of the corridor, were hung portraits of individuals he assumed to be her ancestors. He read a name.

Antonio Giovanni, Marchese dell'Orobianchi.

Logan certainly knew how to slum it.

Grazziella dell'Orobianchi stopped before a gold-patterned door. "Your room," she told them. "When would you like to be woken up?" She was looking at Logan. She stifled a small yawn. "Oops. I must be tired too. I think I'll take a little sleep too. I was going to have coffee, but later with you, I think. Yes?"

Logan nodded. "That will be fine, Grazzi. Thanks so much."

She hugged Logan. "Hey. I was happy to do it. My house is yours. Always." She kissed Logan, looked at Pross. "Am I allowed?"

"Of course," Logan said, straightfaced.

He collected a warm kiss at the corner of his mouth.

"Hmm," Grazziella said. "He is nice. Guard him well."

"I will," Logan said with feeling. "We'll be up about eleven, and ready to move on."

Grazziella gave a knowing smile. "I can tell when you're being protective about a man, Sian. Hah! She's blushing!"

"Get off, Grazzi." Logan would not look at Pross. She pushed the door open, entered. Then her head poked round. "Still here?"

Grazziella winked at them both. "Have fun." She walked jauntily away, glanced back, waved just before she turned a corner.

Pross shook his head slowly, entered the room. He looked about him slowly. His eyes took in the huge, ornate four-poster.

"This room's big enough to land a chopper in," he commented drily. "On second thoughts, I think the bed would serve just as well. My God. The size of it!" He stared up at the stuccoed ceiling. "Beautiful."

He pushed the door shut. It was heavy, and seemed to cut off all outside sounds. He went over to a commode that most antique dealers would have sold their families for, put their cases down next to it.

Logan was standing in a far corner, looking at him as he continued to study the room. It was almost a perfect square, with large windows on two adjoining sides. There were long low radiators, for central heating. The Marchese's descendants didn't like roughing it. The floor, like the corridor, was covered by a vast carpet whose probable value he would not have tried to guess at.

He went over to a window, looked out through its vast pane of sparklingly-clean glass. It was like looking straight down a precipice. That part of the building seemed to have been built straight into one of the many steep slopes that supported the mountain city.

Logan said: "It was the most convenient story to give her. I felt she would find it easy to believe. She's an incurable romantic. Something like this appeals to her."

"As long as she's not hoping to see me get shot." He looked round at her. "Don't worry about it, Logan. I think you've done very well." He smiled at her.

"Then you don't mind?" She seemed worried by it, despite what he had just said.

"No. Of course not. We're here, safe from leaks, and pursuit. We're just an ordinary couple . . . well as ordinary as anyone can be in a place like this. As I've said, you've done well. I certainly couldn't have pulled off something like this, and so quickly. They must be going spare in Rome." He looked out again. "This is really beautiful." He turned back to her. "But it feels empty. Apart from that little man, are there any other people around here?"

"Oh there'll be more staff, but none of the family. Some are in France, others in New York. God knows. They're always travelling."

"What it must be to be so rich. Her parents?"

"Dead."

"You mean this place really is hers?"

"Yes. She's an only child, and inherited."

Pross said: "Logan, you amaze me. When you said you had a friend who could help, I never expected a member of the Italian nobility. Do you have more surprises?"

"That depends."

"On what?"

"On whether Grazzi manages to reach her cousin in time."

"And what's his part in this game of ours?"

"Our ticket to Hong Kong. I hope."

He shook his head again, in wonder. "I can see why Fowler picked you."

"We're not out of the woods yet. Tell me that when we get to Hong Kong."

There was a strange look of preoccupation on her face that Pross could not quite understand.

"Are you alright?" he queried gently.

"Just tired, I suppose. I'll be okay after a snooze."

"Ah yes. Well. Tell you what. You take the bed . . ."

"Don't be ridiculous, Pross. This bed is more than king-sized. There's plenty of room. I've told you before. I don't bite. I'm off to the bathroom. You can do what you like." She went through a door that was close to the bed, taking her bag with her.

He stared at the closing door, stood for a moment irresolutely. What the hell, he thought. Dee would understand.

Thinking of Dee brought with it a sudden rush of homesickness. He had managed to push thoughts of her and the children far down into the recesses of his mind to avoid any distractions that might affect the job he had to do. Now, they had surfaced, bringing with them the unpleasant associations concerning what Ling would do to his defenceless family should he put a foot wrong.

Logan came out of the bathroom, a large blue towel wrapped

about her. She was barefoot, and her shoulders were also bare. The towel reached to just above her calf. She held the towel together with one hand, while the other carried the bag. She'd kept her watch on.

"Don't look at my legs," she said. "They're horrible."

So of course he looked. They were fantastic, he thought. She put down the bag, went back towards the bathroom.

"There's nothing wrong with them," he said.

She re-entered the bathroom, came back out with her clothes on a hanger. She put them into a wardrobe that looked big enough to hide an army. He wondered what she'd done with her garter-worn bullets.

"They're fat," she said, walking past him and round the foot of the bed. She'd kept the rings on too.

His eyes followed her. She sat down on the edge of the bed. The towel fell away slightly, revealing a generous length of full, firm thigh. It hadn't been done deliberately, he thought, for there was no clumsy attempt at modesty. She left the towel alone. Her attention was on the bag which she was now digging into.

She took out the magnum.

"Your legs are alright," he said. Why did she need his approval anyway? At least she wasn't going to get into bed with her bullets on.

She said nothing, as she checked and double-checked the weapon, then placed it on a small, marble-topped table near the bed. It would be close to hand when she was in bed.

She looked at him then. "Thank you, Pross," she said, so seriously, he frowned questioningly at her.

She ignored the look, climbed into bed, towel and all; then she pulled the towel from under the bedclothes, dropped it to the floor.

She said: "Are you going to stand there forever? We've got about four hours of rest. I think we should make use of them." She smiled suddenly. "Don't look so stricken. I meant, to sleep."

"Look . . ."

She turned onto her side, looking away from him. "Oh come on, Pross. The bed's big enough. Before you come in, could you draw the curtains, please?"

He did so, the heavy curtains plunging the room into total darkness. He had to grope his way back towards the bed. He wondered whether she had asked him to draw the curtains to deliberately spare him embarrassment as he undressed. Her next words proved him wrong.

"If anyone we don't want to see comes in," she said, "I'll see him long before he sees me . . . long enough to blow his head off."

Pross thought drily that if he'd had any designs on her, those words would have cooled him off in no time. He undressed, climbed into bed. Logan was right. The bed was big. She could have been on the other side of the world.

"Pross?"

"Umm?"

"Do you really think my legs are alright?"

"Yes."

He did not try to fathom her reasons for asking. He was too busy wondering where Ling was, whether they'd make Hong Kong in time, and whether he'd see his family alive when it was all over. He fell asleep at last, with these things troubling his mind.

NINE

At about the time that Pross closed his eyes, Mary Chi came out of her office building on the other side of the world. She was a little late for her meeting with the man from the People's Republic, but that had been deliberate. Something blazed within the blue eyes behind the glasses; but they could not be seen. The glasses had darkened themselves in the bright sun. There was a slight breeze, gusting playfully.

A Mercedes taxi pulled up almost immediately. The roly-poly man was driving. His companion was nowhere to be seen.

The man got out, opened a rear door for her. For a moment, she stood there, irresolute. She was taking a serious risk, she felt. This man could take her anywhere. She could disappear forever, the way her father had. The playful breeze tugged at her skirt, baring an elegant leg.

She decided she would not go. She'd tell the police everything. She began to turn away. The man's voice stopped her.

"That would be very foolish, Miss Chi," he said in English. "What you cannot see is that a high-powered rifle is trained on you. My colleague is an excellent shot. I believe at this moment he is aiming at a spot in the centre of your forehead."

She paled visibly, seemed to rock backwards as if blown by a strong wind. "You wouldn't dare!" The words were a mere whisper, full of real fear. All her stubbornness, so carefully built up during the morning, had suddenly evaporated.

"Of course I would. My colleague would be very far away by the time the police got here. And I? I would vanish within the crowd which would inevitably gather. Will you please get in?" The man's eyes were cold, reptilian. His voice, though civil, was chilling.

She climbed into the back.

"That is very sensible." He shut the door, walked round to the driver's side.

He looked just like any other taxi driver; floppy trousers, sandals, loud short-sleeved shirt worn over the trousers. He climbed in, shut the door with a bang, drove slowly away. Nothing about him had been hurried. To anyone watching, it would have seemed like an ordinary fare pick-up.

He drove out of Central, turned into Harcourt Road, headed for the Causeway Bay area. He didn't speak to her until they were cruising on Victoria Park Road, with the park itself to the right.

"We shall have a very discreet talk, Miss Chi," he began, continuing in English, "then I believe we shall come to an agreement."

"Agreement?"

The car seemed to have slowed down, less than the traffic appeared to warrant. Was he going to take her to the park? No. The car surged forward suicidally between two cars, scraped through. He appeared to know the rules of dicing in Hong Kong traffic. She wondered how long he had actually lived in the colony.

"Agreement," he echoed, glancing back.

The brief look of his eyes sent shivers chasing along her back.

"What do you want of me?"

The car left Causeway Bay, went on to North Point. Where was he taking her? She stared out of the window, at people, buildings going past; familiar things that had now suddenly become alien. She felt almost as if being in the fake taxi with this man had suddenly transported her to another country where everything, though looking the same, had changed. The car was strange, but the familiar people and things had changed too. It was almost as if she could not hear or see them.

North Point went by. The man chose not to speak until Aldrich Bay was passing on the left. A big jet was coming off the Kai Tak runway, three kilometres to the northwest, across the water. She looked at it wistfully until it had disappeared overhead.

The man said: "What do I want of you? Service. A particular service, which I am confident you will be able to perform."

"What kind of a service?" She did not like the sound of it at all. Not that it mattered. She was for the moment, his captive, as if she had been bound hand and foot.

"One well within your capabilities."

He fell silent again. It was unnerving talking to the back of the round head. The head swung right and left, gauging traffic. The movements were robotic in their regularity. Every so often, he gave a little wheeze, keeping time to the turning of his head.

He said: "During the period of your affair with the Phantom pilot . . .

"It was not an affair."

The man chuckled his scepticism. "You were seen with him, Miss Chi."

She had spoken the truth. It had not been an affair, not in the strictest sense. True, they had seen each other a few times, and had gone into the countryside together, gone swimming, and fishing, and boating. They had hugged each other, held hands. Nothing else had happened. No one else knew that. Everyone had assumed they had become lovers. The simple fact was he had not wanted to. Left to her, it would have happened within a very short space of time. Her mother would have been shocked to know this. As for her father . . .

"Does being with someone constitute an affair?"

"You were observed in very close contact with him."

She was suddenly angry. The blue eyes sparked with an enraged fire. "You were spying on me? You were following us?" She felt the rage go through her as she remembered the times she'd thought had been private.

These people had no scruples about invading the privacy of others. They had no scruples about the taking of life too. They invented countless ways of justifying it. Anything to give respectability to the sordid nature of their trade.

"You were being monitored, for a specific purpose. I have no interest in your sexual activities."

The cold way in which the words were spoken made it even worse. Being observed like a specimen beneath a microscope somehow made her feel as if her dignity had been stripped from her.

There had been no sexual activities to speak of. For some reason, though it had been obvious he had liked her, he had not wanted to make love to her. At first, she had felt rejected. He had never explained why; but she had detected a strange hurt within him and without knowing the reasons, had understood. She had warmed to him even more. Then he had gone out of her life. Now, this obscene man was bringing the memory back, soiling it.

"We would like to know," the man was saying, "the nature of your conversations with him."

"I've already told you. We talked about nothing that would interest you."

"There are always interesting things that a Phantom pilot . . ."

"He was not a Phantom . . ."

"Do not interrupt me!" The voice had become hard, commanding. The eyes stared ferally back at her from the rearview mirror.

She felt the hate mount and glared right back at him.

The eyes glanced from the mirror to the road and back again. "Do not waste your anger on me. It is futile. I could have you killed now. What good would your anger do? It is a waste of energy. A car has been following us from the moment you were picked up. My colleague is in it. Should I decide you are becoming tedious, I have but to stop and leave you to him. He has taken it as a personal affront that you have slept with that man. Unreasonable, of course. But in every culture, there are men who seem to think they have proprietary rights to the woman and no foreigner should touch them. Primitive, but effective in the right circumstances. For example, my colleague would consider that only by forcefully having sex with you could he hope to expiate the insult he feels has been dealt him."

Mary Chi felt her knees press closely together in an involuntary act of protection. Her entire body shivered with horror. The eyes in the mirror noted it.

"Precisely," the man said. "It is not an experience I would recommend. He is known to be quite brutal. A woman such as yourself, and with blue eyes! I think he would be quite transported. There would be no boundaries he would not attempt to cross in his enjoyment of you."

"*Stop it!*"

The cry was wrung out of her as she listened to his words being repeated with cold satisfaction within her mind. Unknowingly, she had crossed her legs tightly, so tightly they hurt. She was trying hard not to give in to the tears she felt coming. She must not let him break her will. She must not.

The man said, in his deadly calm voice: "I, however, will be quite reasonable. My colleague is only one of the actions we can take should you disappoint me. You are the daughter of traitors. I am being kinder than I need be."

She listened to him in disbelief. "Kind? You call what you are doing to me *kind*?"

"What am I doing to you, Miss Chi? You are riding in my car, into which you came of your own free will. You were not abducted. Eyewitnesses would confirm this, should such confirmation be needed; which I strongly doubt. You would not show such a criminal lack of sense."

"You are torturing me!" she said, her voice full of frustration, despair, and fear. The fear had come now, to stay.

He chuckled. "Torture? If I were to let you out now, which of course I will not be doing, where are the signs of torture for you to display to a sympathetic audience?"

"This," she said in a small voice. "What you are doing now is torture."

He drove on in silence. The taxi was now cruising along, past Tai-Tam reservoir.

She waited, fearfully, for him to speak. When he still remained silent, she tried to imagine what he could possibly be dreaming up for her to do. She could not see how she could be of any use to him. She had already told him she knew nothing; yet he persisted. She felt a quiet terror at the thought of his associate violating her body. Her hands gripped the seat on either side of her thighs, nails digging into the cloth cover that had been stitched over it. She could not believe that a few days ago, all she'd had to worry about was making sure her reports were accurate, concise pieces of work; that her car ran smoothly, that her flat had nothing going wrong in it, that her mother always got a telephone message from her, that Tommy Ho was kept at gentle arms-length, that . . .

"You once met a man," he was saying into her rambling thoughts, "at a party; another Englishman."

The eyes were again on her, through the mirror. She looked back at them, puzzled. Then she thought of the man who had pestered her.

"Ah. I see you do remember. Not a pleasant incident. One of my . . . colleagues – oh yes. We do attend parties. Much can be reaped from small-talk. We know what your admirer said to you. You must sleep with him."

"*What?*" Her eyes grew wide with the shock of it.

"You will sleep with him."

"You cannot make me do that," she said in a dead voice after another long silence. "I am not a whore. Because you have me at your mercy does not mean you can insult me so crudely." She was trying to regain her pride, and had spoken with some of her old fire. "I am not something cheap you have picked up from the waterfront. I am the daughter of respected people. We are not common."

Abruptly, he switched to Cantonese, firing it rapidly at her. "You are not common." She did not have to see his mouth to know it had been turned down when he's spoken. The eyes kept glancing from the road to the mirror. "You and your people are worse. Your mother believes herself to be descended from Alexander's people, from the days when Westerners, barbarians, crossed into the northwest for silk and for plunder. I know all about her ridiculous belief. She believes your blue eyes are confirmation of that. *I* believe that somewhere in her ancestry, a Russian pig strayed into a border village and slept with a common whore. He left his mark to stain you with.

"I am a Han. There are no outsiders in my veins; and I am loyal to the People's Republic. Your mother was once a Comrade, until

141

she became seduced by the trappings of capitalist wealth and your father, a follower of the corrupt Kuomintang. He . . ."

"My father shared the original ideals . . ."

"Do not interrupt me!" he screamed. "You will not be told again! The next time you do so, I shall stop, my colleague will catch up, and you will be left at his mercy! He will not kill you, because you must be left in a sufficiently healthy state to sleep with the Englishman; but you will be returned to him to do with as he sees fit."

She glanced fearfully out of the back window. She saw no car that looked remotely like a shadowing vehicle. But would she have known which, anyway?

"He is there," the man said. "You can be sure of it." He was still speaking Cantonese. "Your father," he went on, "was a Kuo spy, masquerading as a businessman. It is a common enough cover; as common as cultural attachés have become. But they never learn."

They were now going into Repulse Bay and the taxi was momentarily baulked by a red Leyland lorry with an open, tarpaulin-hooded body. The man blew his horn imperiously. The lorry took its time, eventually allowing them to pass. Soon after, a motorcycle policeman roared past. Mary Chi watched him go in despair.

Her companion said: "It is no use hoping. They cannot help you."

She made her hands into fists, sat on them. She wanted to scream.

The man said: "You will be invited to a party tomorrow, where this Englishman will also be. It has been arranged. The invitation is at your home. You would have received it last night, had you gone there. The Englishman is attracted to you. He has been heard to talk about you. You will see to it that his attraction is reciprocated."

She had ceased to be surprised by what this offensive man could do; but everything within her was rebelling against what he was asking of her. She tried not to show it, failed.

"Do not even contemplate not doing it," he said chillingly. "Apart from some exercise with my colleague, there is also your

142

mother who could be taken back to the Republic and tried for innumerable offences against the revolution. She could be taken at any time; in a day, a year, ten years. She would be told, then be left to fear its occurrence, never knowing when it would take place. It would be like waiting for death.

"You, Miss Chi, could be handled even more satisfactorily. You have built yourself a reputation in business. You are respected by your male colleagues, and by Western business people. Let us suppose it became known that you were less than discreet about your personal affairs; that you slept with all and sundry . . . my colleague is very good at giving details . . . I believe even your tame pet Tommy Ho would shun you. Your career would begin to die. Gossip is a terrible weapon. It is a form of death for the victim. For one so young, that would be a tragedy."

At last, she felt the tears she had tried so hard to stem come pouring unheeded down her cheeks. She cried quietly, for, having finally succumbed, she did not want to give him the added satisfaction of hearing her as well.

"There is no need to cry. The Englishman will be much gentler than my colleague. The Englishman will treat you like a flower of the East, while my colleague . . . ah. I believe I know what your choice will be. It will be painless, and in the end, I am sure it will be enjoyable. That is all you need to do. You will either take him to your place, or he will arrange something. If he does, you will agree to go with him. We shall attend to matters from there."

"What . . . what will you do to him?"

"That is not your concern. Since you have been able to tell us nothing about your Phantom pilot, it is necessary that you meet with this man. They are involved in some action against the Republic. It is your duty, in reparation for your mother's defection and your father's treachery, to do this."

"Did you . . . did you kill my father?"

The taxi was approaching the sprawling harbour of Aberdeen, with its closely-packed carpet of sampans. She liked Aberdeen, but today, it held no pleasure for her. The tears blurred her eyes. All the sampans became one vast mix of colour that turned opaque. Everything had changed.

"Did you kill my father?" she repeated.

He did not reply. Instead, he stopped the Mercedes. "You may get out." He had spoken in English.

She stared at the eyes in the mirror.

"You may leave, Miss Chi. Find your own transportation to Central. We shall be in touch."

Hardly daring to believe her ordeal was over for the time being, she slowly climbed out.

"Miss Chi." He was looking up at her. "You do not believe I have shown you respect. You have chosen to live away from the traditional ways. You cannot be expected to be treated traditionally."

Something rebellious suddenly welled within her. She threw caution to the winds. The blue eyes flared behind the glasses.

"Traditionally? As traditionally as a footbinder?"

His eyes sparkled meanly. "You will attend the party."

The taxi squealed away, scattering cyclists and pedestrians.

She felt a brief satisfaction. Her parting shot had struck home; but it was not going to help her later on.

Ling was in Hong Kong.

He had arrived quite openly, on a British Airways flight from Heathrow, at 15.30 Hong Kong time. The name Ling had not been on the passenger manifest, and the passport scrutinised by various officials at the beginning and end of the flight was not the same one that had ushered him into Britain.

Now, as Pross lay deep in sleep in the vast bed in Macerata, Ling was driven slowly to an address in Causeway Bay. The car arrived, stopped. Ling got out, went to the address. He pressed the doorbell. No one answered. He was early. He was prepared to wait. He went back to the car, told the driver to leave him. The car would be back later.

He went to a small, nearby restaurant, took a seat that would give him a perfect view of the approach of the person he had come to see.

He ordered a small snack, and unhurriedly ate while he waited.

Mary Chi parked her BMW with a sense of dread. She remained sitting in the car for long minutes, reluctant to climb out. She was

144

not looking forward to finding the envelope with its enclosed invitation waiting for her.

In the silence of the car the wind, that had been growing stronger all afternoon, made itself heard. She listened to its hissing with a preoccupied mind. She was remembering the afternoon meeting in the boardroom. She had been well below her normal form, and Tommy Ho had given her several concerned glances. When he had asked her afterwards, she had pleaded monthly sickness.

She smiled grimly. What a good little standby that so-called curse was. The wind rocked the car gently. A storm coming? There had as yet been no official warnings, in this the season of storms.

She got out of the car. The wind wrapped itself about her, tugged at her clothes, her hair. She staggered a little as she locked the car. The wind, she thought, felt wet. Few people in Hong Kong did not know a wet wind. More rain to come. She wished it would wash out the party she did not want to go to.

She walked to the block of flats where she had her very comfortable home with its two bedrooms and wide lounge, all beautifully furnished and modern. She did not see the man behind her.

"Miss Chi?"

She stopped suddenly, turned, heart pounding. They had followed her even here? Hadn't she already agreed to go? She felt a despairing sense of outrage.

But it wasn't the fat man. A wave of relief passed through her. This person was pleasant-looking, diffident almost, despite the expensive cut of his lightweight executive suit. He was Chinese, but did not look Hong Kong. The suit was American in cut. Having dealt with international businessmen for the past two years, she could practically tell where they came from before she'd heard them speak, merely by looking at their clothes. She could even tell their executive level, and would plan her approach accordingly. It always gave her the edge.

This man, she decided, despite his apparent diffidence, was a top executive. What did he want with her, outside office hours? She liked out-of-hours wheeling and dealing. If someone wanted to see you so badly he came all the way to your home to talk, you were already halfway there. The advantage was all yours. Your protagonist was eager, and therefore malleable to bargaining.

All this went through her mind in fleeting moments as she said: "Yes." She felt no apprehension.

"Could we talk?" He was definitely American. Hawaii?

"Well . . ." she began hesitantly. Always show reluctance. "I've had a very difficult day, and as you can see, I've only just arrived. I usually like some time to myself . . ."

He was understanding personified. "I do appreciate that. I promise to take up very little of your precious time. I am sure you are a very busy lady."

She could hardly be rude to such graciousness. She gave him a smile that was not quite formal. "You are . . .?"

"John Ling, Miss Chi. I knew your father."

She felt a bolt of fear go through her. She did not know who John Ling was. She had never heard of him. This perfect stranger had waited for her or followed her home, to tell her that he had known her dead father, on the same day that she had been abducted by a fat madman in a fake taxi. She was terrified. She hid behind her glasses, hoping to hide her fear. The wind swirled about her.

Ling said: "You look frightened, Miss Chi. You need not be frightened of me. Your father worked for us."

"Us?" she said weakly. First the fat man, now this one. He could be anyone, even working for the fat man, trying to trap her.

"I see you do not believe me," Ling told her in his most reasonable voice. "Very well. I shall tell you what has been happening to you. A round man, whom I shall call Qi Fung, has been pursuing you, demanding information about things of which you know nothing. He has threatened to have your mother returned to the Republic to stand trial for crimes against the revolution." Ling continued into Mary Chi's growing look of surprise: "He has probably threatened to destroy your reputation if you do not obey him, perhaps even to turn his thug upon you. You are surprised, Miss Chi. Do not be. Qi Fung and his methods are well known to me."

"How . . . how do I know you do not work for him? He could easily have told you everything you have just said."

"You are truly your father's daughter," Ling said. "You take nothing at face value. That is good. Your father was a much-admired man. I am pleased to see his daughter . . ."

"You could be anyone, Mr Ling, if that is your name. You could be as dangerous to me as the man you call Qi Fung."

"I am dangerous, yes . . . to Qi Fung, possibly . . . not to you. I am on your side, Miss Chi. We both want the same thing."

"We do?"

"Yes. You would like to be rid of Qi Fung. So would I."

Mary Chi looked into the eyes of the reasonable stranger, and did not know what to think.

Ling said: "We must get out of this wind."

"I am not taking you into my flat."

"An understandable, though unnecessary precaution. May I buy you tea?" He seemed quite undisturbed by the refusal of hospitality. "I suggest the small restaurant over there."

"Is that where you waited for me?"

"Yes," he admitted shamelessly.

She decided to go with him. He could hardly attack her in the restaurant; but if there was the slightest truth in what he had said, then she would be rid of Qi Fung for good. It was worth having tea with this stranger with the American accent, and the American suit.

She was terrified of what Qi Fung could do to her, and as she had begun to believe increasingly that Qi Fung or his colleagues had been responsible for her father's death, the thought of some kind of revenge was beginning to smell sweet.

There was hardly anyone in the restaurant. Ling took her to a secluded corner, ordered tea. They did not speak until the hot, scented brew had been placed upon the table. Ling poured.

"For whom did my father work?" she asked, continuing the conversation as it had started, in English. "The CIA?"

Ling smiled. "Those seem to be everybody's favourite initials these days."

"The Kuo?"

Ling said, after a long pause. "He worked for you."

147

"For *me*?"

"Yes. In working for you, he worked for Hong Kong. In order to work for Hong Kong, and therefore for you, he worked for us; for Taiwan."

Mary Chi looked down into her cup, stared at the leaves nestling beneath the pale, fragrant liquid.

"What did you ask him to do?" she demanded quietly. She did not look up.

"We asked nothing dangerous of him; merely to observe and listen. We wanted to know what was really going to happen about Hong Kong, since that is directly linked to what action may eventually be taken against us by the People's Republic. Your father was one of many who are willing to help us."

"If what he was doing was not dangerous, then why is he dead?" She still did not look up.

Ling said: "We have assumed he heard, or saw, something highly sensitive. I am certain that whatever it was, was accidentally done. Your father was not a spy, whatever Qi Fung might have told you."

"It was enough to cause his death." She removed her glasses, rubbed the bridge of her nose. She looked up. The eyes fastened upon Ling. "Exactly what is a spy, Mr Ling? Exactly what did my father do for you?"

Possibly for the first time in his life, Ling was taken aback by the unexpected. He almost jerked away from her in his surprise.

"Such blue . . . eyes. In *you*?" Softly, a scientist inspecting a rare specimen.

"Exactly what, Mr Ling?" Pushing her advantage.

But Ling was no ordinary executive floored by a startlingly beautiful woman. He had rapidly got over the intitial shock.

"Are you attempting to interrogate me, Miss Chi?" It was said with an almost caressing softness, and Mary Chi was aware of a menacing quality to his voice that had not been there before.

She stood her ground. "I just want to know what my father did for you. I want to know why it was so important that it caused his death."

Ling said: "Quite fascinating." He was staring into her eyes.

148

"A throwback. You are Kazak, with a touch of ancient Greek, perhaps."

"Qi Fung decided it was a wandering Russian."

"He would. Russians are everyone's favourite bogeys too. Ironic."

"You have not answered me, Mr Ling."

"Do not get bold with me, Miss Chi, though your father was greatly respected. In his memory, I am prepared to help you, and remove a nuisance from your life. I have not answered you simply because there is no answer that can be given.

"Your father was not a spy and, I repeat, he was given nothing dangerous to do. Whatever he saw or heard, did not get back to us. He was killed before he could pass it on. Your eyes do not believe me."

"In my place, what would you do?"

Ling sighed. "Miss Chi, let me tell you about the realities of life. I am told the Kazaks are warriors; but this is not the high frontier, and you are not a full-bloodied warrior. This is Hong Kong, where things you have never dreamt of can happen to someone like you, should I leave you to the pleasures of Qi Fung. However, if you are of service to me, I shall be of service to you. First tell me what Qi Fung requires of you."

Command of the situation had shifted irrevocably to Ling. In fact, she admitted to herself ruefully, it had never truly shifted from his hands. She was a terror in the boardroom, but in the streets, in the murky world of Ling and Qi Fung, she was but a minnow. She told him all that had happened to her. He listened expressionlessly.

He nodded slowly as she came to the end. "Exactly as I thought. His pattern never varies. All I require of you, Miss Chi, is that you do not go to the party."

"I don't want to go. But if I do not, he will come for me."

"Precisely. And I, shall be waiting . . . for him."

TEN

Pross opened his eyes.

For the first few seconds, he forgot where he was; then the vast dimensions of the bed impressed themselves upon his vision. He wondered why he could see so clearly with the curtains all drawn, until he saw that one had been opened a little. A bare sliver of light had forced itself between the thick folds, but it was powerful enough to illuminate the entire room.

He turned his head slowly to his left, looking for Logan. She was not in bed.

He sat up immediately, propping himself on his hands, not sure what to think. All sorts of reasons sped through his mind. Had she deliberately brought him all the way up into the Italian mountains only to leave him to his own devices? Had she been the one not to be trusted? Was he even now being guarded by someone outside the door? Who had moved the curtains?

He leaned across to her side, felt it. It was still warm. So she hadn't been gone for long. He leaned further. The gun was not there; but the bag was. The towel was missing too.

The gun was gone. Logan was gone. He did not think she'd be walking about the place with a gun in her hand. He began to fear the worst.

He was just about to get out of bed, when she entered. She'd been in the bathroom. She was wrapped in the towel, and her hair seemed damp. A smaller towel hung from her neck. She was also carrying the gun.

"Sleep well?" was the first thing she said.

"Yes. Yes I did." He felt stupid.

She walked round to her side of the bed, put the gun down. "Thought I'd left you to it, did you?" Even in the bathroom, she maintained her guard. She began to towel her hair, did not look at him.

"Go on, Pross," she said teasing. "Admit it. You thought I'd walked out on you."

"I wouldn't say that . . ."

"Hah!" She towelled vigorously, shook her head like dog coming out of water.

"I didn't know what to think. Then I saw the gun was missing and I began to worry about you."

She put the towel down, turned to look at him. The green eyes were dark in the light of the room.

"You must stop worrying about me. I can look after myself. You have a job to do. You cannot afford to cloud yourself with worries. You've already got a family to think about. Don't add me to the list."

He decided he would never understand her.

In the ensuing silence, she turned away again.

"Sorry," she said quietly. "I didn't mean to sound so harsh."

"Forget it."

"Pross . . ."

"Forget it, I said."

There was a barely perceptible sigh. "Right," she said after a while. There was a stiffness to her back, which remained turned towards him. She began towelling her hair once more.

He climbed out of bed, picked up his clothes, went to the bathroom. It was almost as big as the bedroom, marbled, with mirrors everywhere. He had seen smaller flats.

When he'd come out again, dressed, Logan was also dressed, hair brushed and gleaming. She had drawn all the curtains open. She stood looking at him, almost like a child awaiting censure. It was almost noon.

"We must keep up our act for Grazziella," she said.

"Of course."

"I didn't mean to make you angry."

"I'm not angry." Which was true enough. "There are too many things to worry about; like getting to Hong Kong, for starters."

She stared at him, the freckly pattern on her face making her seem even more childlike.

"Right," she said, picked up her bag. The gun was obviously in it.

She'd probably belted on her loaded garters too, he thought drily as he picked up their cases.

She went to the door, opened it carefully, paused for a moment before stepping out.

He followed.

As they walked along the corridor, she said: "Did you really sleep well?"

"Like a log." He was feeling greatly refreshed.

That seemed to please her. "If everything goes well today, you'll be able to catch up on some more sleep. Depending on when we get to Hong Kong, there may be little time for you to rest before you go on the mission."

"Do you expect any hitches?"

"In my business, in yours too, I'm certain, it's always wise to expect hitches. But I know Giorgio. It will be alright."

Giorgio. "Grazzi's cousin."

"Yes."

"Ah."

They went down the staircase and into the great hall of golden marble with its tall columns. At one end of the hall was an alcove within which was a bust on an onyx plinth. Pross did not have to look closely to recognise the late Marchese, in Dragoon uniform.

A set of double-doors were opposite the staircase. Logan went up, pushed them open. She certainly knew her way around.

He followed her into an opulent room. They went through that into yet another. There wasn't a soul to be seen, though voices could now be heard. As they approached a third door, Pross began to recognise Grazziella's hoarse, sultry tones. She was giving orders, in Italian. Logan opened the door, causing

152

Grazziella's voice to rise suddenly. The miffed old man, and a young woman, were with her. Pross nodded at them.

She stopped in mid-flow at their entry. "Aah! There you are. I was about to send someone to you." She had been sitting at a lavishly set breakfast table. Now she stood up, rushed over to them, a huge grin on her face. "The fugitive lovers!" She kissed Logan, winked at Pross, kissed him too. "Sit down, children. I want to know the story. Why do you think I am up so early?" She showed them to the table.

Grazziella looked ravishing, as if she'd been up for hours getting ready. She was dressed in an expensive lemon-yellow trousers and blouse outfit that seemed afraid to stray too far from her skin. Her blonde hair shone. A necklace that sparkled with green and gold hugged her throat.

The breakfast room, Pross saw, was only marginally smaller than the bedroom he'd just vacated, and had the same golden marbled theme of the building; but something else took his breath away. One entire wall had been turned into a vast french window which opened out onto a full-width terrace. Beyond the terrace was a spectacular view of the mountains and valleys of the Marche. A high stone rail bordered the terrace.

Before taking his seat, Pross went out into the warm sunshine, looked down. It was a sheer drop for several hundreds of feet into the valley below.

God. What real money could do.

He turned, to find both Grazziella and Logan studying him with interest. The old man and the young woman had gone.

"Well?" Grazziella began. "What do you think of my Renaissance painting? Better than a gallery, eh?"

He joined them at the table. "Priceless."

She laughed, said to Logan: "He appreciates it, Sian. Be careful. I shall want to steal him."

Logan said. "Grazzi divorced her last husband because he hated the view. It gave him vertigo."

If you wish to marry an Italian countess, first make sure you're not susceptible to vertigo.

"You are smiling, Damian," Grazziella began. "What do you find amusing?"

Damian? He glanced at Logan who was deeply occupied with a croissant. What, he wondered, had she used as a surname?

Pross said: "Vertigo."

"He was funny, anyway," Grazziella said, peering undecidely at a piece of toast. "He was German." She made it sound like a condemnation. "But quite harmless." She made a dismissive gesture with a flutter of an elegant hand. "Enough of him. I want to hear about you and Sian. *That* is much more exciting."

Pross said: "I think the lady should tell you herself. Shouldn't you, Sian?" It was the first time he'd used her name. He stared at her pointedly. "Then I think we ought to be getting on."

Logan had her mouth full. She did not look at him. They waited for her, Grazziella with barely controlled eagerness.

At last, Logan said: "Don't fret, Damian." She used the name shamelessly. "Everything's being arranged."

Then Pross listened in amazement as she spun Grazziella a tale about a dinner party where it was all supposed to have begun, followed by a hurried, quiet wedding at a register office, culminating in a murderous chase by a hotly jealous ex-boyfriend's thugs. He almost believed it. Grazziella's mouth hung open once or twice when Logan, warming to her theme, elaborated some of her fabricated details. Logan appeared to be enjoying herself.

Pross wondered how Grazziella would react if she knew the truth; that her dear friend Sian had shot and killed people at Heathrow, and would kill again if the need arose.

She'd probably pass out with excitement, he thought sourly.

Sitting in a fairytale palace high in the mountains having breakfast at noon, he found it hard to equate the beauty before him, and the splendour which surrrounded him, with the true reasons for this being there. When he was long gone to whatever fate awaited him in Hong Kong, Grazziella dell'Orobianchi would be waking daily to her Renaissance landscape, for breakfast at noon, or later; and looking for husbands who did not suffer from vertigo.

Some people had it all made.

The phone rang into his thoughts. It was an ornate, sit-up-and-beg model. Pross had no doubt it was an original.

Grazziella left her chair to go to it. She lifted the receiver off the stem.

"*Pronto!*" She listened just long enough to identify the caller before launching into a stream of fast, but haughty Italian. She was talking to an equal who was well-liked, for her face became animated. Every so often, she glanced at the table.

She was clearly speaking about them; then Pross heard Logan's name mentioned. Grazziella paused, nodded vigorously, gave a crow of delight before putting the phone down.

She returned to the table, grinning at them. She did not sit down. "It is all arranged. The plane will be waiting when we get to Ancona."

Plane? Pross stared at Logan. *Logan could get hold of a plane?*

Grazziella smirked with pleasure, said: "May I leave you for a moment? I must cancel some people I had to see today, in Rome."

"Rome?" Pross queried. "You're supposed to meet people in Rome *today?*"

"Half an hour ago," came the unrepentant reply. "I must ring to make abject apologies. To spare you, I shall do so in my rooms. I leave my landscape to you. Enjoy it."

She left them with another of her conspiratorial winks.

"She seems to be having fun," Pross said after the door had closed behind Grazziella. "So Logan," he went on. "You're a story-teller too. You've even got a *plane*. Logan, you're a wonder."

"I'm in the field without cover. I have to do what I can."

"So who's complaining? Although . . . I wish you had chosen something better than Damian, for God's sake."

She was not looking at him, but his words brought a brief smile to her lips. "I used the first name that came into my mind."

"Damian? You knew a Damian?"

"His parents were family friends when I was a child. He liked fishing. When they came to visit, he used to put worms down my back. I hated him."

"Well thanks."

She looked at him then. There was a strange guardedness in the green eyes. "It doesn't matter anyway."

"What doesn't?"

155

"The name. The one on your passport's worse." She grinned briefly, but the eyes were still not in it.

"What have they given me?"

"Paul Pettigrew."

"I like your comedians."

They ate in silence for a while. From time to time, Pross admired the remarkable view. Imagine waking up to that every day, he thought.

"Christ!" Logan exclaimed suddenly. "I'm not bloody thinking!"

Pross stopped, watched her.

"Grazziella," she went on. "She's on the phone to Rome, telling the world we're up here. I forgot to tell her to say nothing."

Pross didn't think it would matter that much.

He said, quite calmly: "The chances of anyone finding out in time to do anything are pretty remote, and even they can't bug every phone in Italy."

"A chance is a chance. The Department's leaking. Whoever's doing it may have access to my file and may find out that I know Grazziella. Just suppose they do find out, but too late to get us here, they could work on her to find out which way we've gone. I think I'll tell her to stay away for a while; at least until the job's done."

"How can you do that without blowing your story?"

"I'll tell her I don't want the gunmen to reach her. That will scare her off."

"She ought to know what I know, then she *will* be scared."

Logan stared at him with concern. "You're alright, aren't you, Pross?" she queried gently.

"Oh I'm fine. I just want to get to Hong Kong and get it over with."

She touched him briefly. "I'll get you there."

Grazziella came back into the room then.

"Grazzi," Logan began immediately, "did you tell your friends about us?"

"Not a word. Do you think I want to share this? I shall talk about it *after* it is all over."

Pross saw Logan look visibly relieved. "Perhaps not even then, Grazzi," she said quietly.

156

Grazziella was clearly puzzled. "Why not?"

Logan said: "I would not like those men to know about you."

Grazziella's brow furrowed. "You mean they would come *here*?" She was scandalised and anxious at the same time.

"Perhaps. I don't want them to pull you into this. It might be an idea for you to stay away for a week or so."

Pross watched as the need for juicy gossip gave way to the stronger need for self-preservation on Grazziella's pretty face.

She sighed. "It is a pity that I will not be able to make my friends jealous with such a story, but perhaps you are right. I can stay with Giorgio. Those men, whoever they are, would not dare go to his house. Giorgio is very powerful these days. He is not the young boy you used to know, Sian."

Pross glanced at Logan, who did not meet his eyes.

Hmm.

Logan stood up. "Do you feel up to the drive, Grazzi?"

Grazziella's eyes sparkled. "Of course!"

Pross groaned inwardly.

"Right then," Logan said. "Let's go."

Grazziella charged out of the building, shouting rapid orders to Alberto, who trailed behind with as much dignity as he could muster.

Pross and Logan followed, Pross fixing the Ferrari with a distinctly jaundiced eye as he put their cases in.

Grazziella had already slid herself behind the wheel, eager to be off. She was still raining orders about the unfortunate Alberto's head. Alberto kept his dignified silence, nodding only when he thought it appropriate. He'd obviously been through it all before, countless times.

Pross and Logan climbed in. The Ferrari began to move, and Grazziella continued her one-sided conversation with Alberto who was trotting along with the car now. He had a unique trot, a sort of shuffle and skip; but he managed to hang on to his dignity. The Ferrari gathered speed. Alberto decided enough was enough. He stayed put. With a final yell, Grazziella pulled away from him.

The Ferrari plunged downhill.

Grazziella said: "I will get you to Ancona very quickly."

In the back, Pross shut his eyes. *Oh God*, he thought.

It was 10.00 pm in Hong Kong, and Mary Chi sat in her flat dreading the passing of each minute. Each one that did not bring the sound of the doorbuzzer, was greeted with relief.

She had spent the evening in fear. The phone had rung several times. She knew it had been Qi Fung checking to see if she had obeyed him. He would have learned long ago that she had not done so. So she had sat in the flat, waiting on his vengeance. She hoped the man who called himself John Ling had meant what he had said. If not, it was already too late to call the police. Perhaps she should have done so right at the very beginning; but she had been terrorised into keeping quiet. There was nothing she could do. Qi Fung would do his worst, unless John Ling, whoever he really was, intervened.

Mary Chi looked about her. She hoped they weren't going to shoot anyone in her home.

Jack Wisyczyk watched balefully from his perch on an ammunition box as two civilians poked their noses all over his beloved Lynx. They had been sniffing about all day and now well into the evening, doing all kinds of weird adjustments, getting in his way. He sat in the lighted hangar fuming. He hated civilians.

He turned to the Chief Technician who was his immediate boss, but who outside the Chief's hearing was also called his keeper. Being in charge of Wisyczyk was sometimes not unlike being in charge of a wild, unpredictable gorrilla.

"Chief," Wisyczyk began, "how fakking long are these fakking people going to fart about with my fakking Lynx?"

"Yours, old son? Her Majesty gave it to you did she?"

Wisyczyk did not answer the question; which was normal. "I've got a lot of fakking work still to do. At this fakking rate I won't get to my fakking pit tonight."

"You'll get a week's leave after this is all over, Jack. You've done well. CO's really pleased with you."

"Fakking CO."

The Chief let the insubordination pass. The paperwork alone was too much trouble to put him on a charge. Besides, he needed Wisyczyk on the flight line, not cooling his heels uselessly in the guardhouse entertaining the snoops.

The Lynx looked menacing in its dull matt colours. It was a very beautiful machine, the Chief had to admit to himself. It looked beautiful, and lethal.

"So when's this fakking civilian pilot coming then, Chief?" Wisyczyk asked. He was impatient, wanting to get on with it. A bad sign.

The crew chief looked at him. "What civilian pilot, Jack?"

"Aw fakking come on, Chief! Everybody fakking knows."

As military intelligence officers had found out since intelligence gathering began, when the first scout went ahead of the first primitive hunting party, the bush telegraph of the other ranks was the best network in existence.

The Chief said: "I wouldn't spread rumours if I were you, lad."

"Who's spreading fakking rumours? I'm fakking asking, Chief."

"I know nothing, lad. Neither do you."

"Fakking hell," Wisyczyk said in disgust, and stared hatefully at the men in the Lynx.

It really was going to be a late night. Outside, a strong wind blew.

The phone rang in Mary Chi's flat. She stared at it, mesmerised. It rang and rang. She continued to stare at it. She sat in the comfortable lounge of her own home, feeling trapped.

She could hear the wind howling as if enraged, wanting to get in. It sounded particularly hostile, as if she were the source of its ire.

The sudden, brittle noise of a window breaking made her jump. She looked from the ringing telephone to seek out the damaged window as the noise of the wind rose dramatically. A gale blew through the flat, scattering everything that was light enough and not fixed or weighted down.

She was in the act of rising, when she froze, dumbstruck. The wind had not broken the window of her first-floor flat.

Qi Fung had just entered. His mean eyes were fixed upon her as he approached. His round face held no expression, but what the eyes said chilled her. Incongruously, he was dressed in a dinner suit. It was too tight for him, and was exceedingly rumpled. He stopped before her, eyes alive with a terrible anger. She stared at him, transfixed. A wisp of paper, blown from a shelf by the wind coming in through the shattered pane, smacked itself against his cheek. He ignored it. It hung there for some moments, as if craving attention; then giving up, it fluttered away. Never once did Qi Fung take his eyes off her.

She found the ignored distraction of the slip of paper more terrifying than if he had shouted at her.

Without warning, he slapped her hard across the face with the palm of his meaty hand. The unexpected blow made her stagger backwards until she came up against a low table. She fell, her cheek stinging with unbelievable pain. She never thought a slap could hurt so badly. She had not been wearing her glasses, and was thankful for that, certain they would have been smashed by the blow, sending slivers into her eyes. The thought made her shudder.

Qi Fung was picking her up, grabbing her roughly by the shoulders. His grip was painful and she cried out. He hit her again, this time with the back of his hand, across the other cheek. The pain was even worse and again she cried out as she fell for a second time. The skin on her cheek felt as if it were being lifted right off, tightening as it did so, across her entire face.

Where was the man who called himself Ling? Why hadn't he stopped Qi Fung as he'd promised? He had fooled her too.

Qi Fung was stooping towards her, his bulk looming above her. He did not attempt to pick her up. Instead, he hit her again, this time with a partially closed fist. The blow took her on the recently wounded cheek, lower down. She tasted blood at the corner of her mouth.

She felt a nameless horror. He was ruining her face! Where was Ling? Where was Ling? She must do something, do something . . .

The wind hurled itself dementedly through the flat, enjoying

160

itself, slamming doors, smashing breakables off shelves. It was almost as if Qi Fung's brutish colleague had joined him.

Qi Fung was screaming at her: "You have dared to make a fool of me!" he bawled in Cantonese. "You were warned about the penalty for doing it!"

She began to squirm away from him, but he reached down, picked her up roughly and slammed her against a cane settee. She felt a sharp edge jab into her thigh. Tears sprang to her eyes. She tried not to sob, but the pain was excruciating. It felt as if the cane had penetrated deep into her flesh, though she did not feel the warm wetness of blood.

She was too afraid to look; too afraid of what she might see, too afraid to take her eyes off Qi Fung.

His hateful eyes glared down at her. "I will not damage you too badly, for the moment. My colleague would like to enjoy you whole, little blue-eyed spawn of a Russian barbarian. Since you were not prepared to take the way offered you, we shall be forced to take what information we can from you. Then we shall have to do something about those obscene eyes of which you are so proud."

Her face paled with the terror of it.

"Ah!" he said softly. "That truly frightens you. Perhaps I should have threatened it before. Perhaps then you would have believed my promise to you."

The fear screamed out of her. "*I know nothing!*"

"It is a matter of belief with the police of many countries," Qi Fung began conversationally, "that something is always known, even when you believe you do not. There is always a small item hidden deep in the mind which by judicious encouragement, can be made to surface."

"I have told you! *I know nothing!*"

She found herself cringing on the settee, trying uselessly to keep away from him. She hated the now sobbing creature she had seen herself turn into; hated it, because she had not realised it existed within her. What would her father have said?

The wind answered her, and it told her nothing.

Qi Fung was saying, almost gently: "I believe you *think* you know nothing. I am certain you are not trying to deceive me, now."

"I have never tried to deceive you!"

"Oh Miss Chi!" Qi Fung favoured her with a look of benign scepticism. The wind raged about him, continuing to wreak its havoc on the flat. He ignored it, his interest focused exclusively upon her.

"Why won't you believe anything I say?" she asked pleadingly.

"I am of a naturally suspicious nature."

"How can I tell you anything if I know nothing? Whatever you say, I know nothing! How can I tell you what I do not know?"

"We shall try to make you."

She buried her wounded face in her arms and sobbed as she lay tightly curled up on the settee, waiting for a resumption of the beating.

Qi Fung said: "You spent a great deal of time with a foreign pilot. We know you were not aware of this, but it alters nothing. The pilot was with you, and you are the daughter of a man who was known to have been an agent of the enemy of Taiwan. The enemy continues to offer great financial inducements to potential traitors so that they may defect with aircraft of the People's Republic. Recently, one such tried. He did not make it. Another tried, and did succeed. The enemy believes that such flights prove discontent among out pilots. Three and a half million American dollars in gold is meant to be the proof of such discontent."

Qi Fung gave what was meant to be a laugh of derision. It turned into an unnerving giggle which died just as unnervingly.

"Miss Chi," he went on, "your pilot friend crossed illegally into the Republic for reasons more dangerous to the revolution than the mere scuttling away of a few greedy pilots. Why, Miss Chi, is what we wish to know from you."

"I know nothing," she repeated over and over again.

Qi Fung said to her soothingly: "Do not distress youself. We shall soon relieve you of that burden."

Where was Ling? her mind asked itself despairingly. No one would hear her screams in this wind. Perhaps if she moved quickly, she could surprise Qi Fung and make it to the broken window. How had he come up? A ladder. That must be it.

She continued to whimper, planning her moves. He was

hampered by his fat, whereas she was strong and healthy, and should be able to outpace him. She might even be able to delay him sufficiently. There were many heavy things she could use to hit him with.

Then she was overcome by a new bout of despair. Where would she go to? Where could she hide? They had got her father. They would get her too, whatever she did. Only if Qi Fung were put out of action would she be safe.

But the man who had promised to do so, had not. She felt an intense bitterness towards Ling. She could not believe her father had worked for such people; but her own mother had said he had.

Qi Fung or Ling. Was there really much difference between them?

She rose suddenly off the settee, taking Qi Fung so completely by surprise, he took a step backwards.

"If you're going to kill me," she yelled at him, "you'll have to do it now!" She picked up a heavy-based lamp that had fallen during the time he had been attacking her, brandished it. Now she was fighting back she felt better, even if it meant she might lose. "I am leaving, and I shall hit you with this if you try to stop me! There will be no information for you, because you'll have to kill me to stop me." She edged towards the window as she spoke, still brandishing her new-found weapon.

Qi Fung moved sideways, matching her movements, light on his feet.

Keeping her eyes on him, she continued towards the window. The wind howled at her, threatening, gleeful. A real storm, she thought. Would the ladder hold? Was it even still there? She tried not to think about that.

"It is no use, Miss Chi," Qi Fung said within the wind. "Your efforts are quite futile. You will not get away, and we shall have what we need from you."

She backed away, he followed, but going nowhere near her. She felt triumph. It was obvious he fully expected her to strike at him. Good! Let him be wary of her for a change.

She reached the window, back to it. The wind tugged at her dementedly. Then suddenly, a host of things happened all at once.

163

The wind abruptly lessened, the lamp was taken out of her hands, and Qi Fung was smiling.

She turned in shock. Qi Fung's colleague was grinning at her.

"It is a great pleasure to make your acquaintance again, Miss Chi," he said in mocking Cantonese.

But something else was happening. The man's eyes were widening first in surprise, then in fear, then in horror as his perch was whipped away from under him. He tried to do several things at once, failed. The hand holding the lamp let go in a desperate attempt to find some kind of purchase. What it grabbed was a jagged piece of glass sticking up from the window-frame. The glass pierced his hand like a dagger.

He screamed, tried to free it with his other hand, robbing himself of his only means of support by so doing. Gravity took over.

His body fell for exactly six inches. It was halted abruptly when another knife-like piece entered below the chin, ploughed upwards through the jaw, through the tongue and into the roof of the mouth. He made the most appalling sounds that Mary Chi thought she would ever hear in her life as his body struggled, embedding this new dagger of glass even deeper.

It moved inexorably towards his brain.

Qi Fung had also moved. He rushed forward to help his stricken colleague.

Mary Chi seized her chance. She picked up another lamp, brought it heavily down upon Qi Fung's unprotected head, screaming as she did so. She hit him again and again, smashing him into the lethal shards of the broken pane. She was a maddened creature, the wind swirling her hair about her head, her blue eyes raging with a momentarily insane fire.

The blows pushed Qi Fung's head through the window and he too was spitted upon the gleaming, brittle teeth of the window.

Still the blows fell, and still Mary Chi screamed as she dealt them. The wind howled about her, adding its own mindless accompaniment.

The door to her flat burst open. She stopped, arms raised with the weapon of destruction held above her head in preparation for another blow. Blood dripped from the base of the lamp. She stared.

Ling was standing there, a gun in his hand.

"*Where were you?*" she screamed at him in English. "*Where were you!*"

The wind slammed the door to. People began to gather outside it.

Ling came forward, avoided her, stared at the two men. Qi Fung was clearly dead. His colleague was still struggling and going slowly, painfully. Ling did nothing to help.

He said, calmly: "You almost didn't need me. You did very well."

Mary Chi let the lamp fall. It shattered. Her eyes stared wildly.

Ling looked at the pieces. "Which proves his head was much softer than the floor." He looked up at her, scrutinised her puffy face, the congealed blood by her mouth. "I am sorry I am late, but I had to wait for his friend."

She didn't know whether to believe him.

"A friend of mine pulled his ladder away," he went on. "As you have so efficiently demonstrated, it gave you all the chance you needed."

"They could have killed me!" She began to tremble, breathing quickly. Reaction to what she had done was beginning to set in. "They could have killed me!" she repeated, yelling at him.

He was still calm. "Not Qi Fung. Not until he had finished with you. I knew there was time. I am sorry that you were subjected to a beating while I waited. It was unavoidable."

"*Unavoidable*? Have you ever taken an unavoidable beating, Mr Ling?"

"Yes," he answered seriously. "I must leave now," he went on. "The police will be round soon and I must not be found here. You may tell them all you wish, except about me. You will make no mention of me whatsoever." The dark eyes bored into her. "I am not as easily overcome as Qi Fung when I am displeased." He put his gun away.

He went to the door. She shivered. His menace was palpable. She sank to the floor, put her head in her hands.

Ling pulled the battered door open. A babble of voices greeted him. Heads tried to peer in.

"Police!" he snapped imperiously in Cantonese at the sea of curious faces. "Get back into your homes and keep out of the way!" They shrank before him as he ploughed through them.

Some stared at the door, but none dared enter.

Ling made it safely out just as the first police were going in.

In the Authorised-Personnel-Only hangar at Shek Kong, Wisyczyk looked at his watch, said: "Fakking hell, Chief. How much fakking longer do I have to fakking hang about here? It's fakking gone eleven. Be fakking midnight soon."

"You wait, Jack lad. That's what you do. Don't you know by now that's what you do in this man's service? And you were once a sergeant?"

"Yah well. Fakking CO had a fakking brainstorm, didn't he, making me a fakking sergeant. Give it to anyone, he fakking would."

"Don't you have any ambition, Jack?"

"Yah. I have. I want to get my fakking Lynx then off to my fakking bed. And listen to that fakking wind out there. Fakking typhoon, if you ask me. Even a fakking Lynx can't fly in a fakking typhoon."

"This one's not a typhoon, Jack. It will be gone by tomorrow."

"You fakking hope."

"Met says."

Wisyczyk made a noise that consigned all Meteorological personnel to a favourite hell-hole in his mind. He hated Met.

"Met! That fakking lot wouldn't know a wind if it fakking came and ponged under their fakking noses." Wisyczyk stared at the Lynx. "Climatic Evaluation Trials. You don't really fakking believe that, do you, Chief?"

"That's what it says on the sheets."

"Fakking sheets," Wisyczyk, a man wise in the ways of service doublethink, said with profound scepticism. "Let me tell you a fakking story, Chief. I got told once I was going on a fakking exercise. Next thing I fakking knew, I was on riot duty in Cyprus.

A *real* fakking riot." He snorted. "Climatic Evaluation Trials. I'll believe that when I fakking see it."

The Chief said nothing.

For reasons known only to herself, Grazziella had decided to eschew the autostrada, and take the coastal road to Ancona; not the main trunk road that ran almost parallel with it for much of the way, but a narrow road that had begun at Porto Recanati. It was one of those beauties that maps liked to term "other" roads. Today, it had the added refinement of being crowded as well.

From his position in the back, Pross did not mind the go-slow. In fact, he welcomed it. Grazziella had called Riccardi's office in Ancona, to tell him they were on their way due to a hurried departure. She had not told him why, but he had said the Lear would not be ready for at least two hours. They had plenty of time. The slow pace was therefore a relief to Pross.

Unfortunately, Grazziella disliked being baulked by slower traffic and every time a gap – which Pross would vow a Mini could not get through – appeared, she had the disconcerting habit of using all of the Ferrari's three hundred and ten rampant horses to burn through the seemingly infinitesimal space. Miraculously, she would get through every time, sometimes accompanied by a wild yell and a blast of the car's fanfare horns.

Now they were leaving Numana, and the road began to twist with a vengeance. Grazziella was in her element. Grudgingly, despite his constant expectations of disaster, Pross found himself admitting she was as good on twisty roads as she was on the autostrada.

Grazziella said, suddenly: "Sian. Where will the plane be going?"

Pross waited with interest to hear Logan's reply.

After a while, Logan said: "Giorgio will tell you."

"He knows?" Grazziella was surprised. "He said nothing to me."

Pross was himself surprised, but said nothing.

Grazziella was baffled by Logan's silence. It did not stop her from pouring the power on round a bend and nearly clipping a little Fiat down a steep slope that seemed to go on forever.

The Fiat squealed its fear.

"There's was plenty of room," Grazziella said indignantly. "What is the matter with him?"

Bowel trouble, Pross thought grimly. *Like me*.

Logan said, at last: "I called him from Rome to give him time to prepare."

"Prepare for what?" Grazziella was curiosity personified.

"All in good time, Grazzi."

Pross thought he detected a strange tightness in her voice, but assumed he must have been mistaken, for Grazziella did not comment on it.

She said: "As long as I am told, I will forgive you."

Logan made a strange sound, suspiciously like a giggle.

Grazziella decided to glance at her while veering round a corner. Pross forced himself to keep his eyes open. Might as well see the end coming.

The bend was mercifully empty.

Grazziella said: "Is something wrong?"

"Oh no," Logan answered. "I remembered something funny, that's all."

"Damian," Grazziella called.

"Yes?" Pross answered.

"Did you know that when Sian was a teenager we thought she and Giorgio would get together?"

"No. I didn't" He watched Logan keenly. Nothing about her posture told him anything.

"Of course, they did not. Giorgio was too busy with silly little girls. You know . . . models, starlets. He is so stupid sometimes. It takes a fool in some ways not to see what is in someone like Sian. Do you not agree?"

Pross was still looking at the silent Logan. "I agree absolutely."

Logan was giving nothing away.

Grazziella chose another corner to take her hand off the wheel long enough to give Logan a pat on the thigh. "There. You see? You've got yourself a champion. He is a good man. Not jealous."

"I know," Logan said. She had spoken very quietly.

ELEVEN

Giorgio Riccardi was sickeningly handsome. He had carefully cut blond hair, deep, brooding brown eyes, and a fine Roman nose that somehow managed to give the impression that the smell of the entire world was of singular offence to it.

Despite the predilection in Italy for the kidnapping of the rich, Riccardi preferred to be his own chauffeur. He always carried with him a Beretta 93R automatic, with which it was said he was quite competent. There could be other reasons why he was left alone. Rumour had it that he could be far nastier than anyone who dared go up against him. Whatever the truth of it, the fact was Riccardi enjoyed a life that was remarkably free of such annoyances.

He was extremely rich, some of his wealth being inherited, while unkind suspicions hinted at a fortune amassed on the wrong side of the law. No one spoke them aloud.

Riccardi was just thirty, and owned a Learjet. As he drove to Ancona airport in his brilliant white, special-bodied Mercedes 500SEC with total disregard for anyone who dared use the same stretch of road as he, he pondered upon Logan's request. There was a smile of anticipation upon his fine lips as he aimed the big car through the traffic. He drove the car as if it were a gun; as if he were shooting people out of his way.

He wore a white lightweight suit with a pale-blue shirt that had a white collar. In the breast pocket of his jacket, a pale-blue handkerchief nestled boldly. On his left wrist was a thick gold bracelet that would cost a junior executive a year's salary.

Giorgio Riccardi was a prime shit, but he would help Logan for his own very personal reasons. The car pulled up in his reserved parking space. He shut down the engine, and waited.

They arrived at the Ancona airport with some time to spare. They saw Riccardi's car almost immediately. Grazziella pulled up next to it with a suicidal flourish. Pross, eyes closed, waited for the bang. He opened them reluctantly when nothing happened. He stared at the white car disbelievingly. It should have been wrecked.

Grazziella was already out, greeting her cousin, who had climbed out of his Mercedes, almost like a long-lost lover.

Pross watched the gleaming blond head, decided he disliked it on sight. But he needed the man's plane – a *Lear*, of all things, Logan had said in the car – and vowed to be on best behaviour. She had pulled off an amazing coup. He would not ruin it for her. A Lear would get them to Hong Kong on time. He hoped this man would not be coming.

Riccardi came forward to take Sian's hand to help her out of the car, but she managed to occupy herself with taking her case from Pross.

Riccardi looked confused, but not put out.

Pross hid a smile of satisfaction as he climbed out.

Grazziella was saying: "Giorgio, this is Sian's husband, Damian. Damian, my cousin, Giorgio Riccardi." She was looking from one to the other with an air of mischief. "He is not a jealous one, Giorgio."

Riccardi said: "A good virtue."

Pross knew a sugar-coated insult when he heard one and was glad he did not like Riccardi. What the hell. He only wanted the man's plane.

Riccardi said: "I would like to speak to Damian and Sian alone."

Grazziella looked hurt. "You are hiding things from me, Giorgio?"

"I will tell you about it later."

170

Everyone saw that he wouldn't. He seemed to treat Grazziella like a spoilt child. She gave him another hurt look before climbing resignedly back into the Ferrari.

Riccardi walked a little way from both cars. Logan and Pross followed. He stopped, turned to face them.

He said: "I know you two are not married. Don't try to tell me I am wrong. I am not a fool. Sian, you may be able to make my feather-brained cousin believe your ridiculous story, but not I. I insist on knowing what this is all about before I turn my jet over to you."

"I cannot tell you, Giorgio."

Riccardi stared at them for some moments, then nodded slowly. The fine lips curved in a slow smile. "I think you have just answered me. Who would believe the girl who once went for midnight swims with me would be doing such work?"

"What work, Giorgio?"

"I repeat. Do not take me for a fool." Riccardi stared at Pross. "I would like a moment with Sian. Alone."

Pross stared right back, but moved away. He watched as Logan and Riccardi talked animatedly for some minutes; then Riccardi came up to him.

Riccardi said: "I am doing this for Sian, not for your Government."

"I am grateful," Pross said with studied civility. "You will, of course, be reimbursed."

"We will not talk of money now," Riccardi said. "The aircraft has been fuelled, and all documentation completed. The crew is already on board. You will have no problems going through customs. I will not be coming with you. My affairs take all my time."

Pross said: "You have been very helpful, Mr Riccardi. I realise what pulling out your aircraft at such short notice must mean. I'll make sure you're not deprived of it for very long."

Pross thought he was sounding very pompous, decided it was the best way to handle a prideful macho like Riccardi. Riccardi was doing his best not to look down upon him, and was barely succeeding. There was the merest hint of a smirk on Riccardi's face.

171

Logan, Pross saw, was being hugged by Grazziella who was trying not to cry. He wondered what she'd had to offer Riccardi.

Riccardi said: "If the aircraft is lost or damaged, or the crew injured, I shall demand full compensation."

"Understandable."

Riccardi stuck out his hand. They shook hands briefly, silently. Riccardi went over to Logan. Pross saw her look at him neutrally, then his attention was distracted as Grazziella came up. She gave Pross an unrestrained hug.

"Look after her, whoever you are," she said quietly. For Grazziella, she was being very serious. "She is very special."

"I know," he said.

The whole scene, he thought, to anyone watching, would appear normal; normal to those who didn't know who they really were, not to pursuers. He hoped there were no pursuers.

"And you be careful driving back," he went on. Her arms were still about his neck, body lined against his. Telling Grazziella to be careful was like whistling into wind.

She tossed her blonde head, stared into his eyes. "The Ferrari knows me. Tell me, is there really anything between you and Sian?" Her smile warned him about his choice of answer.

"Well . . ." he began.

But she did not let him finish. "It's alright. I can see she has some feeling for you." She paused. "I am not as foolish as my cousin thinks."

Shit.

Grazziella moved reluctantly away, glanced to where Riccardi was standing talking to Logan.

"Don't worry about Giorgio. He hasn't a chance. He is too late."

"I wasn't worried."

Pross looked at Logan. Riccardi made to hug her, but she stuck out her hand. Riccardi took it, looking surprised.

Odd.

But Logan seemed to be smiling. Riccardi had no choice but to smile too; but Pross could see his pride had taken a little dent. He wondered with some dread whether Riccardi would pull a sulk and call the Lear off; but no. It seemed to be alright.

"Grazzi!" Logan called. "Get off him!"

Grazziella winked shamelessy at Pross. "You see?" she began in a whisper. "That is the sound of a woman warning a trespasser."

"Grazziella," Pross said, "you're impossible." He was beginning to like her.

"But of course. How else could I be me?"

"Thanks for everything."

"I am glad I have been able to help. You must make Sian bring you back when there is time."

"We shall see," Pross said, knowing the chances were pretty slim.

"Grazzi!"

Grazziella said: "You must go before she scratches my eyes out." She smiled, kissed him chastely on the side of the mouth.

He picked up his case, went over to Logan and Riccardi.

Riccardi said: "My business calls. I shall take my leave of you. Have a good flight." He gave a brief nod, walked away towards where his car was parked.

Pross said: "Everything alright between you two?"

"Yes." She was busy with her bag, shifting the shoulder strap to a more comfortable position. "Why?"

"I just thought he looked slightly pissed-off about something. I told him he'd be reimbursed. I hope you don't mind. God knows what he'll sting your Department for."

They heard Riccardi's Mercedes start. The engine raced. Pross turned to look. The white car screeched out of the parking area.

"No. I don't mind," Logan said from behind him. "We reached agreement on his reimbursement."

Something about her voice nagged at Pross, but it was elusive. He let it go. It didn't matter. They had a swift, private plane to take them to Hong Kong, and were well ahead of any pursuers.

No one would catch up with them now.

"Logan, remind me when it's all over to tell Fowler how bloody marvellous you are."

"If you say that too often, I'll start believing it."

"Believe it."

They waved to Grazziella who was still standing by the Ferrari, biting her lower lip, and looking like a mother sending her little ones off to boarding-school.

"I wonder if I'll ever see her again," Logan said quietly.

"You will."

They turned away. Behind them, the Ferrari snarled into life. It screeched away even more loudly than Riccardi's Mercedes. Pross smiled to himself. Grazziella being careful.

They did not look back

The Gates Learjet Longhorn 50 lifted on upturned wingleted wings into the clear Adriatic sky, heading for 24,000 feet.

"Well," Pross began, "we made it. A whole plane all to ourselves. You should be running your firm, Logan, not just working in the field."

She gave him a tired smile from her seat across the aisle. "I'd hate it."

She probably would too, he had to agree. Logan was the kind of person who operated best in the field, under pressure; just like the man he was going to rescue.

Now that it appeared they were well on their way to a smooth flight to Hong Kong, he felt all his paranoia about Ling return. Had Fowler's people continued to maintain a tight screen about Dee and the kids? Had Ling's people managed to penetrate yet again?

And of course, there was Hong Kong itself. Ling had said he would be contacted. How? Ling did not know when he'd be arriving.

Logan said: "Something up? You're looking worried again."

"What?" Pross came back to his surroundings. "Oh no. No. I was just wondering who'd be meeting us. No one knows where we are."

The uncomforting thought suddenly occurred to him that if the Lear decided to nosedive into the sea, it would be some time before Fowler and his lot found out.

Not that it would help us, he thought drily.

Logan said: "I'll work something out."

He knew she would. By now, he had every faith in her.

Riccardi had even had the plane stocked with food and wine

for the long flight; not cheap stuff either, but the kind Riccardi himself would have deigned to eat. They were to help themselves to whatever they wanted. Pross supposed the Department would receive the bill eventually. Some little financial gnome, buried within the depths of the Department and whose job it was to keep a beady eye on expenses, would probably let out an almighty squeal when the bill hit him.

Pross did not feel guilty. Fowler and his people had uprooted him from his home, placed his family in jeopardy, so that he could pull their burning chesnuts out of the fire. It was the least they could do.

The Lear passed Flight Level 240, step-climbed to 33,000 feet, and hit Mach 0.81 as it began the first leg of its long flight east.

Fowler was in the office of the man who had replaced Kingston-Wyatt as his immediate boss.

The man said: "Well Fowler? According to this report you've given me, your operative took it into her head to steam off on her own without letting you know."

Knowing more that the man did, Fowler said: "Her job is to get Pross to Hong Kong. I assume that's just what she's doing."

"You *assume*? You're supposed to be running this show, Fowler. Am I to tell the Minister you make assumptions about the activities of your field personnel?"

Fowler refrained from saying what the Minister could do with himself. It was obvious to him that his new boss, already a knight, was angling after new and dizzy heights and believed the best way to achieve this was by keeping the Minister happy.

Perhaps he dreamed of being an ambassador, Fowler thought sourly. He hoped that would happen and that the new man would get a posting to some dreary hell-hole. In the short time that he'd spent with the Department, he'd proved to Fowler that if ever there had been a case of a disastrous appointment, this man exemplified it. Fowler had not wanted the job himself. Kingston-Wyatt, for all his faults, was a difficult man to replace. Machiavellian in the extreme, he had nonetheless been an astute strategist.

The new man was saying: "Didn't what's-his-name set this up some time ago?"

What's-his-name. Address the man by his name, damn you. The poor sod's dead. At least show him that respect.

But Fowler did not speak his thoughts. "Yes," he answered. He hadn't liked it, but it had been running before he'd known about it.

"Bloody dicey."

Of course it was. "We thought there was a good chance of success."

We? Why the hell am I defending him? I remember bawling him out about it, telling him how risky, dangerous, and bloody mad it was, especially if something went wrong. I know why I'm defending him. It's because I can't stand this little berk.

The man said: "Success." He tapped the report impatiently. "We had better achieve success, Fowler. *You* had better achieve success. Why your unit chose to go off on her own is beyond me."

Unit? Logan was not a bloody unit. She was a person, shaping out into a top-class operative.

We're leaking like a downed chopper, Fowler didn't say. That's why.

He waited for more. It wasn't long in coming.

"And what about that mess she left lying around at Heathrow?"

"She had no choice. They were waiting for her, after first having taken out our own people. Instead of panicking, she kept her head, assessed the situation correctly, went into action. Forget Heathrow. She did bloody well to neutralise those people. She had to be quick, *and* accurate."

"I'll grant that." Grudgingly. "Ling's mob, do you think?"

"No identification has as yet come through. There was precious little left to identify. They could have been working for anyone who wants to stop our operation. I can think of many, some of them so-called 'friendlies'; in quotes."

"The report says he could be Taiwan. Why would Taiwan be wanting to take our people out?"

"Perhaps they think we're going to walk out of Hong Kong in a secret deal and leave them to face the sleeping giant."

"Don't be facetious, Fowler. We're not going to *walk out* on Hong Kong, as you put it. And there are no secret deals."

"I can certainly understand them wanting to know what we're up to."

"Our necks in sewage, if this thing blows," the man said sourly.

Fowler said nothing. He thought of Logan, glad she was running independently. He would say nothing to Hong Kong. She would make contact when she felt it safe enough to do so.

In his mind, he wished her luck. She had done well so far. He wanted that luck to continue. He was beginning to feel quite proud of her.

He took his leave of his new boss, went back to his office. A decoded priority signal was waiting for him. He took it from the person who had brought it, thanked her, sat down to read. He was on his feet almost immediately. He hurried back to the office he had just left. He put the signal down on the man's desk.

Sir John Winterbourne looked at the signal, looked up at Fowler, looked down again and began to read.

"This is very brief," he said when he'd finished. "Two men found dead in a flat belonging to a Mary Chi, in Causeway Bay, Hong Kong. One tentatively identified as Qi Fung. Such strange names, these people. This Mary Chi apparently acted in self-defence. Why should that merit a priority? If the Hong Kong Chinese want to do themselves to death, let them. What has it to do with this Department?"

Fowler stifled the retort of distaste he felt coming. No one should expect him to work with such an idiot. He decided he'd resign after this, live quietly in his home in the Cotswolds. The Department could find another house for its returning wounded and out-going warriors.

But he knew it wasn't as easy as all that.

He said, patiently: "Qi Fung was a senior man in the security services of the PRC . . ."

"PRC?"

Good God. "The People's Republic of China," Fowler supplied, biting back on his exasperation.

"Why didn't you say so in the first place? I dislike this *penchant* for talking in groups of letters. We're not Americans, nor are we computers. Always hated it, even in the service."

Winterbourne was not ex-RAF, another factor that rankled with Fowler. The Department was being fragmented.

He went on patiently: "Qi Fung was very, very good. This is the first time we've been able to put a face to him. We knew the name, but that was all."

"This Chi woman identified him as such. How reliable is that source?"

"Mary Chi was the daughter of a man killed in a supposed boating accident last year off High Island. He used to do little jobs for the people in Taiwan. We believe he was found out, and taken out, by Qi Fung's people. It is reasonable to suppose that Qi Fung would go after her for information. How he came to die in her flat is a mystery until we receive further details. I'm also surprised he told her his name, be it a cover, or real."

"Then who would have told her?"

"The only person who would want Qi Fung neutralised, and would also be interested in Mary Chi because of the Taiwan connection."

Winterbourne was fast on that one. "Ling?"

"Ling," Fowler said grimly. "Which means he's already in Hong Kong."

He thought of Logan and Pross. Nothing could be done to help them until he knew where they were.

In the building in Wan Chai, Ling stared at the man sitting across the room.

"Those were supposed to be good men," he said. His voice was accusing, cold with suppressed anger. "They could not take *one* young girl, despite having the advantage of surprise." Ling shook his head in disbelief. "You were supposed to be of help to me. Yet now we hear the people you recommended are dead, and Pross is still covered. I've got to get to him when he arrives here, without drama. How am I to do that with this woman who seems to shoot by instinct, covering him? She is liable to start a war on the streets of this city."

"Think she may be able to take you on, Ling?" the other said,

178

deliberately goading. He had an American accent; the same man who had accompanied Ling in the red Porsche.

Ling's glowing eyes narrowed. "No one takes/me on. This young woman has been dealing with incompetents."

The hard-faced man said: "Be careful. I'm not even supposed to be with you. My people pull me out, and you've had it. The Brits are supposed to be our allies. We're helping you get hold of their man because you want to know what they found out in China, and how it's going to affect you on Taiwan. People get splashed in this game. You started zapping theirs before they hit you. They're still not hitting you first, only hitting back. So don't start bitching me, Ling."

Ling's anger was a cold fire. "And what about you? When the British move out of Hong Kong, are you going to make peace across the water and leave us to rot? It has already begun, hasn't it?"

"What the goddam hell are you talking about? What has already begun?"

"Plans. Plans to dump us. Don't you think we know? Do you believe us to be so stupid?"

"Jesus H. Christ, Ling. What the hell is this? What is this sudden paranoiac crap?"

"*Paranoiac*?" Ling shouted, uncharacteristically. "Is it paranoia that stopped us from getting the F-16 and the Tigershark? We needed those planes, but you listened to the PRC."

"What is this shit? You've got over two hundred Tiger 5Es. You'll have two-fifty soon, two hundred and fifty of the best little interceptors this side of Beijing. I don't call that a bad deal. The 2nd and the 455th Wings are up to strength. So quit bitching and let's think of how to get this guy off the Brits."

Ling retreated into silence, then as if ashamed of his temporary loss of control, said: "Hey look. I'm sorry. I had just hated losing out to the woman. I've worked hard and long for this and I don't intend to lose."

"Okay, guy. I understand. It gets to you sometimes. Happens to all of us."

TWELVE

Thursday morning at Shek Kong dawned bright and windless. The raging gale of the night before had gone as if it had never been. At eight o'clock, Jack Wisyczyk reluctantly opened an eye, decided he was entitled to more time in bed because of his late night, went back to sleep again.

Most of his fellow inmates of the barrack block had already clattered off to their various duties. A few stragglers were still hanging around, but Wisyczyk was oblivious to them.

At nine o'clock, the crew chief was by his bed.

"What's this then, Jack?" the crew chief said with deceptive softness.

Remarkably, Wisyczyk heard with absolute clarity. Both eyes came open. He stared.

"Chiefy? Fakking hell!"

"Don't Chiefy me, lad. Why are you still in bed?"

"Fakking hell, Chief! I didn't get to bed till fakking three o'clock!"

"All the sleep you want when the exercise is over, lad. Not before. You knew that. Up you get. There's an airtest at ten hundred. Be there, Jack, or you're on a charge. I'm not joking lad." The crew chief left.

Wisyczyk knew his superior well enough to know he would indeed be reported for failing to turn up for duty. Charges did not worry him. He'd been on too many to care. He also knew he was needed on the flight line. No one would charge him now; but later, when the exercise was over, they'd hit him with a charge. Right in the middle of his leave.

He got out of bed.

"Fakking bastards!" he said with feeling. Then he brightened. The Lynx was going to fly.

At 09.45, Cado Rees appeared on the flight line in full gear. The Lynx had been wheeled out of the hangar. Wisyczyk, fretting round the aircraft like an anxious mother-hen, watched him approach.

"Don't fakking bend her," was the first thing Wisyczyk said.

Rees wore no badges of rank, but that would hardly have mattered to him. The mournful face looked at him from beneath its matt green, integral flight helmet.

Rees said: "You must be Jack Wisyczyk. I've heard about you."

"Oh yes? Who fakking from?"

"Just about everyone. You're famous. Will this thing stay up?"

"If you know how to fakking fly it, it fakking will. Are you the civvy pilot?"

"No. I'm here to test it for him. Making sure it will stay up when he gets here."

"Can *he* fakking fly?"

"Oh yes. He can." Rees climbed into the right-hand seat, strapped himself in. He began to do his checks.

Wisyczyk watched him. The civilians who had worked on the aircraft throughout the night had not yet appeared.

Rees completed his checks. Wisyczyk moved out of rotor range. The crew chief was standing a little distance away, facing the front of the aircraft. Everyone watched anxiously, even people in the hangar.

Rees started the twin uprated Gem-60s. The blades began to rotate slowly, before disappearing in a blur. The Lynx sounded powerful. Rees held it down for a while, then he lifted it, slowly at first, as if trying it out for feel, until its lifting motion metamorphosed into an increasingly swift vertical climb.

Wisyczyk let out a sigh of relief.

The Chief came over. "Well, Jack. It flies."

Wisyczyk stared at the receding Lynx, said nothing.

"Don't worry," the Chief said. "He'll bring it back."

"He'd fakking better."

Rees put the Lynx through its paces for half an hour, occasionally carrying out manoeuvres that had Wisyczyk, watching every alteration in its flight attitude, patting his pockets for non-existent cigarettes. By then, the two civilians had come onto the apron to watch.

Rees brought the Lynx back down. The civilians promptly went to its flight recorder, removed that, inserted a new one. Rees asked for certain changes. Wisyczyk, the rest of the ground crew and the two civilians, worked right through the lunch period.

Rees took it up again.

Watching, the crew chief said to Wisyczyk: "Well, Jack. He knows how to fly."

Wisyczyk rubbed an oil-stained nose with an oil-stained finger. "Where's he fakking from?"

"Blighty. Came in yesterday."

"Raf?"

"Army."

"Fakking pongo," Wisyczyk said dismissively. He watched the Lynx with the concern of a man who had just lent his prized car to someone in whose driving abilities he had little faith. "Any more news on that Wessex?"

The bodies of two soldiers had been found, one headless, by fishermen near a tiny lump in the sea called Round Island, a good nine kilometres east of Starling Inlet; while part of the tail of the Wessex, complete with rotor intact, had been found by marine police on another tiny island, Sai Ap Chau, almost at the mouth of the inlet itself. No one had as yet come up with a valid reason for the cause of the crash.

The crew chief said: "Not a sausage. It's going to take a while before we find out what really happened to that one. I don't envy the CO having to write all those letters home to the families. What can you really say? Dear Sir/Madam, your son/husband died bravely carrying out his duties and is now feeding the fishes. Poor sods."

"Yeah. Fakking rough, that."

Wisyczyk watched critically as the Lynx did a wing over, pivoted, swooped in to land. The let-down was done beautifully. The Lynx settled, rocked only a little.

"I've seen fakking worse," Wisyczyk said. From him, it came perilously close to an accolade.

Rees climbed out, walked up to the civilians, spent some time with them; then he came up to Wisyczyk who had already been inspecting the aircraft for damage.

Rees removed his helmet. "She's a sweet ship," he said to Wisyczyk. "You've done a good job. We'll do one more test a little later."

Wisyczyk did not look round from what he was engaged upon. "The Chief's the fakking boss around here."

Rees was not offended by the blunt put-down. "Everybody says to talk to you. I know how hard you've worked on this Lynx. The Chief told me."

"He fakking did, did he?" Wisyczyk still did not look round. "About fakking time somebody fakking appreciated me around here."

Rees' mournful face broke into a smile. "Keep her nice and tight, Jack. The man who's coming can make choppers walk on water."

"This I've got to fakking see."

Wisyczyk defiantly kept his back turned. Rees smiled again, and left him to it.

It was Thursday afternoon, 2.15, Hong Kong time. In England, it was 07.15 on the same day.

Fowler had slept in his office, but he managed to look as if he had had the best night's sleep of his life, instead of what had arguably been the worst. He was worried about Logan. He was worried about Pross and Pross's family. He was worried about Ling. He was worried about the success of the operation. There was little point in worrying about failure. The flak would be too widespread for him to care.

None of this showed in his face as he drank the coffee that had been brought to him. He grimaced at its taste, but continued to drink despite it. He read the long signal that had also been brought, for the second time. It had come during the early hours, and he had sent an early call to Winterbourne. Winterbourne, he knew, would have hated that. Too bad. The crunch was coming. Winterbourne should be there.

Winterbourne arrived, irate, just under an hour later. Fowler was in his office with the signal, within five minutes. There was another signal too.

"Why the early call, Fowler? It's not World War Three, is it?"

Fowler said nothing, handed over the first signal. Winterbourne read it, looked up when he had finished.

"More details about the Chi woman. Gory affair, what with this colleague of Qwee . . . er Qi Fung spiking himself like that, then Qi himself having his head smashed open. I see no mention of Ling."

"Which convinces me he was there."

"But there is no mention, as I've said."

"Ling would have warned her to say nothing, or else. He can be very persuasive."

"Is that bitterness I detect, Fowler?"

Call it what you will, Fowler said to himself sourly. "Ling," he went on, ignoring the jibe, "would have had someone on hand to move the ladder . . . I know the report says the strong winds caused the man to lose his footing, but I don't believe a word of it. It was Ling's handiwork. He's frightened Mary Chi into keeping her mouth shut. She would have had to have been extremely lucky to have caught Qi Fung off guard. People like Qi Fung are not caught out by female executives living the soft life."

Winterbourne stared at the signal. "There's something here about the Wessex . . ."

Fowler handed over the other signal. "This came soon after. It explains about the Wessex. They say they're guessing. I think they're absolutely right. We could have the first cousin to World War Three."

Winterbourne read the signal once, twice, face paling with each reading. He stared up at Fowler.

"My God, man! This can't be true!"

"I'm afraid it is."

"Then this operation is madness. You must call it off! We're in deep trouble!"

"We'll be in worse trouble if we do. We might just get away with a skirmish. We must make the pick-up."

"Is Pross to have support?"

"None whatsoever. That way, we might be able to contain things. He will be told that if the pick-up seems like failing, on no account must our man be left on the ground alive."

Winterbourne's eyes were red with anger. "Fowler, did you know the details of all this?"

"No." There was real bitterness now. "It was dumped in my lap to sort out."

"It was madness to set this running!"

"Someone thought it was in our interest."

"Not if the Chinese army pours into Hong Kong, it isn't." Testily. "What's the strength in that area?"

"Two army corps in Guangdong. The one facing Hong Kong had been moved to the Vietnam border, but it's back; or most of it. There are three in Fujian, with two facing Taiwan, including the 31st, which had also been sent to Vietnam. That's back too, but probably spread out. What we're doing would have been too fast for any preventive action to have been taken."

"But they've found out, dammit! That's why your man's running too soon. If this thing blows, the Taiwanese might think it a good idea to pitch in, then of course the Americans, then the Russians . . ." Winterbourne sighed as if the weight of the entire world had suddenly descended upon his shoulders. "I have the strange feeling, Fowler, that I have still not been told everything. Tell me, Fowler, what is the average strength of a corps in the Chinese army?"

"About 42,000, give or take a few hundred."

Winterbourne stared at him. "Are you being flippant?"

"That," Fowler said, unperturbed, "is our most recent update."

Winterbourne rubbed a palm against his forehead slowly: "My God," he whispered. He stared at his desk. "If my head goes, Fowler," he went on tightly, "so does yours."

185

Fowler looked down on him with naked contempt. *All that matters is your miserable career.*

As if aware of the look being thrown at him by Fowler, Winterbourne kept his own eyes stubbornly averted.

Fowler took the signals off the desk, walked out of the office without another word.

The phone in Ling's office in Wan Chai rang. He picked it up, his hand reaching for it with the speed and grace of something lean and venomous in the act of striking.

He put the instrument to his ear, listened. He didn't speak, simply putting the receiver down at the end of whatever his caller had to say. To anyone watching, it was obvious he wanted to bang the phone down, but the tight coil of his control prevented him.

He looked at his companion, the American. It was as if they had been there all night but in fact they had returned bare minutes before, and had taken the same places. They had spent the entire morning and early afternoon at Kai Tak, watching for arrivals. The wasted time did not serve to improve Ling's humour. He had left some people to continue the surveillance, but the call had just proved they were doing no better.

The American said: "When's the next flight from Italy?"

"Not till tomorrow. Too late. It must be today."

"Unless they're already here."

"Impossible. I would have known."

"I don't see how. Your contact himself doesn't know where they are."

"I know they are not here!"

"Well fine, Ling. All we've got to do is get to them when they do get here."

Ling's eyes held no emotion. "You believe me to be mistaken. You believe they have already arrived and that my contact has failed to inform me."

"I didn't say that. I said your contact just goddam well doesn't know."

Ling said: "Pross knows he must make himself available to me or his family will be dead."

186

The American seemed perturbed. "Take it easy, Ling. It's one thing to threaten the guy's family to frighten him, or to waste guys in our trade. They're armed, and they know the score. It's another thing to actually go after the woman and the kids."

Ling said coldly: "After Vietnam, don't you dare give me any of your puritan morality."

The American stood up. "Well that's just dandy, Ling. Throw it back in our faces. You know, you guys sometimes get me up to here. You all come running to Uncle Sam to give you guns, ships, planes. And what do we get for it? Goddam ingratitude!"

The skin on Ling's face tightened. "Perhaps," he began in a voice that was barely above a hiss, "if you stopped trying to play God, you might get somewhere!"

They glared at each other.

Finally, the American said: "To hell with this. I'm going out for some air."

Ling said: "Going to report that the Taiwanese bum is getting uppity?"

The American turned. The taunt had stung. "Don't get funny with me, Ling. I've backed you all the way. My neck's on the goddam block for it, waiting to be chopped off if this thing fouls up. Okay? So don't give me any of that bullshit."

After long seconds, Ling breathed deeply. "Yes, yes. Alright."

The American said: "I'm still going out for some air. Now take it easy, for Chrissake."

Ling watched him go. When the door closed, he looked strangely content.

He picked up the phone, began to dial.

The Learjet arrowed itself into a beautiful curve as it prepared for the let-down into Kai Tak.

Pross looked across at Logan: "Well, we're nearly there. Looks as if we've made it this far. What's the time?"

She looked at her watch, smiled at him. "Four-thirty, Hong Kong time."

It had been a smooth flight. There'd been three stops for fuel, and that had been all. Every so often, one of the pilots had come back for a chat. There had been no alarms. No one had tried to shoot them out of the sky. The pilots had said they would sample the delights of Hong Kong for a while before returning home.

The landing gear came down, locked.

"What about the gun?" Pross enquired softly. "How will you get that through?" No one would be meeting them, which meant no one to smoothe the way in.

She didn't seem worried. "I'll work it out. How do you feel?"

"Fine." He'd had a good sleep during the flight. "You?"

"I'm alright."

He still had not asked her about the little parting scene with Riccardi. They'd talked about all sorts of things, except the mission. He'd found out she liked music, both classical and mainstream jazz which, she insisted, was making a come-back. She also liked dramatic plays, and modern art; and she'd studied archaeology. From archaeology to magnums.

Why archaeology? he'd asked.

"Because it teaches you more about us than anything else," she had answered. She had no time for history books which she believed were too biased to be taken seriously. She'd come to that conclusion after studying a particular incident from four sources, and had found none of them had agreed on any of the salient points. They might have been writing about four entirely different incidents. Archaeology, unless deliberately faked, was not a good liar, and it was pretty difficult to fake every site in the world; whereas most history books were quite good at lying, or at least, bending the truth so far it met itself coming the other way.

Pross watched her now as the Lear levelled its wings, set itself up for the run-in. Her eyes were closed, face in repose. The freckly pattern seemed once more prominent, and again she looked too young and too vulnerable.

She opened her eyes suddenly, looked at him. The eyes seemed blank, as if she were not looking at him at all; but he knew she was. The eyes were searching deep into him. Then the look was gone. She turned her head, closed her eyes once more.

The Lear sank towards the ground.

Pross looked out of the window at Hong Kong clawing its way skywards. He found he could not appreciate what his eyes saw. His mind was on the mission, and on Ling. Here was Hong Kong. It was all real, and Wales was very far away indeed.

He turned to look at Logan again. A quite formidable young lady. She had said she would get him to Hong Kong, and she had done so. Now, it was over for her. She could relax, go home, take a well-deserved spot of leave. It would be goodbye. He would never see her again.

He felt strangely sad about that.

The man watched the sleek shape of the Lear as it touched down. He was bored. He'd been checking the arrival of every scheduled airliner that had landed. The lack of anything to report was making him too relaxed. It was a relaxation forced upon him by the sheer monotony of his task.

He watched the Lear interestedly, but only because it was so different from all the other aircraft. That, however, was the extent of his interest. He watched it as it hurtled down the runway like a little winged missile. It turned off, disappeared behind a huge Boeing 747. It was so small by comparison, he could see sections of it through the Boeing's massive landing gear.

He wondered what kind of people had the money to own and fly those things. He knew he wouldn't be able to see because the door was on the side hidden away from him.

He left the rich people to their plane, returned his attention to the dreary task of checking out the more mundane aircraft.

In the Lear, the senior pilot came down the aisle, grinned at Pross and Logan. He had sleek black hair, and a pencil moustache. His name was Paolo Fortunato who, according to Logan in a whispered aside during the flight, fancied himself as a ladykiller. But Fortunato was pleasant, and had been hospitality itself.

"I hope you enjoyed the flight," he now said to them. "Not too bumpy?"

Logan said, as she got out of her seat: "It was wonderful, Paolo. We'll certainly tell Mr Riccardi."

Fortunato's grin widened. "Thank you, Miss Logan." He took her hand, kissed it. Logan raised an eyebrow at Pross. "I hope you enjoy your stay in Hong Kong." He held on to the hand.

Logan eased it gently away, ignoring Pross's amused smile.

She said: "Don't get snared by all those oriental lovelies, Paolo."

He shrugged, as if to say who would complain. The prospect seemed to please him.

Logan went on: "We'll be leaving now. Our people are waiting."

Pross shook hands with him. "Thank you very much. It was a great flight."

The other pilot came out, shook hands with them.

"*Arrivederci!*" both pilots said as Logan and Pross left the aircraft.

They turned, gave Fortunato and his co-pilot brief waves.

"*Arrivederci!*" Logan called up, then she and Pross began walking towards the terminal buildings.

The Lear had come quite close and, within seconds, they were under cover.

Logan's eyes had done a swift scan.

"Anything?" Pross queried.

"Nothing yet." She had their passports in one hand, her other was deep in her bag.

Pross carried their cases. He knew her hand was on the magnum.

They reached the customs desk. Logan showed their passports. The customs officer took them, looked at Logan's, looked at her sharply, shut the passports, handed them back, nodded that they could pass. It was as simple as that.

Pross said: "What the hell did your passport say?"

"I'm a special attaché," she replied, straightfaced. "You too."

"I'm certainly coming up in the world."

"Let's get a taxi."

They were walking quickly now, to get away from a possible ambush. They found a cab almost immediately, dumped their things in it, climbed into the back. Logan gave the name of a hotel on Hong Kong Island, in Central. They did not speak in the car.

Pross paid little heed to the heat and the scents of the colony. His mind was focussed on Ling. When and how was Ling going to contact him? What would happen to Logan if she were around when that occurred? He knew he would not stand by and watch her get hurt. How could he weigh the lives of his family against that of Logan? He hoped he would not be faced with such an agonising decision.

The taxi plunged into the cross-harbour tunnel. The taxi-driver plucked up courage to speak.

"First time Hong Kong."

"Yes," both Pross and Logan said. They looked at each other, smiled.

The driver giggled. "Very nice place, Hong Kong. You like."

"I'm sure we will," Pross said. He looked at Logan, as if with adoration.

The driver took the hint, smiled at them in his mirror.

They paid him off in front of a very impressive-looking hotel, watched him leave. A doorman stood by to usher them in. Someone came for their cases.

"It's alright," Logan said. "We're not staying."

They stared at her as if she were mad.

"Let's go," she said to Pross.

They found another taxi. She gave the name of another hotel. The taxi went into the cross-harbour tunnel.

Pross said: "Didn't we . . ."

"We did," Logan interrupted.

Pross said nothing more. The taxi eventually stopped before another prestigious hotel, this time on Salisbury Road in Kowloon.

"We'll book in here," she said as the taxi left.

"As what?"

"Mr and Mrs Pettigrew, of course."

"But the passports . . ."

She got two out. "Magic. Those are for us as husband and wife. But we're not staying."

"Naturally." He shook his head slowly at her. "Logan, I'm going to miss you."

"Naturally," she said, and went in.

Pross followed her, was forced to surrender the cases to a determined hotel porter. They were put on the tenth floor.

In their room, which had a splendid view of the harbour and Hong Kong Island, Logan said: "So far so good. No ambush. All we've got to do is get to the airfield without alerting Ling . . . which means no calls whatsoever. We must simply arrive."

"How?"

"We hire a car. I know where to go."

Pross said: "How well do you know this place?"

"Quite well. I lived here when I was younger. My family were out here."

He smiled at her. "A service brat, were you?"

"Not quite." But she didn't tell him what. She went on: "I'm going for the car. I won't be long." She picked up her bag, went to the door.

"Logan."

She turned.

"Be careful."

She gave him a hesitant smile. "I'm always careful."

He stared at the closing door.

Unaware that the people he wanted had passed through his area twice within the last half-hour, Ling watched as his American companion returned.

Ling said: "Have you paid a visit to Lower Albert?" He meant the road where the consulate was.

"No, Ling. I've not been reporting to anyone, so quit it."

The phone rang. Ling grabbed it, eyes alive, body alert. He relaxed almost immediately, clearly disappointed. He barked a stream of Cantonese at whoever the unfortunate at the other end was. The sounds he made were not friendly.

Suddenly, he stiffened, listening. He asked sharp questions, then he was shouting into the phone. He slammed it down.

"There are times when I am convinced I am surrounded by fools," he said to the American, switching back to English.

"Something come up?"

"Something certainly has. A Learjet came in over an hour ago. The idiot who saw it paid little attention because he was told to watch the scheduled airlines. The fool misinterpreted his instructions. I have told him to check the registration. If it's Italian, we'll know."

"That was pretty goddam clever of them. So you were right, Ling. I eat my hat."

Ling actually smiled. "You're not wearing one."

"So what's a hat between friends?"

Ling said: "An hour. If it's Pross and Logan, they've been here an hour. Customs would have let them through . . ." He paused.

The American said: "Got anyone who could find out without raising suspicion?"

For answer, Ling picked up the phone, made a quick call. Within seconds of his putting the phone down, it rang again. He listened. Now he was once more alert. He chose not to bawl out the man on the other end. He put the receiver down once more, this time, gently.

He said to the American: "The Lear is Italian."

"So that's it!"

"Yes." Softly. "Now I must find them before they get to their destination."

The phone rang again. By the time Ling had answered it and returned it to its cradle, he knew part of what he wanted.

"They were let through by Customs."

"So they're at the airfield?"

"No. I believe not." Ling was speaking almost to himself. "Taxis! They'll have used a taxi."

He grabbed the phone, made four calls in quick succession. The first return made him stiffen, then smile grimly. It was more of a spasm that twitched across the tight skin of his foxy face.

He ended the conversation, said to the American: "A taxi took them to what was meant to be their hotel, in Central."

"Meant to be?"

The spasm twitched again. "They never went in. The doorman said they took another taxi, and went somewhere else. He was so curious about this odd behaviour, he had a good long look at

193

the taxi. He knows the driver, who is one of their regulars." Ling went on dreamily: "To think they were actually here in Wan Chai. We shall soon find out where they are."

Logan was back fairly quickly. "I've got the car. Let's go. If Ling is here, he's probably found out by now we've arrived. I would expect him to start trying to find us. He's probably got a good network."

Pross was up with the cases, ready to leave.

Logan said, drily: "We're always doing flits from hotels."

Pross said: "When this is all over I'm going to book into a room and stay there, just for the hell of it."

She made a face at him for reply.

They went out, headed for one of the three lifts in their particular wing. There was one available. They took it to the ground.

Logan said: "You take the cases to the front while I make the receptionist happy."

He nodded.

The lift stopped. Logan got out first, went to the desk.

A man got into the lift quickly, punched the button.

Ling.

Pross felt his stomach plummet as the doors began to close. Ling stood squarely in his way, a gun pointing at his stomach. He saw the sudden turning of Logan's head, her reading of the situation, the horror on her face.

Then he heard her single, anguished cry of: "*Pross!*" before the door shut on her.

She'd been running back, magnum coming out. He'd seen it, heard its powerful roar as the lift whisked him back up.

Ling said quickly: "I am not here to kill you, Mr Pross, but you know I can. I have put something in your pocket. Upon it, are the co-ordinates of your second pick-up. My man will be waiting. Do not let me down. If he is still over the border when you have completed your mission, you will never see your family again. I shall not kill you. It would be a greater punishment to leave you alive, knowing you were responsible for their deaths."

The lift was coming to a halt.

194

"I must leave you," Ling went on with dry amusement. "Your amazon downstairs is probably decimating my men."

Or they're decimating her, Pross thought with mounting anxiety.

The lift stopped. Ling stepped quickly out. Pross hit the button frantically. The doors began to close, too slowly for his liking.

"Come on! *Come on!*"

They closed. The lift started its second journey down. Pross wanted to scream at it to increase speed. God oh God. Logan could be lying down there, dead or dying in a pool of blood.

The lift arrived, doors opening.

"Logan!"

"Pross!"

Without realising it, he was hugging her, so pleased was he to find her alive. Then suddenly embarrassed, they released each other as if they had handled something that was too hot to the touch.

Only then did he see the two bodies, and the staring ring of horrified faces.

"Ling's on his way down!" he said urgently. "Let's go!"

"He's already been. I missed him!" She sounded disgusted with herself.

"Did he shoot at you?" he asked worriedly. Ling never missed.

"Yes, but I was too quick. I think I threw him off his aim. I hope I meet up with that bastard again."

"Bloodthirsty, aren't you?" He smiled his relief at her. The lift doors were beginning to close. He reached in, grabbed their cases. "We'd better leave before they wake up, don't you think?"

The people were all staring. No one seemed prepared to move. The dead men, both Chinese, lay sprawled across hotel furniture. Those who had gathered to watch kept looking from Pross and Logan to the bodies, trying to decide which was the more horrific: the bodies, or the person who had turned them into bodies.

Logan said: "Good idea."

People parted for them like chaff in a strong wind as they ran. They tumbled into the car, a BMW 316, and Logan had it moving before Pross had fastened his seatbelt.

"That will set the cat among the pigeons," Pross said.

"By the time the police get to know what's happening, the mission will be over. Then it won't matter. How did you escape from Ling?"

He'd been expecting the question. "He didn't want to kill me. He wanted his men to get you, but he wanted me out of the way."

"Why?" She concentrated on her driving, not looking at him.

"He knew I'd try to help. Then I might have got shot. Not what he wants at this stage."

She said quietly: "Would you have intervened?"

"Yes," he said, surprised by the certainty he felt.

She glanced at him then. "Oh, Pross," she said softly.

The Datsun 280ZX moved sedately along Hong Chong Road. The American was driving.

He said: "I can't believe it, Ling. You met her and she bested you?"

"She did not best me," Ling said calmly. "I am still alive. However, I am forced to admit she is very good. Those men she took out were picked by me. They were not slow, but much too slow for her. She is a natural. I was very surprised to see them dead, and that gave her the edge. I could almost admire her. In that hotel foyer, many people would have hesitated. She did not. Perhaps our paths will cross again, one day. I would very much look forward to that. Stop!" he commanded suddenly. "Stop here. I shall get out."

"Get out? Why?" The 280ZX came to a halt by the HK Polytechnic.

"Because, my friend, I have been seen twice in public, in rather unfortunate circumstances. At the Chi flat, I was lucky. No one was able to give a description of me. They were too busy trying to see into the room. I may not be so lucky a second time. I have decided to change my operating base; keep out of circulation till this is over."

"Change? Why? What about my principals? We're supposed to share . . ."

"Share?" Ling said. "Why should I share anything with you?" And he shot the American.

He climbed out of the low car calmly, walked unhurriedly until he came to the railway station.

THIRTEEN

Logan brought the BMW to a rubber-burning halt before the camp gates. It had been a hairy drive, and Pross decided she could teach Grazziella a few lessons.

An RAF policeman came hurrying up to them. His colleague remained watchfully at the gate, near the barrier.

Logan had her special passport out. "Diplomatic service!" she said as soon as the man had lowered his head to look in. "The Station CO. *Quick*!"

The man's eyes widened perceptibly. "Yes, ma'am! We've been told to expect you two at any time." He saluted, jumped to it.

The barrier was raised with alacrity. Logan powered the BMW through. She seemed to know just where to go. For Pross, it was again like a feeling he'd had at St Athan. An RAF station had a certain feel about it. Wherever you were, it was familiar. There was a built-in sameness that ensured you felt at home once you'd passed through the gate. It was either clever psychology, or a numbing lack of imagination.

He said: "Logan."

"Yes?"

"When I first saw you at Fowler's house, you went all Irish on me. The slight Irish is still there, but not the street sound you used on me. Why did you do that?" It was something he'd been meaning to ask her.

He glanced at her, noticed a tiny smile.

"My way of giving you a look-over. Seeing me merely as staff made you more yourself. As I was detailed to mind you to Hong Kong, I needed to study the subject to see if I would have felt at ease with you." A bigger smile. "There's nothing more disastrous than being forced to mind merchandise that's not compatible."

"Merchandise?"

"Well . . . you know."

Merchandise. Great.

The BMW screeched to a halt before the station headquarters. The first person Pross saw was Sanders, in civvies. He was followed out of the building by Rees, who grinned with a real pleasure. Rees was also in civilian clothes. Behind Rees came Brimms.

Pross was surprised. Had Fowler been playing safe? Was Rees here to do the pick-up – with Brimms sent to mind him across to Hong Kong – in the event of Pross and Logan not making it?

It seemed quite likely to Pross, but it made him feel uncomfortable to know his expendability had been taken into the calculations.

Sanders was saying: "They called from the gate to tell us you were on your way. Logan, you're amazing!" Sanders' face was creased in a smile. He looked at Logan with some fondness.

Brimms said: "Pretty good job, Logan."

"Thank you, sir."

Rees came round to Pross as he hauled their cases out. The mournful face gave a semi-mournful smile.

"Didn't expect to see you here, Cado," Pross said.

"Didn't expect to see you either, after what we've been hearing."

"You can thank Logan. That's a one-woman army over there."

Logan smiled at him as they all trooped inside.

Pross said: "How's the ship?"

"You'll drool," Rees said. "Makes the one at St Athan look and feel like a wreck."

"You're joking."

"I joke not. You'll also come up against a strange phenomenon called Wisyczyk . . ."

"Wisy*what*?"

"Wisyczyk. An SAC who runs this camp, can't say two words without his own special punctuation, but is a bloody magician when it comes to choppers. Oh yes. Every chopper he works on is his own property, or so you'll think when you meet him. The Lynx is top of the list. Be warned."

"You make it sound almost as if he's worse that what's across the border."

"People have been known to think so."

They entered an office where a tall man with an ascetic face and silver hair rose from behind his desk to greet them.

"Group Captain Chalmers," Sanders began, "this is Logan, and this is our pilot."

Pross noted the fact that he had not been introduced by name. If anything went wrong, the Group Captain would be able to deny all knowledge of him. They shook hands.

Chalmers said: "I've seen you, now I shall leave the lady and you gentlemen to it. First, I must give something to Miss Logan. I was instructed to ensure only Miss Logan received it." He handed a white envelope over.

Everybody else had a look of surprise on his face, with the exception of Pross. As for Chalmers, the Group Captain left the room with the eagerness of one who wanted to be out of it. Cloak and dagger stuff was not his game. The thoughts could almost be seen chasing across his face.

As the door closed behind Chalmers, Logan tore open the envelope, moved a little distance away from the rest of them. She pulled a sheet of paper out, stared at it.

"It's in bloody code," she said. "I'll have to work on it. I need a pen." She zipped open her shoulder bag.

What happened next took everyone by surprise.

It was not a pen that came out of the bag, but the magnum. It did so in a seeming blur, the sheet of paper and its envelope falling to the floor as Logan pointed the massive weapon two-handedly at *Brimms*.

"Brimms, you bastard!" she said in a tight, soft voice. "I'm putting you under arrest! Go for your gun, and it will be the last thing you ever do. I just need the excuse." The green eyes blazed with a bone-chilling fire.

200

Pross could not believe a pair of eyes could look so cold. He looked interestedly at Brimms.

Brimms.

The inside man. The man who was close enough to Fowler to know everything. The man with access to Logan's file. The man whose hounds would have succeeded at Heathrow had Logan not been so good. The man who had tried to engineer Logan's death.

It was a wonder she was not killing him on the spot.

It was touch and go, however. The magnum looked hungry, and it would need the tiniest of wrong moves from Brimms to seal his fate.

"Why don't you try to deny it?" Logan said to Brimms in her cold voice. "Why don't you try, you bastard?"

Sanders and Rees were standing as if someone had put eggshells beneath their feet. They seemed hardly daring to breathe.

Brimms stared at her watchfully, said nothing, did nothing.

"Pross?"

"Yes."

"Pick up the paper. It's in code, but a code only I can under-stand. There are a group of figures at the bottom. Those are your co-ordinates. That's the target area. The pick-up will be waiting. I shall tell all of you what the remainder of the message says. It's very short. 'Arrest Brimms'. It's from Fowler. Take off your gun, Brimms. Very slowly." The magnum never wavered.

Brimms did as he was told, the out-of-true eyes never leaving the magnum.

"I now have command of this mission."

No one seemed to want to argue with her.

"Sanders, get on the phone. Have Brimms locked up, under armed guard. If he looks like breathing the wrong way, tell them to shoot him."

Brimms glared at her, but remained silent.

Sanders stared, but he went to do her bidding. A short time later, two RAF police arrived with sidearms. They took Brimms away. It was only then that Logan relaxed. She let out a great sigh of relief, put the magnum away.

"God!" she said. "I was so scared."

"You could have fooled me," Pross said.

"*I* was bloody scared," Sanders remarked. "Of that damn magnum."

"Brimms," Logan said, "is very, very good. If he'd been sure, he could have taken me, even going for his gun. But he wasn't sure, thank God! I was banking on that. I had to use the trick about the pen. If he'd suspected I was going for the gun, I'd have had it." She looked at them in turn. "And so would all of you."

They believed it.

"Do we pull the mission-time forward?" Sanders queried.

"Yes. Fowler said six o'clock tomorrow morning." She told Sanders and Rees about Ling, and the shoot-out at the hotel. "All things considered, I think we should, now that Ling knows we're here. At least, he hasn't got his inside man now." Her mouth turned down briefly with distaste. She looked at Pross. "Pross, do you feel up to a test?"

He said: "The sooner I get to know the feel of this new ship, the better for me. Yes. I'll take her up."

"Right. I'll leave you to Rees and Sanders, then. I'll wait here."

Pross looked at the eyes and the freckles. She was suddenly very young, and very vulnerable again.

"Gentlemen," he said without looking at them. "Could you leave us for some moments, please? I want to talk to this young lady alone."

He heard them go out of the room. He opened his arms as he would to a small child. She came to him, put her arms tightly about his waist, pressed herself against him.

"Oh, Pross," she murmured against his chest. "This is the first time I've had to do a job like this, and sometimes, I get very, very frightened."

He held her tightly. "Logan, you've done an exceptional job. If that's what you're like when you're frightened, I'd hate to be around when you're not."

He felt her body shake with suppressed laughter. She looked up at him.

"You always say the right things, don't you, to stop me making a fool of myself."

"You're not making a fool of yourself," he told her gently. He kissed the curve of freckles beneath her right eye. "Now I'd better go or those two out there will get the wrong idea." He released her. "Take care."

She smiled. "I always do."

He went out to find Rees and Sanders.

"You the fakking genius, then?"

Pross looked down at the rumpled mess before him. This must be the notorious Wisyczyk.

"Am I?" he queried mildly.

"Everyfakkingbody seems to fakking think you are."

Incredible form of speech.

Pross was in full combat gear, as was Rees who would be accompanying him on the test flight.

"In that case," he said to Wisyczyk, "I'd better see your pride and joy."

"Just don't fakking bend her," Wisyczyk said ominously, and left the hangar office that served as the Lynx's crew room.

Rees said: "What did I tell you?"

"I agree. He's worse."

Rees grinned as they followed Wisyczyk out, carrying their helmets.

Pross stared at the Lynx as they approached it. He did not stare at the four armed RAFPs who stood some distance away, at its four quarters. He did not stare at Sanders, nor at the two civilians with him near the aircraft. He was staring at the twin cannon, mounted Harrier-like in ventral pods beneath the nose. The cannons were bigger than the one on the St Athan Lynx. The cannons were mounted close, on either side of the twin nose-wheel.

He continued to stare at the external stores, mounted on specially-strengthened pylons on either side of the fuselage. They carried a full complement of Stinger air-to-air missiles, and twin 2.75 inch rocket pods, one on each side. There was a mast-mounted sensor too.

"What am I taking on?" he said to Rees. "A battalion?"

Rees said nothing.

203

The civilians with Sanders had moved away by the time he reached the Lynx. He stared after them before turning to Sanders.

"Do they know what's going on?" he asked.

Sanders said: "To them, this is a Climatic Evaluation Exercise."

"They're that stupid?"

"It's what they want to believe. They certainly don't know the true reason."

"And what about me, Sanders? I've just come halfway across the globe being chased by homicidal maniacs . . . for what?"

Sanders looked at Pross with narrowed eyes. "You know for what, Pross."

While Pross and Sanders were behaving like a pair of stags sizing each other up, Rees chose the time to do a ground check of the aircraft.

He was checking the tail rotor when Pross said: "This is a fly-off, isn't it, Sanders? A bloody fly-off against another ship. A fucking competition. What have they got over there, Sanders? What is it that worries you people so much? Eh? Tell me!"

"It's not like that at all," Sanders continued to insist. "Your friend is waiting over there for you . . ."

"I am not a dummy, Sanders. I know I am here to pick up my friend. But this is a *brand new* Lynx; a variation on a theme with many variations. There is enough service experience behind me for me to know an experimental mark when I see one. I know there are all sorts of Lynx variants being tried. This little angel smells of anti-chopper ship to me. *Well*?"

"If that's how you feel, Pross," Sanders said angrily, "don't go!"

"Don't you give me that mealy-mouthed bullshit! You know damed well I didn't come all this way, after Logan's nearly got herself killed to get me here, just to pack it in. I don't need your hypocrisy. So come on, Sanders. Give. I want to know what I may be up against."

Sanders said: "I don't know."

Pross looked at him with contempt. "You lying bastard. Cado!"

"Yes!"

Rees came round the nose.

"Checks complete?"

Rees nodded. "All clear." He put on his helmet.

"Right then. Let's take her up." Pross put on his own helmet, opened the door to the right-hand seat. All doors had been left in place on this Lynx.

He climbed in, settled himself comfortably. There was a subtly different feel to the aircraft. The seat felt better. The whole air of the ship was much more purposeful; more lethal. Outside, they'd added flare dispensers; inside were some fancy new avionics.

Rees climbed into the left-hand seat; the gunner/observer's position.

"Better target acquisition, and better imaging for night and bad weather," he said. "I didn't think they could have improved on the one at St Athan. These are beauties. All offensive and defensive equipment are fully pilot-operated. The cannons are 25mm. Good punch."

"So it's still a one-man job."

"Yes."

"Fine."

They went through their checks, then Pross started the twin Gems. He felt the power flow through him. He put all thoughts of Dee and the children, and Ling out of his mind. From now on, he would be the aircraft, and the aircraft would become part of him. It was the way he had operated on Phantoms. There was little point in getting into one of those things if your mind was going to be cluttered with all sorts of distractions. It was a good way of getting killed.

"There's something I ought to tell you," Rees said.

Pross looked at him, waited.

"A few days ago, a Wessex with a full load of crew and troops disappeared. They've been finding bodies and bits of aircraft in the Starling Inlet area. No one knows exactly what happened, but the locals claim they heard an almighty bang and saw a brilliant flash over there one morning. The Wessex was in the area about that time."

Pross kept looking at him. "Fuel? Somebody being careless with his ammo?"

"Or a missile."

Great.

"What from, and why?"

"That's what everybody would like to know."

Great.

Pross looked at his instruments, then brought his head up for lift-off. "Right, Cado. Let's take her up and see what she can do for me."

Wisyczyk watched with alarm as the Lynx seemed to fling itself skywards. For the next half-hour in the failing light, he saw the Lynx put through manoeuvres he had not dared think possible. He suffered heartache each time his beloved machine seemed about to break through the limits of its flight envelope. He put his hand in his mouth.

The crew chief, who with most other people had come out to watch, said to him: "Jack. I haven't heard a word from you."

Wisyczyk made a strange sound as the Lynx whirled overhead, upside down. It went into a soaring loop. Wisyczyk gagged.

"You sound as if you're in bad shape, Jack lad."

The Chief was rewarded with another gagging sound as the chopper spiralled downwards. Wisyczyk was sure it was going to crash.

It went into a sudden hover, continued to descend, alarmingly quickly it seemed. Wisyczyk waited for the inevitable. His beloved Lynx was soon to turn into a ball of expanding fire. He even began to edge away.

The landing was an anti-climax. The Lynx simply settled down on its wheels without fuss.

Wisyczyk couldn't believe it. Then he found his voice as he slowly removed his hand from a mouth that was hanging open.

"Fakkingfakkingfakking hell!" he crowed. "I like him!"

The Chief was shocked by such blasphemy.

The rain began to fall at about midnight. By one o'clock, it was a deluge.

From his bed in the Officer's Mess, Pross listened to it. Perhaps the rain would be a friend, he thought, if it lasted.

He had checked the Lynx out as minutely as he possibly could. There had been nothing more he could have done to improve things. The ship was tuned to fine pitch. He had also been stunned by the hero worship suddenly conferred upon him by the strange-looking Wisyczyk. If he'd said bark, Wisyczyk would have.

Pross smiled in the darkness. He thought of Logan. She had been watching his performance in the Lynx and he had seen an even more disturbing look in her eyes. He put it out of his mind. That she was in the next room did not make it any easier.

Strange, he thought. They'd slept together in Italy; but here, separated by a wall, he felt more uncomfortable. He tried not to think of Dee and the children under a sentence of death if he failed. He forced that out of his mind too.

He listened to the rain, and fell asleep.

At five o'clock, it was still raining as heavily as ever. Pross felt pleased. The rain was good cover. It would also keep unwelcome attention away. No one liked being out in the rain; soldiers especially.

He started to put on his gear. Finished, he picked up his helmet, went to Logan's room. He knocked. There was no reply. He knocked again. Still nothing.

Wondering, he tried her door. It came open. She was not there; but the bed had been slept in. He felt relief. She was alright then. His relief changed to a strange feeling of disappointment. It would have been nice to have said goodbye to her.

Perhaps she hadn't wanted it.

He walked through the silent Mess. There would be hot coffee in the hangar. That was all he wanted.

An RAF Land-Rover was waiting. He got in. He grunted a good morning to Sanders who was in the driving seat. Sanders grunted back. That was all they said to each other. He wondered where Rees was.

The Land-Rover set off in the pouring rain. Visibility was practically nil. The new day looked as if it would never come. The rain drenched the vehicle, shutting out the world around it.

Sanders drove it faster than the visibility afforded by the over-worked wipers allowed. Pross said nothing. They made it to the hangar, dashed into the make-shift crew-room. Rees was there

Pross gratefully took the cup of coffee offered him by Rees, peered through the glass partition into the hangar. The Lynx was not there.

"It's already out," Rees informed him. "Wisyczyk's with it, getting wet."

"Dedicated."

"More so today. You've done something no one's been able to. You've made him like you." Rees grinned. "That could be worse than being hated."

"Seen Logan?" Sanders asked of Rees.

Rees stifled a yawn. "Not since last night."

"Oh well. She's not necessary for this, anyway."

Pross put down his empty cup. "I won't shake hands, Cado."

"Nor I," Rees said. His eyes were strangely lively.

"Let's go," Sanders said.

They went back to the Land-Rover. Pross felt Rees' eyes on his back

The Lynx appeared out of the deluge, looking even more menacing in the half-light. A solitary figure in what looked like a hooded ground-sheet stood by the pilot's entrance.

Wisyczyk.

Further in the gloom, Pross could make out two more figures. So the RAFP were still on guard.

Pross looked at Sanders. "Well, Sanders?"

"I'd like to see you back in one piece."

"I must be crazy, but I actually believe you do."

Sanders stared at him. Pross got out quickly. He heard the Land-Rover drive off as he dashed past Wisyczyk who was opening the pilot's door for him. He climbed in, felt a pat from Wisyczyk on his back. The door was pushed shut.

Then he saw the person in full gear in the next seat.

"*Logan!*"

Her eyes looked huge in the gloom, beneath the helmet.

"What the hell do you think you're doing?" Pross yelled at her. His concern for her safety made him raise his voice louder than he'd intended.

"I thought . . . I thought you'd need help," she said lamely.

He was angry with her. The idiot. What did she think she'd be able to do? What bloody help?

He pointed to the array of instruments and avionics. "Can you operate these?"

The helmeted head shook from side to side, the green eyes wide.

"Then of what possible use do you think you could be to me? It takes a skilled person to operate these things. Rees can do it. He is not here because the risk may be too high. He's army. We don't want an army man caught there, do we? So Rees is not here. Now *you*, you can't take Rees' place. Furthermore, I'm going to have my hands full. I don't want to worry about you as well. Got it? Remember Heathrow. This is my patch now. Everything else is excess baggage. Whoever heard of the mission controller going on the mission?"

"Fowler is the mission controller. I'm just the field controller."

"What I've said still stands. Get the hell out and let me start this thing up. Wisyczyk's getting soaked out there."

As if to confirm his words, there was a bang on the door.

"Come on, Logan. You're holding things up."

"I have left authorisation for Sanders. Control is now his."

"Jesus Christ!"

"And you're absolved of any blame too. It's all written down."

"Do you think I'm worried about blame?" He was thinking about the laser exercise at Southerndown. In that very position, Rees had taken a simulated fatal hit first time round. The second time, they'd lost the pick-up. Such statistics did not encourage confidence.

"Logan, for God's sake . . ."

"Start up, Pross. I'm coming with you. As you said, let's not keep poor old Wisyczyk out there for much longer. Someone else is getting wet too, waiting for us. The rain belt is drenching the target area."

She had changed again. The little girl had gone, now that she knew she'd got him over a barrel. The efficient Logan was back.

Shit.

There was another reason, a very important one, why he'd wanted no one with him. In a left pocket, he carried Fowler's co-ordinates; in a right, Ling's. Logan had given him a complication he could well have done without. What would she do when she realised he was making for a second rendezvous?

There was another bang on the door.

Pross started up, switched on the electronics, let everything settle. The wipers fought the rain which streamed down the split screen. Logan was doing something with her hands. He looked.

She was checking the magnum.

She smiled at him. "You never know." She looked like a vulnerable child once more, made so by what looked like a disturbing belief in his ability.

Christ.

He lifted the Lynx off the deck. The instruments glowed at him. The world disappeared in the rain. He took the ship straight up to 800 feet, activated the thermal imager. He could see. He had a 45 degree field of vision. He took the Lynx higher, and still in rain, took a direct course for Tsung Yuen Ha, fifteen kilometres northeast of the airfield, and within spitting distance almost, of the border.

A few minutes later, he violated Chinese airspace.

A new tenseness had descended within the cockpit. Even Logan, peering through the murk, looked subdued. There was no contact with base now.

"Wishing you hadn't come?" Pross asked her.

She looked at him, freckles startlingly clear. They were beacons for her emotions, if one knew how to read them.

"No," she said. She looked out. "I think this is beautiful."

Beautiful? It probably would be if the Chinese weren't tracking them, and if whatever had got that Wessex wasn't even now sniffing them out. Rees hadn't said whether the Wessex had strayed. Had the doomed helicopter been a deliberate feint to draw fire? If so, no one was talking.

They travelled on in silence. Nothing showed on the screens. No one following, no one ahead. Pross armed all weapons, except the Stingers. Imagine shooting down an airliner, in Chinese airspace.

210

"We're nearly there," he said. Was it going to be easy, after all? He'd fed the first set of co-ordinates into the navigation computer and the target area was coming up. He began his let-down.

The screens were still mercifully empty. The rain shrouded them. He decided he would not settle to the ground. Fat lot of good he would do if he bogged the Lynx.

He came down cautiously, vertically. The imaging gave him a clear view of the landing area. It was awash. No chance of putting down. He held the machine at the hover, one foot above the deck.

"Can you see anything?" Without helmet-mounted imaging, she'd be seeing even less than he was, but he wanted to know what it looked like.

"It's soup out there."

Which was good news. He scanned the area for a human body. Nothing. Nothing moving.

Logan was doing something. He looked briefly.

"What the hell's that?" He had to concentrate on maintaining his hover and couldn't look at her. It had looked like a cut-down assault rifle, with its folding stock extended.

"A Beretta," she answered. There was a smile in her voice. "More firepower."

Jesus.

"We don't need more firepower. We've got enough here to sink a battleship."

"If someone's chasing our pick-up," she began reasonably, "you'll have to remain at the hover until he makes it. You can't turn the chopper until he's aboard. We'll need suppression fire."

It was good reasoning, but he didn't think one assault rifle would be much use against a bunch of determined troops.

"Where did you hide it?"

"By my seat. And before you ask, it came in my case. You carried it all the way " She sounded as if she was trying hard not to laugh.

Bloody marvellous

"You were going to do this all along," he said accusingly.

No one coming. Where the hell was he? How long had they been waiting. Impossible. Only two minutes?

"Yes," she answered, unrepentant.

Three minutes. Four. Five.

"I swear Logan, when we get back I'll . . ."

"Yes?" Teasing.

"I'll . . ." Wait a minute. Something moving, stumbling, splashing. "He's here! Open the main door!"

She was already moving out of her seat to slide the wide door open. She was useful, after all, he admitted reluctantly. He could never have done it. With the chopper on the ground, yes. But not like this.

Logan was back in her seat, her door partially open, rifle poking out to give covering fire if necessary. No one appeared to be chasing the stumbling man.

Pross turned the Lynx to give her a better field of fire. The running man was now coming broadside on.

Pross frowned. The man seemed to be Chinese. What the hell was going on? He got ready to take the Lynx up in a fast climb. No. He wasn't Chinese, just wearing Chinese clothes, and bedraggled.

But . . .

The man scrambled aboard, pulled the door shut.

"Thank Christ!" he said, sobbing for breath. "Never thought you'd make it. Let's get out of this bloody place!"

The helicopter didn't move. Logan shut her door, pointed the rifle at the man.

He stared. "What . . ."

Pross said, harshly: "You're not Gallagher."

"Of course I'm not bloody Gallagher! I'm Searle!"

"I don't care who the fuck you are, mate. I'm here to pick up *Gallagher*. Logan, do you know this joker?"

"No." The rifle was aimed with deadly intent.

Searle said: "You were never to pick up Gallagher Gallagher's not even in China."

"*What?*" Both Logan and Pross spoke at the same time. The Lynx danced alarmingly, like a suddenly frightened horse Pross made soothing motions with the controls, yanked the Lynx upwards.

He was fuming Bastards Bastards, bastards, *bastards*.

212

Logan was saying: "I'm sorry, Pross. They fooled me too. I had no idea they'd cooked this up. They wanted you because you're the best, and they didn't know how to persuade you. This was the only way they knew, to con you.

He was raging inside. All that he'd gone through; all those people dead; Dee and the kids; Logan on the firing line . . .

Bastards.

"I don't understand it. This was a simple pick-up. No one was here. It was a good rendezvous. A novice chopper jockey could have made it."

Which was an exaggeration. The weather was foul. No novice would have survived for more than a few seconds, and if he had, he would have bogged the Lynx.

Logan said: "You know that's not true."

"Even so. Rees could have done it."

So what else was there?

"What's so important about you Searle?"

"I . . . I can't tell you."

"Don't give me any crap!" Pross shouted. The Lynx danced again. "Logan!"

"Yes."

"Keep your rifle on him."

"It is."

"Good. I'm going to ask him once more. If I don't get an answer, shoot the bastard and throw him out."

Christ. Is that me?

"Gladly."

"You can't do this!" Searle sounded as if he felt he'd been trapped with a pair of lunatics.

"Who's to know? We didn't find you. Had to leave because of pursuit."

"You wouldn't!"

"We would," Logan said.

"I'll report this!"

"How?" Logan asked derisively. "As you're falling to earth?"

"You're interfering with highly classified material! This work has taken months. The information I have is ministerial, Cabinet stuff. You can't expect me to . . ."

"I've been put on the line, you bastard!" Pross raged at him. "My family's been threatened with death, and you give me some bullshit about Cabinet secrets? I have two kids, Searle; tiny little people. Your stinking Department conned me out of my home with a story that hung me out to dry on my loyalty to a friend. In doing that, they put my wife and kids at risk. Right now, Searle, I want to know what my family's life was put on the line for. If you don't tell me, you're going back where you came from. The fast way."

"That's murder!"

"Tell that to my kids."

"For God's sake, man! You're one of us!"

"Never, Searle. Never one of you." Pross sighed. "Okay, Logan. Shoot the bastard."

"Alright! Logan, are you with the Department?"

"Yes!"

"Then you're in deep trouble."

"Watch what you say to me, Searle. I'm controller in the field. I killed a lot of people to get your helicopter to you. Don't push it."

Pross could almost hear Searle take a swallow. God. She could be a hard little number when she wanted.

Searle began to speak. "The Russians," he said. "The Russians are in China."

Pross went cold. Logan was too stunned to say anything.

"They've taken over?" Pross asked at last.

"No, no. They could never take China. They can't even take Afghanistan. They'd die in China, as would anybody stupid enough to try it. The Chinese may not have very modern forces at the moment, but any invader would be facing the biggest guerrilla army on earth. After Afghanistan, a lot of people are learning new lessons. The Russians," Searle went on, "are arming China If you can't beat them, join them."

"My God," Pross said, softly.

"Which, of course," Searle carried on, "is what we in the West have been trying to do. It's a question of who has the best arms for China's needs. We're wary about giving them sophisticated arms, but we're even more worried about letting them get Russian arms again. Russia feels exactly the same about us. One bride,

214

two grooms. The Russian groom seems to have got his feet under the table." As if suddenly exhausted by all he'd said, Searle collapsed into the single seat in the cabin.

Pross suddenly felt as if the shrouding rain about him had become inimically hostile. They were still over Chinese territory.

"Searle!"

"Yes." It was a tired voice.

"Have you proof of all this?"

"I've seen them: advisors, technicians, the aircraft, the tanks, the guns. Unless we can do something quick, we can forget China. Imagine Hong Kong turned into a full-blown naval fortress, shared by China and Russia."

"Could that really ever happen?" No wonder Ling wanted to get his own man out. Taiwan would be hauled in like a fish.

"If I hadn't seen the stuff with my own eyes, I'd have asked the same question a few months ago."

Pross took out Ling's co-ordinates, swiftly hit the data-entry keyboard, punching them into the nav computer. Logan was staring out at the murk, and had paid no attention. He returned the paper to its pocket.

He altered heading. She took no notice.

The dark, unmarked Mil Mi-24 Hind E gunship prowled through the heavy rain. It had found a target, but as yet, the target did not know this. The target was not onscreen; not yet. But it had been heard, its sound analysed, its direction plotted. The Hind knew it was hunting another helicopter that was not of its own kind. It followed.

FOURTEEN

Pross began the let-down through the pouring curtain, doing so in a wide spiral. The imaging showed him nothing to worry about, and both offensive and defensive radars were clear. Nevertheless, he was glad his weapons were armed. If something went wrong with Ling's pick-up, he had no intention of hanging around and would blast his way out of whatever the situation developed into.

He hoped.

He looked at the ground. It did not seem as waterlogged as the last site. A full landing? It looked safe enough, though skids would have been better. He continued his descent.

Neither Logan nor Searle appeared to realise what was happening. Perhaps they thought they were landing at base. Logan could not see through the rain, and Searle was in the cabin, probably dozing easily for the first time in God knew how long.

Logan woke up when Pross was committed to the landing.

She stared through the windscreen at a low hill. "Where is this, Pross?" She did not sound worried, trusting him implicity. Not being totally aware of what this particular Lynx would do, she would think he had landed for some aeronautical reason, Pross decided.

He said: "A brief stop. Getting my family off the hook."

She turned to look at him, at first puzzled. Then: "Ling! He got you to do this! Pross! Why?"

216

"My *family*, Logan! He was going to kill my family! All I've got to do is pick up his man and we're away. I'll drop him off before we return to base. No one will be the wiser, and my family will be safe."

Logan stared at him, conflicting emotions chasing across her face. "You lied to me, Pross."

"And everybody else lied to me! That's why I'm here! It's alright for you. When people point guns at you, you shoot them. What do I do when they point them at my family? Can you answer that, Logan? Can you?"

He kept his eyes on his instruments, on the approaching ground, and did not see her bite her lip as she turned to look out through the windscreen.

"I did not lie to you when I said I would have tried to prevent Ling from shooting you. I would have risked it, even unarmed."

She looked at him once more. "I'm sorry," she said. "I was being unfair."

The helicopter settled to the ground. The rain lashed at it. Pross kept the blades turning.

Searle was suddenly on his feet. "This is China! Why aren't we back at your base?"

Pross said: "A brief stop."

"A brief stop? In *China*? For God's sake, man! Get this thing off the ground! Don't you know where you are? Don't you know what this is?" Searle was becoming very agitated. "Even in this rain, I recognise that hill over there. I was on it some weeks ago! This is a training area for special combat troops!"

Pross was stunned. There was nothing on the radars.

"There's nothing on the radars."

"You may have been lucky. Perhaps no one's seen or heard you, or there are no troops in this particular spot. I would not guarantee that state of affairs lasting for very long if you remain here. Get off, for God's sake! Get off!" Searle was practically shouting with fear.

Logan had picked up her rifle again.

"Logan?" Pross said tentatively.

"Give it a couple of minutes." She stared out at the rain, eyes trying to penetrate it.

"A couple of minutes!" Searle was nearly going wild in his mounting terror. "You people are *insane*! You're jeopardising a whole operation that has taken months . . ."

"We'll be leaving in a couple of minutes, Searle," Logan said with a deadly calm.

Searle was nearly weeping. Pross couldn't understand it.

Searle said: "I have detailed information in my head. If I'm caught, they'll do anything to get it out of me. You don't understand! I've been running from them for weeks. Ling . . ."

"*Ling*?"

Searle was taken aback by both Pross's and Logan's combined yell. "Why yes . . . yes. You know him?"

"Do we know him," Pross said grimly. "Bloody Taiwanese . . ."

"*Taiwanese*! Ling's no Taiwanese. He's one of the Republic's top men. He's been after me for weeks!"

"Jesus Christ!" Pross said. It was all falling into place. He hauled the Lynx off the ground; or attempted to.

He had done what only a novice would. He had bogged it

"*Pross*! Look!" From Logan.

"I know!" He tried again to drag the Lynx off from the mud. He had seen the figures in the imager. Jesus. Some had come out of the ground.

It occurred to him that he had been neatly suckered into landing at this particular spot. The ground had been specially prepared. The Lynx appeared to be sinking.

"What's happening? What's happening?" Searle was looking from one to the other.

"The ship's in a sea of mud! It's dragging us down." Pross told him.

Logan suddenly opened the door and jumped down.

"Logan!" Pross screamed. "*What are you doing?*"

"Less weight! Get off, then pick us up again."

"Us?"

But she was opening the main door. "Out!" she said to Searle.

"*No!* You can't!"

"*Out!*" she screamed at him. "Or I'll shoot you where you stand!" The rifle was pointed squarely at him.

218

Searle gave a defeated, despairing sob as he climbed out of what he'd thought had been sanctuary.

Logan grabbed him. She glanced down at her feet. "Pross!" she yelled. "This is not mud! It's some kind of concrete mix. Get off as quickly as you can!" She disappeared into the rain with Searle.

A concrete mix. They wanted the helicopter to show the world. That was why they weren't shooting yet; but they would, if he looked like escaping.

In the imager, he could see a swarm of people approaching.

He urged the Lynx to lift-off, willing it to fly. The Lynx struggled valiantly, like a bird caught in oil. Slowly, slowly, it began to shift; then like a cork popping out of a bottle, it launched itself into the rain-soaked sky.

Pross knew he had the uprated engines to thank. He had got out of there because of their sheer power. The Lynx seemed to shake itself like a dog coming out of water. Pross could feel pieces of the stuff falling off it.

His mind went to Logan, trying to find some kind of cover down there. He thought of Southerndown, and the way he had lost both Rees and the pick-up. He was determined it would not work out the same way in real life. He was not going to leave Logan down there, no matter what.

He looked through the rain, went back down in a wide spiral. The soldiers had stopped, seemed undecided what to do. Had they missed seeing Logan, after all?

Pross stayed hidden in the rain. He still had to find her.

Then his warning radar went berserk.

He threw the Lynx into a hard turn to the left, winging over onto his side and diving. The noise stopped.

What had that been?

Someone else was in the rain, hunting him.

He turned, looking. A fleeting something in the imager. They had not tried missiles. Why?

He did not waste time wondering about it. This had to be ended quickly, and he had to get back to Logan.

Logan hugged the wet earth with her body, tried to keep Searle from whimpering. Up above her, she could hear the Lynx. She heard something else too: a heavier, more ominous sound; another helicopter. They sounded as if they were hunting each other. She prayed in her mind for Pross.

She kept her helmet on, and although it filtered out some sounds because of the drumming of the rain on it, she was reluctant to discard it. It would only betray their presence. The soldiers had apparently not seen her leave the aircraft with Searle. Carrying the helmet was out. She needed both hands free.

She waited with Searle, in their hide of bushes, in the blessed incessant rain.

Something flashed past in the imager. Pross couldn't believe it. A *Hind*! He'd seen enough pictures of the big gunship to recognise its profile. The tandem bubbles of its nose were unmistakable, as was its great hump and its stub wings. But what had happened to its nose gun?

Searle had been right.

So now I know.

If the Hind had no nose gun, that meant fixed ones on the fuselage sides. Anti-chopper.

Right. Let's see what you can do.

The Hind, Pross knew, had a very good turn of speed; but it was big, too big for a turning fight, even though the stub wings helped it to out-turn other choppers. The Lynx was another thing altogether. Other choppers couldn't loop. They couldn't roll like the Lynx either. As for the Hind, it would go straight down if it tried one of these manoeuvres. So. The answer was to make the bastard as unstable as possible, then blow the hell out of him.

Pross had metamorphosed into a fighting machine. Nothing existed outside his present universe: not Dee and the kids, not Logan down there in the wet, not Ling, whoever he might be. All that mattered were the Lynx, the Hind, the rain, and the air within which one of them had to kill the other to survive.

The tail radar was screaming. He flung the Lynx over, sliding sideways to the left, going down, then up and over in a wide barrel roll. He rolled upright at the top. No noise. No Hind. The mast sensor showed nothing. At least he was neither up top, nor behind. So he was down there somewhere; but where?

The driving rain had washed the Lynx clean of whatever substance had been used to snare it. It felt light, eager to do battle. Pross could swear it made the sound of its animal namesake; but that could have been his mind.

Did the Hind have comparable avionics? The side guns denoted it as an E, but that meant nothing. As with the Lynx, this one could be a variant of any kind. It didn't matter. He would get the big bastard.

He spiralled down, dropping like a stone. And there it was. He halted his spiral, eased back up. He had dropped past. Now it was a nose-on job. Had it seen him in the rain? His imager showed them clearly. Five hundred metres and closing. If it hadn't seen him, he would go for the slash.

If it had, it would probably wait for him to commit himself to a pre-climb accelerative dive before turning into him and bingo, they'd be into a corkscrew, trying to get behind.

There wasn't time for all that. It had to be quick.

Pross reasoned the Hind hadn't seen him. He took the Lynx into a fast dive, lifted it into a heart-stopping cyclic climb, rolled over onto his back, brought the nose up.

Beautiful.

Without his imager, the rain would have blinded him completely and the manoeuvre he'd just carried out would have been insane. But the imager was magic. There was the fat Hind, just below and in front, waiting to be taken. The sights pulsed.

Pross took him.

The 25 millimetre twin cannon barked in the rain, making the Lynx shudder as the armour-piercing shells punched into their fat target. Pross eased the Lynx round so that the strikes started from the rear three-quarter, marched into the engine hump and on towards the cockpit.

He pulled the Lynx away just as the Hind simply exploded, its fireball lighting the rain. Then there was nothing.

Pross did not feel elated. It was, he thought, as if the Hind had never been. In the dreamscape of the rain, that was how it felt.

Logan heard the bark of the cannon, followed by the astonishing roar of the explosion. Something heavy landed only a short distance away. She heard the noise of other falling pieces. None came near.

Then there was an eerie silence in the rain.

She had decided to remove her helmet, and had forced it down upon Searle's head. Luckily, his head size was quite small, or hers was big, she thought drily. It was still an uncomfortable fit for Searle, but it was one way of getting rid of it without leaving it around to be picked up by pursuit.

She could have buried it, of course. But that wouldn't necessarily mean they would not find it.

She thought of the helicopter that had just exploded. Pross? She daren't think about it.

She could hear the other helicopter, but it was too far away to distinguish above the rain.

There was a new noise too. The soldiers' voices had become silent, like animals in a forest aware of an unnatural intrusion into their secret world. Now, their fast chatter had started up again. She hoped they hated getting wet. They would be less motivated. Perhaps they were truly not aware of her presence, and of Searle's. If only he would try harder not to whimper.

She felt like knocking him out. Which wouldn't help.

"Shut up, Searle!" she hissed.

"I can't help it!" he said reproachfully. At least he'd kept his voice down. "I've been doing this for weeks! Sometimes I got help. It wasn't always easy making my contacts." He bit on his hand.

The soldiers seemed to be getting no closer. Then Logan had a sudden feeling of dread. They would soon begin looking for the remains of the destroyed helicopter. How ironic to be discovered during a routine search.

"If they catch us," Searle was saying, "I wouldn't give much odds on what they'd do to you. They'd have a field day with us."

It would not happen. She'd already decided she would shoot Searle, then herself. If Pross were really gone, it was hardly worth trying to escape.

Pross brought the Lynx down fast. He'd achieved total surprise. He loosed a salvo of rockets, watched them burn the atmosphere as they seared groundwards. They caused havoc among the soldiers, ripping into the sodden earth, flinging mud and bits of human beings into the air.

The Lynx disappeared into the rain.

Logan felt her heart swell within her. "Oh, Pross," she murmured.

She heard him up there, knew he would not leave until he had found her. She stayed where she was. It was not yet time.

She heard the Lynx returning. It flashed about a hundred metres away, across her line of vision, hugging the earth. Its guns were roaring. Then it was gone once more.

She heard the frantic yells of the surviving soldiers as they searched for cover. A body suddenly threw itself next to her. The soldier gaped, opened his mouth to yell.

She was fast. She jammed the rifle into his mouth, pulled the trigger once. The impact took the back of his head with it, flinging the body away from her. She felt something warmer than the rain on her cheek. The rain washed it away.

The report brought a sudden silence with it. Then a voice was calling, first tentatively, then more sharply.

Searle's body trembled violently. "Oh God. We've had it now. They know we're here."

"Will you shut up!" she hissed. "For all they know he could have shot off his rifle accidentally."

"These people are special combat troops. They never take anything for granted. They'll come looking. Sooner or later."

Then the Lynx was back.

Pross let off another salvo of rockets, picking his target well. He hit a large concentration of soldiers. He watched the ripple-fire with satisfaction as it raked the world about them. Great showers of dislodged earth rose into the watery air, blackening it.

What a ship! he thought as he hauled the Lynx up and round for another pass. As yet, he had not taken any ground-fire. He knew that would not last for long.

He was about to start his run when the defensive radar shrieked its warning at him. The digital display indicator screen, its target image quartered by cross-hairs, blinked its pale blue at him rapidly. With each blink, it gave the range of the object on his tail. The outer rings of the target display were disappearing off-screen continually as the object approached, new ones replacing them with equal continuity and rapidity as the range closed. The warning tone kept up its manic shrieking.

The approaching pulse was dead in the centre of the cross-hairs. Its speed was awesome.

Missile.

Pross did nothing for a few seconds, but his mind raced, working out possibilities. He thought only of survival. Time later to worry about where it had come from. Survival need was immediate. A matter of seconds.

Concentrate. *Concentrate.*

Range: 500 metres. It had come on-screen at 2000. Short-range launch. Whatever it was would be close behind.

Pross waited, holding the Lynx steady, giving the missile a fat homing point. He knew that the ship's infra-red signature had been cut right down, but this new missile had either been launched with a perfect lock-on, or it was a super-sensitive sniffer, homing inexorably on the heat of his engines.

Now!

He took the Lynx straight down with a suddenness that brought his body tightly up against his straps and made him wish he had a G-suit. He fought threatening nausea as the aircraft dropped like a stone and prayed they had gone for a hit and not a proximity burst.

The defensive radar had stopped shrieking and he was still alive. He never saw the missile, knowing only that it had passed above him in the rain. Would it turn and come searching for the weak infra-red signature? Would it continue on its way, confused, until its propellant was expended?

Pross kept his eye on the radar as he jinked the Lynx about, his own attack radar hunting for the owner of the missile. Had the missile been a radar-killer? In which case his own radar was virtually saying here I am, come and get me.

Then the shrieking started up again.

Christ. The same one? Another? Where was the bastard who was sending them?

Jesus! This one was dead ahead!

But its track was curving, searching, looking for the weak signature.

Pross felt relief. Infra-red. It was trying to get behind. Right, he thought. Let's feed you. He took the Lynx up in a climbing turn.

He hit the flare dispenser button. Two sunbursts appeared in the rain, searing the gloom above him as he took the Lynx into a savage wing-over and headed groundwards. He felt, rather than saw the subsequent explosion.

The missile, programmed but unthinking, fed itself on the energy of the two flares by committing suicide.

Pross ground-hopped, the imager showing him the obstacles in his path. Had that been the same missile? Another?

No use trying to think it out. Somewhere in the rain, the Hind he'd killed had a brother who was out for revenge. He'd have to find him before he could return for Logan.

He hoped she would still be there, waiting; and alive.

Logan heard the Lynx as it beat furiously at the air. She'd heard the tremendous explosion, and had felt her heart stop, fearing for Pross. She'd felt relief when she'd heard its engines going as strongly as ever.

She heard a rattle of ground-fire; but it was still unco-ordinated. The soldiers were firing at ghosts. That state of affairs would not last for long, she knew. Hadn't Searle said they were special combat troops? Sooner or later, he'd whimpered at her, they'd come looking. She knew he was right.

Come on, Pross.

Then she heard the new sound above her. Another helicopter. She listened with a sense of despair. This one sounded menacing. There was a meanness to it and that gave it the stamp of an implacable hunter. It was almost as if its blades cut the air with a sense of cold glee as it searched out its quarry.

"They'll get him, you know," Searle was saying in a shaky whisper. "I recognise that sound. It's a new chopper they've got, not even seen by the West. I may well be the only person from our side who's seen it. It's been built especially for anti-helicopter duties. I believe it's a Mil-28, a murderous-looking devil, flown by one man. No other crew. I call it the *Hellhound*; which is what you'd think if it ever got on your tail."

Searle raised his head cautiously to listen.

Logan pushed it back down, none too gently.

"Keep your bloody head down, you idiot!" she hissed at him. How had he survived? she wondered bitterly.

Then she suddenly felt less uncharitable towards him. He'd been in a hostile environment for months, collecting prime information. He was a man at the end of his tether. Could she even have lasted a fraction of the time?

She looked at the lowered, cowering head. Pross would have to beat the Hellhound. If not, she was quite determined to shoot both Searle and herself.

There was no doubt in her mind.

Pross took the Lynx to two thousand feet, still in the massive belt of the raincloud. Nothing showed on the radar. The imager showed nothing trying to hide in the rain.

Was it another Hind? Then where the hell was it? Where could it be hiding?

All questions, and no answers.

He thought of Logan waiting for him down there in the wet; but he couldn't go down. Not yet. Not until he had taken out whatever was hunting him.

The radar searched ahead as he did a slow circle. Nothing. He selected look-up mode. Nothing above.

Then the shrieking was back.

Shit. A *third* missile. How many were the bastards carrying? Would there be a fourth? Yes. There it was, close to the other on the target image. They were trying to bracket him.

He danced the Lynx round, hit the dispenser button to give him a spread of six flares, then he plunged down as the swollen sky above him was lit with a painful brightness.

Even as he took the ship down, he wondered what they were using. Swatters, he knew, took 21 seconds to reach 4000 metres, and Spirals took 10 seconds for 5000 metres; but these monsters were much faster, it seemed. Dedicated air-to-air.

226

The shock wave reached him as the two missiles consumed themselves in the flares he had left for them.

He brought the Lynx very low as he hunted for his still undetected assailant. He found himself a hill, scanned it, saw nothing to worry about. He descended cautiously, behind a line of trees. He half-expected small-arms fire; but nothing came at him. He was at least five kilometres from where he'd left Logan.

He waited.

A minute passed. Two.

The radar was in look-up mode. The mast sensor scanned 360 degrees. Nothing.

Three minutes.

He continued to hover.

Four.

Something. Not a missile. Much too slow. Chopper.

Come closer. Let's have you on visuals.

As he lay in wait, Pross suddenly knew how they'd done it. They had stayed low, done a tail-down job, launched their missiles. The missiles had gained height, then had curved towards him. He had just four flares remaining, should they decide to launch more of their nasty arrows at him. He hoped they had used the last of their missiles.

The chopper came closer. The rain drenched the Lynx.

Come on, come on. Let's be having you.

He got an image of it just as it suddenly skidded sideways. He swore. He'd been seen. He felt a surge of pre-combat excitement.

The Lynx accelerated laterally along the line of trees before breaking cover to gain height in a swift cyclic climb. Pross held the other helicopter on visuals. He was not going to lose it. They had obviously used up all their missiles, for none had been launched. This pleased him. He did not intend to use his Stingers.

He stared at the darting image. He had never seen anything like it. It was certainly not a Hind, being much smaller, lighter looking. It was lean, still carried the stub wings and importantly, appeared to be crewed by a single person.

Pross felt his heart flutter. This, he thought, was a true beast for its job. This was a dogfighting anti-chopper ship, a totally

227

new design. Perhaps there were weaknesses that had not yet been ironed out. That would probably help in the coming fight.

The Lynx continued to rise in the rain. The wipers fought at the streaming water. Pross kept the strange chopper in sight, following it now in a climbing turn. Too far for a gunshoot. He had to be spot-on.

Jesus, it was fast. There'd be just one chance.

Abruptly, he lost it.

He threw the Lynx over, rolling left. He hadn't seen the guns. Did it have guns? If so, how many?

What about imaging? Could the other chopper see in these conditions?

Pross brought the Lynx round in a tight turn. Christ. There he was, head-on.

The other pilot was too eager, and fired too soon. Pross saw four flashes, two on each side of the narrow fuselage, before he threw the Lynx out of the way.

Four guns.

It had to happen, he supposed. Only a matter of time before choppers started fighting one another. Dogfighting had moved into a new dimension.

As the black, unmarked chopper slid past, Pross did a lateral shift, got behind him. They both headed earthwards. Suddenly, the chopper broke right in a tight turn, going tighter than Pross would have expected.

Pross did something no fixed-wing fast-jet pilot would do these days if he wanted to live: he went into a high yo-yo, pulling the Lynx up and rolling behind. He was still on the chopper's tail.

But not for long.

The black chopper broke again, turning towards Pross. The bastard could handle his ship, Pross decided grimly. He was very close to the ground now. The fight had so far cost a lot of height.

Pross barrel-rolled the Lynx to gain height while keeping it out of the other's sights. The radar shrieked. Pross rolled opposite, went down again. The shrieking stopped.